THE STOLEN CHAPTERS

STORY
THIEVES

THE STOLEN CHAPTERS

JAMES RILEY

SCHOLASTIC INC.

ISBN 978-1-338-03787-6

Text copyright © 2016 by James Riley.
Interior illustrations by Chris Eliopoulos copyright © 2016 by Simon & Schuster, Inc.
Cover illustration copyright © 2016 by Vivienne To. All rights reserved.
Published by Scholastic Inc., 557 Broadway, New York, NY 10012, by arrangement with Aladdin Paperbacks, an imprint of Simon & Schuster Children's Publishing Division.
SCHOLASTIC and associated logos are trademarks and/or registered trademarks of Scholastic Inc.

12 11 10 9 8 7 6 5 4 3   16 17 18 19 20 21

Printed in the U.S.A.   40

First Scholastic printing, March 2016

Book design by Laura Lyn DiSiena
The text of this book was set in Adobe Garamond.

Dedicated to the fictional. Remember,
you don't have to do what your authors say.

CHAPTER 1

Kiel Gnomenfoot

the Magister

Charm

CHAPTER 2

The library

CHAPTER 3

"WHERE ARE YOU?"

CHAPTER 4

smiling half-robotic girl.

trapped in the nonfictional world

sidekick,

CHAPTER 5

███████████

Bethany!" ████████████████████

████████████

████████████████████████████████

████████████████████████████████

████████████████████████████████

███████ what she'd done ███████

████████████████████████████████

████████████████████████████████

████████████████████████████████

████████████████████████████ she

couldn't face them.

████████████████████████████████

████████████████████████████████

CHAPTER 6

████████████████████

Mr. Holmes ████████████████████████
████████████████████████████████
████████████████████████████████
████████████████████████████████
████████████████████████████████
████████████████████████████████
███
████████████████████████████████
████████████████████████████████
████████████████████████████████
████ A pistol ████████████████████
████████████████████████████████
████████████████████████████████
████████████████████████████████

CHAPTER 7

backup plan,

"Moira Gonzalez,"

CHAPTER 8

the key

Baker Street School

found her dad

CHAPTER 9

CHAPTER 10

Someone was trying to steal Owen's life, and there was nothing Owen could do about it.

"Your life is *mine* now," said the story thief, a brown-haired boy wearing the exact same T-shirt, the exact same jeans, and the exact same face as Owen.

"No!" Owen tried to shout, but he couldn't move or talk. His body just wouldn't respond.

The duplicate leaned in, hands reaching out for Owen . . .

And that's when Owen woke up with a start.

Wait, he'd been asleep! It was just a *dream*! A scary, sweaty, awful dream.

Owen wanted to laugh. "It was all a dream" was the worst possible ending to any story, but right now, it definitely felt comforting. It had felt much too real, though he supposed that was dreams for you. Owen ran his hands over his sheets, happy to still be in bed.

Except his sheets felt a lot like carpet, and he wasn't lying on a pillow.

Also, his carpet-feeling sheets were orange for some reason.

"Uh?" Owen said. He picked his head up a bit from the carpet, only to wince and drop his head back to the floor, squeezing his eyes shut. A huge ache pounded through his temples, and everything smelled weirdly smoky.

He tried opening his eyes again, but even the little bit of light in the room caused his headache to scream at him. But Owen knew that orange carpet. He knew it like the back of his hand. Which, admittedly, he didn't know all *that* well, but still.

This was the library. He was facedown on the floor of his mother's library.

And he had no idea how he'd gotten here.

Gathering all of his courage, Owen opened his eyes again to look around.

"Owen?" said a voice to his side, followed by a painful groan.

"Kiel?" Owen said, and groaned too as he turned slightly to face the direction the voice had come from.

Kiel Gnomenfoot, former boy magician and hero to millions as star of his own book series, looked like he wanted to burst into tears. "Owen," Kiel repeated, as if the word tasted bad. "Why . . . head . . . hurt?"

Owen tried to bring up a word or two, something along the lines of *I have no idea, but it's obviously for evil, evil reasons,* but all he managed to croak out was, "Unnh." Figuring that wasn't enough, he slapped his hand a few times on the floor, then cringed at the noise.

How had he and Kiel gotten to his mom's library? The last thing Owen remembered was . . . wait, what *was* the last thing he remembered? It was like everything in the recent past was just gone. He remembered Kiel being introduced to their class as Kyle, a new student, but that was the last thing. How long ago had that been? And why couldn't he remember anything else?

Thunder crashed, and Owen grabbed his head as it erupted in pain, which made him face-plant onto the floor. After a moment of pure agony, something more urgent than the ache seeped through his brain.

"Do you smell smoke?" he asked Kiel. Owen pushed himself up and over onto his back, so at least he wouldn't hit his face again if he fell.

"Probably," Kiel moaned from his side. "Is something on fire?"

Dark black smoke began to curl into sight above Owen on the library's ceiling, and in spite of the pain, Owen immediately sat up. "Kiel!" he shouted. "The library's on fire!"

"No yelling!" Kiel shouted back, and they both groaned. Kiel slowly pushed himself up too and looked around. "Oh. Fire. That's not a good thing. Hold on, I'll use . . . whatever it is I do. Magic. To put it out."

"Holding," Owen said, gritting his teeth and waiting. "Hurry. *Hurry.*"

A pause, and then Kiel gasped. "They're not there!"

"What aren't?"

"My wand-knives!" he said, then paused. "Owen, I can't remember any magic, and my spell book's gone too. I can't do magic without it or my wands."

"A brilliant observation," said a too-deep, fake-sounding voice from behind them, as if someone was talking into a voice changer. "Which begs the question, what exactly *can* you do,

Mr. Gnomenfoot? What use are you without your magic?"

Owen turned to find himself staring at a short figure wearing a brown overcoat, a Sherlock Holmes hat, and a white mask with a black question mark where the face should have been.

Well. *That* wasn't good.

"Gentlemen," the masked figure said, crossing his arms over his chest. "I would say the game is afoot, but unfortunately, your game is already over."

CHAPTER 11

And you are?" Kiel asked, pushing himself to his feet a bit unsteadily. Owen followed his lead, but the whole room decided to spin at that moment, and he stumbled sideways into one of the library's study tables.

"Doyle Holmes," the masked boy said in the strange voice. "You have, of course, heard of me." He wasn't asking.

Kiel shook his head, wincing at the pain. "No. Should I have?"

Owen shook his head too, but for a different reason. "No," he groaned. "No, no, no, no, *no*. He shouldn't be here. He *can't* be here. Kiel, Doyle Holmes is, like, the great-great-great-something-grandson of Sherlock Holmes. He's a . . . he's like you." Owen winced and lowered his voice so that only Kiel could hear. "Only he's from a book that no one read. I heard it wasn't good."

Kiel straightened up, and his hands automatically flew to his belt, where his wand-knives usually were, before he sighed. "Maybe he's wearing a costume," Kiel said, not sounding hopeful.

"Ah, no," Doyle Holmes said. "I am, in fact, fictional, just like you, Kiel Gnomenfoot. Though that is the only thing I imagine we have in common."

Owen's eyes widened. He knew Kiel was fictional? This was *so* not good!

"Not possible," Kiel said, taking a step toward the boy in the mask. "You couldn't have gotten out. Not without—"

"Your friend Bethany?" Doyle finished. "You're very correct. Which brings up the question: Where might she be now?"

No! "What do you want?" Owen said.

Doyle shrugged, his mask betraying no emotions. "What does *anyone* want? To be the world's greatest detective? To solve the most challenging mysteries of all time? To ensure that no one breaks a law ever again without me catching them?" He paused. "All of those things, of course. But right now I want to see you story thieves pay for your crimes."

"*Magic* thief," Kiel corrected. "Get it right. *Kiel Gnomenfoot, Magic Thief.* It's right there in the title of my first book."

"Don't worry, your stories are now over," Doyle said, and

Owen could almost hear the boy smirking behind the mask.

Behind the detective, a flickering orange glow grew brighter, and the smoke along the ceiling began to thicken. And for the first time, Owen noticed that there were gas cans stacked around the library shelves.

And Doyle was holding a long match. He slowly lowered it to his fingers, snapped them, and the match lit.

"No!" Owen shouted, and grabbed his phone to call 911. Was a fictional character actually burning down his library? He punched in the numbers, but somehow, his phone had no service. Not even one bar, even though it always had service in the library.

"Don't worry," Doyle said, holding up a phone of his own. "I've already made the call. The police and fire department should be here momentarily. I've informed them that I saw two kids of your description setting fire to the library, so I imagine they'll have some questions." He nodded at the gas cans. "And once they discover Owen Conners's fingerprints all over these, I'm fairly certain they'll have all the evidence they need to put you away."

What? He was *framing* them? Why was this all happening? And why couldn't Owen remember anything that'd happened before he woke up?

"You know, I haven't had to fight someone without using magic for a while," Kiel said, stepping forward. "I think I've missed it. Owen, want to hold him down?"

"I wouldn't," Doyle said, pointing his match at the gas cans. "Not unless you want these going up prematurely."

"Why would you do this?" Owen said, pulling Kiel back, away from the boy in the question-mark mask. "And where is Bethany?"

Doyle shrugged. "I wouldn't worry about her." He held up his hand and tapped his watch. "Well, at least for the next two hours or so." He glanced at his wrist. "Sorry, two hours and ten minutes. Don't worry, I've put watches on both your wrists as well. Consider that part of the punishment. As soon as the timers reach zero, you'll never see your friend again."

Owen looked down at the rubber band on his wrist. The amount of buttons and markings on it made the band look far more complicated than just a watch, but the only thing on the face was a timer counting down: 2:10:09.

Kiel pulled his arm out of Owen's grasp and stepped forward. *"Where is she?"* he shouted, angrier than Owen had ever seen him.

"That's a good question," Doyle said, stepping back into the

burning section of the library. "But one you won't need to concern yourself with. No, I'd worry far more about the police if
I were you."

Outside, the sirens grew louder, and Owen grabbed Kiel
again. "What have you done to her?" Kiel shouted, struggling
against Owen's hand.

"It's not what *I'll* do, but what she'll do," Doyle said. "Figure
out where you are, and you'll have half the mystery solved."

"Why are you doing this?" Owen asked. "And why can't we
remember anything?"

"The headaches?" Doyle said. "My apologies. I forced Kiel to
use his little forget spell on you both. Couldn't have you using
what you knew to find Bethany, now, could I? No, this has all
been planned out from the start." He leaned forward, and in spite
of the mask not having eye holes, Owen felt like Doyle was staring
right at him. "Just remember, I did all of this *by the book*."

Owen grimaced. Amnesia? Seriously? What a horrible cliché.

"The police won't capture us," Kiel said, pointing at Doyle.
"We'll rescue Bethany, and I'll find my wands and spell book.
And then you and I will have a pleasant talk, where you don't say
much, and I smile a lot." He winked then, though it didn't look
easy for him.

Doyle shook his head. "Oh, Kiel Gnomenfoot. I'm a *Holmes*. There's nothing you can do that I can't see coming." And with that, he tossed the match into the stack of books right next to the gas cans. "You have about thirty seconds before the fire hits the gas. I'd *run*."

"NO!" Owen shouted, only to have Kiel grab *his* arm and yank him toward the library doors. Owen glanced back as they ran through the automatically opening doors, and he saw Doyle slip out the back way right as the fire reached the gas cans.

Kiel pulled Owen to the side of the building, just as an enormous explosion shattered the library doors and all the windows. The force of the blast sent Kiel and Owen flying, then crashing into the library's bushes.

As sirens filled the air, Kiel groaned, then turned to Owen. "What did he mean, 'a homes'?" he asked.

"That's the great-great-great-great-great-grandson of Sherlock *Holmes*, the greatest detective who ever lived," Owen said, his eyes wide as he turned back to watch his mother's library burn in the night. "And if anything, I think Doyle was written to be even *better*. We're in so, *so* much trouble."

CHAPTER 12

02:04:14 remaining

As the fire grew, Owen pushed his way out of the bushes, staring at the flames in horror. This library was his entire life. He'd spent so many days here, after school, weekends, even vacations, helping out, waiting for his mother, and especially reading all of its books.

The sirens drew closer, and Kiel pulled Owen back into the bushes to hide. Kiel seemed less angry, though he was still breathing hard. "I think this Doyle guy just made things a bit hotter for himself than he realized," he told Owen, then winked. "Don't worry, we'll find Bethany and then make him pay for this."

Owen slowly turned to Kiel in disbelief. "Did you just make a *joke*? The library's burning down! We need to help."

"But we'll be caught if we do," Kiel said, his brow knit in

confusion. "Doyle said the police are coming, and if they're anything like the Science Police, that's a bad thing. This will have to wait, Owen. If we get caught, we might never find Bethany and save her."

"Then we tell the police the whole thing!" Owen said, realizing that tears were streaming down his face as smoke filled the air. "This isn't a *book*, Kiel. This is my real life! We can't just run, not from the police. We need to tell them what happened, and they can help us find Bethany."

Kiel raised an eyebrow. "Think about what you're saying, Owen. You're going to tell the police that a fictional character escaped his story to kidnap your half-fictional friend, then set fire to your mom's library?" He shook his head. "Who would believe you? There's a reason Bethany keeps her powers a secret. This is something *we* need to take care of. By ourselves."

"I don't care if they believe me!" Owen shouted back. "This is my entire life! My *mom's* entire life. She put so much work into this place. I can't have her thinking I did this! I *can't*."

First a fire engine, then two police cars sped into the parking lot of the library, slamming on their brakes to skid neatly to a stop within inches of one another. As firemen poured off the truck and hooked up their hoses to a fire hydrant, four police officers leaped out of their cars, noticing Kiel and Owen instantly. "Freeze!" one shouted, reaching for his gun.

"Hands in the air!" another shouted.

"We didn't do it!" Owen said, his hands flying straight up.

"Descriptions match the suspects," one of the police officers said into the radio on his chest. "Moving to apprehend."

"We're not suspects!" Owen shouted. "And there's no need to apprehend. We're surrendering!"

"This is a terrible idea, Owen," Kiel said, taking a step backward toward the bushes. "I don't have my magic, so I can't help you if this goes badly. You sure you want to do this?"

"*No,*" Owen whispered. Then louder, "The guy who set fire to the library ran out the back. You can still catch him! He's wearing a brown coat and a creepy mask with a question mark on it."

The four police officers moved closer, their guns drawn. "Don't move!" one said.

"Tell it to the judge!" another said.

Tell it to the *judge*? Even with his headache and the fire and everything falling apart, Owen couldn't believe his ears. Who talked like that? Someone had seen too many cop movies.

"We need to get out of here," Kiel hissed, backing away as

the firemen began hosing down the library, not that it was doing much good: The fire was blazing out of control now. "Bethany's depending on us. We have . . . two hours, exactly, to find her. There's no time to waste with this."

"The police will find her," Owen said, not quite as confidently as before. He glanced at his watch and saw Kiel was right: 02:00:00, right on the dot. "This is how things work in the real world, Kiel. Kids don't solve crimes here, the police do. We have to let *them* handle it."

"Cuff 'em," one of the officers said, and two pulled out handcuffs while the others kept their guns pointed at Kiel and Owen.

"We didn't do it," Owen said, practically pleading with the police. "You have to believe me. The guy who did is getting away!"

"Owen Conners, you have the right to remain silent," the police officer said, then began to mumble something about an attorney and a few other things, getting so quiet that Owen couldn't hear any of his other rights.

Handcuffs snapped around Owen's wrists, and he was jerked roughly away from Kiel, who sighed and held his hands out in front of him. A second officer went to handcuff the boy magician, but Kiel didn't take his eyes off Owen. "Sorry, my friend," he said, shaking his head. "I want to believe you, but chalk it up to too many years living under the Science Police."

And with that, Kiel knocked his hands up into the police officer's, reversed the handcuffs, and latched them onto the officer's wrists instead. Then he disappeared into the night, his black cape and clothes cloaking him in the fire's shadows.

"Suspect escaping on foot!" one of the cops shouted into his radio. "We need backup!"

"He didn't do it!" Owen shouted as an officer dragged him by his cuffs back to the police cars. "Why won't you listen to me?"

The officer opened his squad car door and tossed Owen into the back, as even more sirens filled the air, and the whirring of a helicopter sounded from a far-off distance. A *helicopter*? The police officer jumped into the front seat and began fiddling with his computer.

"The guy who did this is named Doyle Holmes!" Owen shouted. "He kidnapped a friend of mine, Bethany Sanderson!"

The police officer frowned, then pushed some buttons on the computer screen. "I'd advise you to keep your mouth shut until you get to the station. Anything you say can and will be used against you, as I said." The computer beeped, and he paused. "Also, there's no record of a Bethany Sanderson in this town, so maybe come up with a better story next time."

"What?" Owen said. "Of course there's a record. She's my classmate! Call her mom, she'll tell you!"

"I have a Stephanie Sanderson, thirty-nine," the police officer said. "No dependents, though." He abruptly shifted the car into reverse and, without looking, slammed on the gas, narrowly missing the other squad car and two light poles. "Base, I'm coming in," he said into the radio on his shoulder. "Have one of the arsonists from the library. Throw the book at this one." The officer turned to glare at Owen. "He deserves it."

Owen's eyes widened, and he turned to the door, only to find it had no handle on the inside. Had Kiel been right? Was this a huge mistake?

And why was there no record of Bethany?

"Please believe me," Owen said to the police officer. "My friend is in danger. This guy, Doyle Holmes, said that we've got two hours before we never see her again."

"You might never see the friend who doesn't exist again?" the officer said. "I'll be sure to alert the FBI."

"I'm serious!" Owen shouted as the officer slammed on the gas again, sending the car bursting out into traffic. Owen quickly grabbed the door's arm rest just to hold on as the car weaved in and out of the few vehicles on the road this late at night, driving at least ninety miles per hour down the street. "She's in real danger! This Doyle guy isn't from around here!"

The police officer looked back at Owen, his eyes not even on the road as he continued to swerve. "Boy, you're just really digging yourself in deeper, aren't you?" he said, smirking.

Owen sighed and collapsed back against the seat, then glanced down at the watch on his wrist: 01:55:46.

Kiel had been right. This was a huge mistake.

But maybe that was okay. Kiel was still free, and he was a *hero*. He was probably out there right now, finding Bethany all on his own. Knowing Kiel, in fact, Bethany was probably free already!

CHAPTER 13

01:55:46

It took Bethany several minutes to realize that she wasn't dreaming the sound of running water. She opened her eyes and immediately gasped.

She was in a room made entirely of cement, it looked like, though it was so dark she almost couldn't see. The only light came from the ceiling, where grates let in streams of water. The room was empty except for large metal shelves against one wall, cameras in each corner, and whatever she was sitting on.

Bethany tried to stand, only to find she couldn't move her arms or legs. Heavy chains were cuffed to her wrists, binding her to an old green chair with the cushions half missing, while her ankles were tied to the chair's legs with rope.

Meanwhile, the water pouring through the grates in multiple waterfalls was starting to collect on the floor.

"Help!" she shouted, everything coming back at once. Owen and Kiel. Kiel's forget spell. *Doyle*. Her heart began beating out of her chest, and she tensed, ready to jump.

"I wouldn't," said a voice from behind her, and a boy in a Sherlock Holmes hat and coat wearing a mask with a question mark, stepped into the light.

"Let me go!" Bethany shouted, pulling at the chains as hard as she could.

Doyle didn't move. "I don't believe I will. But please, feel free to escape."

She bit her lip to keep from screaming at him. "Why are you doing this? I've done nothing to you!"

"Really?" Doyle said quietly. "What about humiliating my family, Bethany Sanderson? You've revealed our secret to the entire world. And maybe worst of all, you've presented me with a mystery I haven't been able to solve. We can't have that, now, can we?"

Bethany just stared at the detective as the water flowed into the room. He was *insane*. "Where are Owen and Kiel?"

"You won't be seeing them again," Doyle said. "I imagine they're both being arrested as we speak. If I were you, I'd be far more concerned with what will be happening to you in"—he looked at his watch—"just under two hours."

"Two hours?" she said. "What happens—" But she stopped midsentence, realizing she didn't want to know.

"That's when this room fills with water," Doyle said, then glanced up at the ceiling. "Don't worry, I had this room specifically modified so I'd know exactly how long it'd take. Of course, the water will rise above your head far before then if you're still tied to the chair, so let's say you have about a half hour, tops."

Bethany's eyes widened. "You're trying to kill me?" she asked quietly.

"Me?" Doyle said, managing to look indignant despite his mask. "Of course not! I'm just providing motivation. After all, you can't have a mystery without a motive. And you, Ms. Sanderson, are my only lead in solving your mystery."

Jump, her mind said. *Get out of here!* Her whole body tensed, but she couldn't. "This isn't a mystery, Doyle. This is my *life!*"

Doyle waved a hand around. "What's the difference? All of our lives are mysteries, Ms. Sanderson. What will we do at any given moment? How far will we go to get what we want? Who will we sacrifice to save ourselves? All mysteries, and I, for one, am excited to see their solutions."

Bethany glanced up at the water flowing in. "You're insane. This is a death trap! You're acting like some kind of villain—"

Doyle leaped forward, his mask stopping within inches of her face. *"Some kind? I'm the greatest villain,"* he hissed almost too softly to hear. "But this isn't a death trap. It's a mystery!" He slowly stood back up. "A true classic, what we call a locked room mystery. How did the victim die when the murderer couldn't get into the room? In this case, the murder weapon is water, and the victim is you, dying from drowning. The fun comes when you're discovered, and the water has been drained." He gestured around proudly. "You'll have drowned in a dry room! Don't you see how fun that'd be to solve?"

Bethany just stared at him in shock. "Why, Doyle?" she asked. "I paid you what you asked for."

Doyle leaned back in. *"Sometimes a story just needs a good villain,"* he whispered, then stood back up. "But don't think of this as punishment. It is, of course, but don't think of it that way. This is an experiment! I'm here to learn from you. Whether you want me to or not."

With that, Doyle turned and walked over to a small door in the wall, the rising water sloshing on the floor as he went.

Bethany yanked on the chains again in frustration, then stopped. He might be crazy, but he still had his family to think about. "This is crazy, Doyle!" she shouted. "You know that. This isn't worthy of a Holmes! What would your great-great-great-whatever-grandfather think?"

Doyle paused, then slowly turned back to her. "Nice try, Ms. Sanderson. I know what he'd think. My family's known what he thought since that day at the waterfall." He shook his head. "A *flying man* saved his life. That's what he claimed, and for the next three years, he searched the entire world for the man, the secret of flight, anything. *Three years.* There's nothing Sherlock Holmes couldn't find in that time, but this was one mystery that defeated him, and he was never the same afterward. We all thought he'd lost his mind, that Professor Moriarty had beaten him." Doyle pointed at her. "But no. It was *you*, you and Kiel's Magister all along."

Bethany's eyes widened, remembering the Magister chasing her through books, and his flying form accidentally saving Sherlock Holmes from a fall over Reichenbach Falls. "We saved his life!" she shouted. "He might have died!"

"Better to die with one's reputation than live without it," Doyle said, and turned his back on her.

"I can just escape!" Bethany shouted, pulling on her chains. "You and I both know I can!"

"Please do," Doyle said, his hand on the doorknob. "And my cameras will record it. Should be all I need." He turned and faced her. "But we both also know what happens if you do. You'll never see them again, Bethany Sanderson. You'll have lost two more, just like you lost your father."

Bethany screamed again in rage, pushing off the floor as hard as she could, almost toppling the chair she was chained to.

"I'd be careful not to fall over," Doyle said, opening the door. "Wouldn't want to drown in just six inches of water, would you?"

"I'm going to get out of this," Bethany told him. "And I'm going to make you pay. Do you understand me?"

Doyle shrugged. "Just remember, *you* came to *me*. So whose fault is this, really? Like I said, life is a mystery, isn't it? I never would have thought you'd break every one of your rules just to get what you wanted, but here we are. Who could have deduced that?"

Bethany gritted her teeth, holding back another scream.

"Good luck," Doyle said, then closed the door behind him. Bethany heard some sort of spinning noise, and a huge lock clicked into place. And for the first time, she noticed she had a black band on her wrist that showed a countdown in red: 1:50:19.

Jump, jump, jump, jump, jump, her mind said.

No. Kiel and Owen would find her. Of course they would. Whatever trouble they were in, they'd find a way out of it. Owen was probably a huge fan of mysteries and had read them all. And Kiel was a hero! He'd know *exactly* what to do.

CHAPTER 14

01:50:07

Kiel Gnomenfoot, former hero to millions as the star of his own book series, current boy magician without any magic, had no idea what to do.

Things used to be so easy. There were keys to find, Charm to help him find them, and Dr. Verity to fight. But now there was this Doyle guy, Bethany was missing, and Owen had surrendered to the police at the very first chance he got, which just felt so wrong that it made Kiel's stomach ache. Back on Magisteria, whenever the robotic Science Police had caught someone, that was it. You never saw them again.

Tended to leave a bad taste in one's mouth about the police.

"We've got you surrounded!" shouted a voice from just a few feet away in the darkness. "Come out with your hands up!"

Usually, this would be the point where Kiel would cast some

fun, probably ironic magic spell, then say something amazing, often with a wink and a grin. Charm seemed to appreciate that sort of thing, so Kiel made sure to push it, even when he was scared or uncertain. Even without magic, part of him wanted to take this police officer down, steal his radio, then spout off something snappy and daring, just so the police knew who they were dealing with.

But this wasn't his world, or even a fictional one, so instead, Kiel inched his way back into the shadows. The roaring fire offered up lots of shadowy hiding spots as it consumed the library where Kiel, Bethany, and Owen had all met most nights to have exciting, dangerous, amazing adventures. Just like the last time, where they . . .

They what? Kiel couldn't remember the last adventure they'd been on. For some reason he thought of the Magister, and . . . and a spell book. He rubbed his forehead, trying to bring that memory to the forefront. Why was it so hard to think of it? Clearly he was just too amazing at magic, if he'd erased his own memories this well.

He heard footsteps go by, and Kiel counted to five, then silently stepped out and made his way in the opposite direction. Overhead, a large flying carlike object with what looked to be a sort of halo above it floated loudly in midair, shi... ...g a light down onto the library's grounds. As the light shifted closer, Kiel dove beneath a car, which had just enough room for him to fit easily.

This was all wasting time, and there was only an hour and forty-eight minutes left before something terrible happened to Bethany. The very idea left a hole in his stomach and made him want to punch something, and hiding when he should be looking for her made it even worse.

Still, it'd waste even more time if he got caught, so Kiel took a deep breath and stayed out of sight.

As soon as the flying car's light passed, Kiel rolled out from beneath the car in what he hoped was an impressive way, then leaped to his feet and took off at a noiseless sprint in the direction he'd seen Doyle go right before the explosion. Bethany could be anywhere, but if Kiel got ahold of Doyle, this would all be over in moments, with or without magic.

Maybe more than a few moments. After all, Kiel planned on enjoying interrogating Doyle. Whoever he was.

Unfortunately, more police were flooding the grounds now, and it took longer than he'd have liked to make his way around to the other side of the burning library without being caught.

Firefighters were also running everywhere, and steam rose from the roof as they sprayed the building with water.

If he still had his magic, he could have put out this fire instantly. Doyle would pay for that, too. While the library seemed to belong to Owen's mother somehow, it still had given Kiel some pretty happy memories. Or at least, he *thought* it had. Granted, he couldn't remember them now, but he was confident that they had been good.

As he moved, he reached out with his mind, trying to sense his spell book. Even when it was lost, he could at least pinpoint its general direction. That was part of the magic, after all. He was connected to his spell book, and it to him.

This time, though, he got no sense of the spell book at *all*. That wasn't good.

Kiel reached the back door of the library and slowed to a stop, looking around for signs that anyone had passed by. The hard surface of the road wouldn't show footprints, though, so Kiel moved on to the woods nearby, where the softer dirt would hopefully be more useful. The darkness obscured almost everything, though. Kiel wanted to scream to whoever was listening in either the fictional or nonfictional world how much he hated having to rely on his own eyes instead of just using magic, like the universe had intended.

The sound of footsteps pushed Kiel back into the trees, and he barely breathed, all his thieving skills coming back to him instinctually. Whoever it was stopped just a few feet from him.

"We got one of them, sir," the voice said, then paused. Kiel waited, but the same voice spoke again. "No, the boy in normal clothes. Owen Conners. The other one, Kiel Gnomenfoot, got away."

Kiel pushed forward an inch at a time until he could just make out the silhouette of a police officer speaking into his shoulder radio as he flashed a science torch through the air. Who was the officer talking to? And how did he know Owen's name? Obviously he'd heard of Kiel, as everyone had. But that raised another question: Didn't nonfictional police officers think that Kiel was just some heroic, amazing wizard from a series of books? This guy didn't even seem the slightest bit surprised to be talking about a fictional person.

"I know you said this Kiel boy wasn't dangerous and that the Conners kid was the one to worry about, but are you sure?" the police officer said, then stopped. "No, of course I didn't mean to doubt you! I apologize, sir."

What? Kiel Gnomenfoot not dangerous? And Owen Conners

was the one to worry about? What sort of upside-down world *was* the nonfictional world?

Kiel loved Owen like a brother, of course, but dangerous wasn't the first word that came to mind. And Kiel had taken down dragons, giants, and fire-breathing unicorns! Not dangerous?! Whoever was on the other end of the line was clearly not dealing with a full spell book.

"We're taking the Conners kid to the station," the police officer continued. "We'll interrogate him there, and . . . no, you're right. Whatever you say. This is your case, after all. Yes sir, I'll keep you updated. Yes, sir, thank *you*, Mr. Holmes."

Kiel's eyes widened. Holmes? *Doyle* Holmes? Were the police working with the boy who kidnapped Bethany? Or was there another Holmes? Owen had mentioned a grandfather, so maybe there were more family members involved.

Of course, the Holmes family was also supposed to be fictional. Or was just Doyle fictional? Kiel shook his head. If Owen hadn't surrendered, he'd be around to answer these questions, instead of letting them give Kiel *more* of a headache.

This would have been the perfect time for any number of spells, but instead, Kiel just waited until the police officer moved out of sight, then went back to searching the ground.

Just as he was about to give up, the fire's light lit up footprints in the dirt, leading away from the library.

Ah. Let's see who was dangerous now, *Doyle.*

Kiel followed the trail through the woods and down through some backyards. The path struck Kiel as a bit familiar, but that wasn't too surprising. He, Owen, and Bethany had gotten used to walking back and forth to the library at night for their adventures. Hadn't they?

And then the footprints ended at a house, and Kiel skidded to a stop, sighing heavily.

Owen's house. The footprints led to the back door of Owen's house. He'd been following Owen's footprints the whole time, probably from the last time they'd all jumped into a book, which was . . . recently? Maybe?

Kiel started back toward the library, then stopped. Doyle would be long gone by now, and the only thing back there were police. But without another clue, how exactly was he supposed to find Bethany or Doyle? Especially after wasting so much time following the wrong tracks?

Wait. He *did* have another clue. The police were working with a Holmes, maybe Doyle. And that meant there was definitely a place he could go to find out more.

And he really should rescue Owen. It wouldn't do to leave his friend locked up, even if Owen had unwisely given himself up. And who else knew the boring, unmagical, nonfictional world like Owen?

With new purpose, Kiel set out for the police station, shaking his head at the idea of having to jog the whole way. Magic was just so much easier for getting around!

Kiel had been without magic before, of course. Both before he'd met the Magister, and then when the Magister had made him forget all of his magic after they'd met Bethany, and his master had gone off the deep end.

But he'd gotten the magic back . . . somehow. Somewhere in the fog, there was a memory of what he'd done.

Kiel slowly breathed in and tried to think of something, anything that'd help him remember.

Bethany's face came to mind, and he smiled in spite of himself.

Then Bethany's face morphed into Charm's, and he gasped out loud as the memory slammed into his head like a hammer.

MISSING CHAPTER 1

Two months ago . . .

"So I'm not real," Kiel Gnomenfoot said quietly, staring at his hands.

"What makes you think that?" the Magister asked, the hints of a smile playing over his face.

"I'm made of science, Magi," Kiel said, shaking his head. "Dr. Verity formed me from that unnatural—"

"Science is about as natural as you could possibly *get*," Charm said, her robotic eye narrowing in irritation. Kiel glared at her, and she turned away guiltily. "But, um, I understand your point," she finished.

"He *made* me!" Kiel said, shouting now. "I was never meant to exist. All I am is a clown—"

"Clone," Charm pointed out.

"Of the man who's currently trying to destroy Magisteria." Kiel sighed. "And Magisteria isn't even *my* world, is it? If I'm a clown—"

"Clone."

"Then I'm actually *Quanterian*." Kiel grabbed his apprentice spell book, his face contorted in anger, and threw it across the room.

The spell book froze as soon as it left his hand, then turned in midair to glare at its owner. Kiel ignored it, dropping to the floor to sit cross-legged with his head in his hands.

"I'm not even *real*," he said again.

The Magister circled around Kiel, then kneeled in front of the boy and pulled Kiel's chin up to look his apprentice in the eye. "You assume that real is something anyone would want to be."

Kiel gave his master a sad look. "Magi, now isn't the greatest time for a lesson."

"What is magic if not forcing unreality to *become* real?" the Magister asked. "So Dr. Verity recreated himself, giving us you. Do *you* want to destroy Magisteria?"

Kiel shrugged. "Only sometimes. When people annoy me."

"And what could be more real than that!" the Magister said, clapping Kiel on the shoulder.

Kiel snorted, then shook his head. "I can't be him, Magi. I *can't*! What if I turn out just like he did? What if I'm destined for evil? And look at him! *That's* what I'm going to look like when I'm older?"

"Ugh," Charm groaned, and Kiel could almost feel her rolling her eyes.

"You will be whatever you *decide* to be," the Magister told Kiel gently. "The idea of destiny is something we made up to justify whatever we wanted to do. You are no more destined to become Dr. Verity than I am to turn Alphonse into a dog."

Alphonse, Kiel's cat, stopped licking his wings for a moment to look at the Magister, then shrugged and returned to his important bathing.

"I'm not sure any of this is helping," Kiel pointed

out as he pushed to his feet. "But I suppose I don't have time to feel sorry for myself. Charm can't get the last three keys by herself—"

"Actually—"

"Even if she's far too proud to admit how much help she needs," Kiel continued. "I'll just have to soldier on and hope that my natural talent and intelligence is enough to keep me from turning into Dr. Verity."

The Magister smiled. "I have the utmost faith in your . . . talent and intelligence."

"Of course you do," Kiel said, shrugging. "We all do."

Charm clenched her fists and slowly took several deep breaths. "If we don't leave *now*, I swear I will ray gun you."

"She has trouble admitting her feelings for me," Kiel whispered to the Magister, who nodded, still smiling. Kiel walked over to stand next to Charm and made an impatient gesture. "Uh, let's *go* already."

Charm's eyes widened, and she opened her mouth to scream at him just as they both disappeared in a flash of light.

The Magister smiled, dropping into his chair. So

Kiel Gnomenfoot had finally learned he was a clone of Dr. Verity. The day the Magister had dreaded for so long had now come, and the boy was taking it about as well as anyone could, finding out that he was the creation of a madman.

But would the boy take the truth about the Source of Magic quite so well?

To be continued in Kiel Gnomenfoot and the School for Wizardry, *book five of the Kiel Gnomenfoot saga.*

"Magi?" said a soft voice from behind him, and the Magister turned around in his chair to find Kiel looking at him strangely, Charm standing just behind him. Oddly, Charm was giving the Magister a look of almost palpable hatred. Usually those looks were directed more at Kiel than himself.

"Back so soon, my boy?" the Magister asked.

"I, uh, forgot my spell book," Kiel said, and held out a hand toward the still-floating, still-angry apprentice spell book. The book floated over to him in a sulking sort of way, then shrank down to the size of a coin, and Kiel slipped it into a pouch on his belt.

"I thought you had moved beyond the need for it?" the

Magister asked. "You didn't need it to find the Fourth Key, after all."

"Can't hurt to have a backup," Kiel said, then slowly took a step back.

"Kiel," the Magister said slowly, "I know why you're here."

Kiel froze. "You do?"

"Because it occurred to you that if you're a clone, then I have misled you about your parents," the Magister said.

Kiel paused. "That's it. You're right. But just hearing you admit it, that's really enough. I should get back to things—"

"I couldn't tell you the truth, my boy," the Magister said, his voice dropping low. "I cannot apologize enough, but you had to find out on your own, when you were ready."

"I'm not sure I was *ever* ready for some truths," Kiel said.

The Magister nodded. "I understand, believe me. Truth is a sword with no hilt. We grab for it at our own peril, at times."

"The truth, like how you're secretly planning on destroying Quanterium?" Charm mumbled, and the Magister blinked. He must have misheard her.

"I'm sorry, what did you say?" he asked the glaring girl.

"Nothing," Kiel said, throwing Charm an annoyed look.

"We really should get going. Keys to find, crazy madmen to fight, that sort of thing . . ."

"Kiel," the Magister said, and opened his arms. "Please tell me you forgive me."

Kiel's eyes widened slightly, and oddly, he looked up at the ceiling. "Seriously?" he whispered to no one in particular.

"Of course I am serious," the Magister responded, a bit confused. He gestured for Kiel to hug him. "Please, my boy. I can't tell you how sorry I am to have deceived you."

Kiel gritted his teeth, then stepped forward and hugged the Magister, who smiled and let out a sigh of relief. Kiel quickly pushed back, then stepped away. "Well, gotta go!" he said, and raised a hand into the air.

"You don't have your teleport button," the Magister pointed out.

"Charm's got it," Kiel said as she took his hand.

"Good luck, my boy," the Magister said.

"Magi," Kiel said, avoiding his teacher's eyes, "if *you* ever find out something that turns your whole life upside down, like I just did, try not to turn crazy and evil. As a favor to me."

The Magister smiled. "You have my word."

Kiel sighed, then disappeared with Charm from the Magister's tower, reappearing in the middle of a dark library.

"I *really* wanted to hit him," Charm said. Kiel mumbled some words and the disguise spell faded, revealing Bethany in Charm's place.

"Did you see him *hug* me?!" Kiel shouted at her, his face contorted with disgust. "UGH. I need to bathe."

"But he's the Magister!" Owen said from where he sat on a nearby table. "You *love* him."

"It's amazing what happens to your relationship when your adopted father tries to kill you," Kiel said with a shrug. "Plus, if he hadn't forget-spelled the magic out of my head, I'd never have had to steal my own spell book in the first place." He reached into his pocket and pulled out the tiny still-sulky book, which quickly expanded into a normal-size still-sulky spell book.

"So you're sure this book has the spell?" Bethany asked, shifting her weight from foot to foot nervously.

"Trust me," Kiel said, winking at her. He tried to open the cover, and the book snapped at him. *"Hey!"* he shouted. "Bad book! Don't do that again." He pointed a finger in warning at the book, and it pouted, then flipped open to the right page.

Kiel held the book up for Owen and Bethany to see.

Illumination of Location, the page said.

"So who wants to find Bethany's father, then?" Kiel asked, grinning widely.

The memory hit Kiel hard, and it almost staggered him.

Just like it did to Owen, who looked around almost in dis-belief, his head throbbing. Where had *that* come from?

CHAPTER 15

01:42:56

Memories weren't supposed to almost knock you over. Since when did that happen? And why had it hit him so suddenly, out of nowhere? For a second Owen almost lost track of where he was, but the sight of a police officer filling out paperwork at the counter of the police station reminded him quickly enough.

Someone bumped into him, and Owen looked up to find a burly man who smelled like burned hair staring down at him. Owen quickly backed up into the police officer, who pushed him back toward the man.

One meaty hand hit Owen's shoulder. "Excuse me," the man said politely. "Sorry about that. Didn't mean to bump into you." And with that, he pulled off a beard and tossed it onto the counter, followed by his stinky overcoat.

As the man peeled off his disguise, he revealed a tailored suit, hair that wasn't even mussed by a wig, and a face with no smile lines. He patted Owen's shoulder once, then dropped the rest of the disguise onto the counter and turned to walk away.

"How'd it go, Inspector?" the officer at the counter shouted.

The man in the suit jabbed his thumb over his shoulder, and Owen turned to find police officers dragging in what looked to be an entire criminal gang, all dressed in black. "Book 'em," the man in the suit said. "These boys are going away for a long time."

Just then one of the officers yelled, and before Owen knew it, the largest of the criminals broke free and grabbed a gun from an officer's holster, aiming it right at Owen. "Let me go or the kid gets it!" the man shouted.

The man in the suit sighed and, almost faster than Owen could see, kicked the criminal in the back of the knees, grabbed the gun from midair, and punched the man in the face. The criminal collapsed to the floor, and the man in the suit handed the gun back to the officer. "Try holding on to this a bit more tightly next time," he said, then turned and walked away.

Wow. Apparently, police stations were exactly like every cop movie or TV show Owen had ever seen. Who knew those were so realistic? Right down to the innocent kid getting threatened when a criminal breaks away. It was almost a cliché, it happened so often.

Like a fictional cliché.

Owen frowned, something small and annoying tickling his brain. There was something off here. Not by much, just—

And then a shove in the back derailed his train of thought.

"Move," said the police officer who'd arrested Owen, pushing him farther into the police station. In spite of everything that was happening, a familiar feeling of excitement came over Owen. It was like when he and Charm had been under fire on the *Scientific Method*, Charm's spaceship. Sure, he was being arrested, but at least it was happening in an awesome way.

The officer led Owen down one of the quieter hallways and into an empty room with two metal chairs, a table, and one lone light—exactly what Owen expected. He was going to be interrogated! Classic.

The man shoved Owen into one of the chairs, which faced a long mirror on the wall, then slammed the door as he left, leaving Owen to stare at himself in the mirror. It was probably one-way glass, with people on the other side watching him, right? That was how it worked in movies. The boss watched as the police interrogated the criminal.

That thought killed the excitement instantly. *He* was the criminal here, and *he* was being framed for his mother's library burning down. The image of the building going up in flames hit him almost as hard as the memory of Kiel returning with his spell book did, and he felt like throwing up. He had to convince the police that he was innocent and get them to find Doyle. If not, Owen would be going to jail, probably for the rest of his life. But, even worse, he'd have to explain this to his mother!

Not to mention that Bethany was missing, and they only had . . . an hour and forty minutes left to find her before, well, *something* bad happened.

Why did this all have to be such a stupid mystery? Owen *hated* mysteries. Why spend an entire book just waiting to find out what had actually happened? It was like the world's longest magic trick, only usually really lame when you found out how it was done.

Okay, so *exactly* like the world's longest magic trick.

He'd read a bunch of mysteries, of course. Sherlock Holmes, Encyclopedia Brown, all the ones his mom recommended, but he just couldn't get into them. Magic was just so much cooler, and involved a lot fewer details and clues and convenient plot devices that revealed exactly what the detective needed to know exactly when they needed to know it.

But since he was clearly living out a mystery now, he might as well embrace it. Doyle had said he'd planned this mystery by the book, so maybe that was a hint. Owen would just have to treat this like a mystery in a book, and maybe he'd be able to figure out what was going on. So first, he needed to list the questions that needed answering.

Where is Bethany? No idea. Could be anywhere.

How did Doyle get out of his book? Bethany had to have done it. Who else could have?

But why would Bethany take Doyle out of his book? Maybe by accident? But how did you accidentally take a freakishly masked guy out of a book with you? Maybe he grabbed her at the last minute. But how would he have known to grab ahold, anyway?

And that led to the next question:

How does Doyle know who we all are? It's not like Kiel's books existed in the fictional world. Did they? Did books also exist in the fictional "real" world, the realistic place where all non–fantasy or science-fiction stories took place? Was there a library in the fictional real world with Kiel's books?

The idea of a fictional real world just gave Owen an enormous headache, so he moved on. Even if Doyle had Kiel's books, how did he know *Owen's* name? He couldn't have gotten that from any book. Maybe he'd learned it when Doyle had escaped, somehow? He just couldn't remember, and that was the most frustrating part.

Speaking of not remembering:

Why did Doyle make Kiel remove their memories? What was so important for them to not remember? Maybe where Bethany was? Even so, Doyle had gotten them arrested, so it's not like he thought they'd be able to run around looking for her. So what was the whole point? Or to put it differently:

Why is Doyle doing this? Yeah, seriously. Why?!

Okay, so those were the questions, none of which had any answers. He did have a guess here or there, but none that helped him. Perfect. This whole detectiving by the book was going *so* well.

And this was exactly why Owen hated mysteries.

Minutes passed, and Owen kept checking the watch Doyle had put on his wrist: 01:38:47. 01:37:19. 01:36:12. Where were the police? Couldn't they just throw him in jail already and get this over with?

At least Kiel was out there, a real hero. If anyone could rescue Bethany, even without any magic, it was Kiel Gnomenfoot. After all, he'd been written to do just that kind of thing, hadn't he? When Owen had tried living Kiel's life, he'd almost died. But this was what Kiel was made to do, beat the bad guys and rescue the good guys. He'd have Bethany back in no time.

Or hopefully in 01:35:34. 01:33:29. UGH.

A knock came at the door, and after a pause it opened, revealing the man in the suit from earlier. The man nodded at Owen, then turned his gaze to the file in his hands. He slowly closed the door, his attention on the file, then sat down in the chair across from Owen.

"I didn't do it!" Owen said as soon as the man's behind hit the seat.

The suited man's eyes briefly rose above the file, gave Owen a look, then went back to reading.

"Listen to me, my friend's in danger!" Owen said, his voice rising. "There's this crazy person who kidnapped her, and said that after an hour and a half I'll never see her again. She might die!"

Again the man's eyes flicked up from his file, but this time they stayed locked on Owen's. "Your friend is this Bethany Sanderson?" the man said.

"Yes!" Owen shouted, just thankful that someone had been listening. "She's *completely* not fake. She goes to my school. She has a library card. How could someone not exist but still have a library card?"

The man just looked at Owen, then glanced back down into the file. He closed it now and laid it on the table, then folded his hands on top of it, giving Owen an unreadable look. "I'm Inspector Brown," he said finally. "From the city."

The city? Which city was that? But that could wait.

"I'm Owen Conners," Owen said, sticking out his hand.

The inspector glanced down at Owen's hand, then shook his head. "I hate to say it, but you're in a lot of trouble here, Owen Conners. We've got a witness claiming you set fire to the library where your mother works. I'm told the lab boys are pulling prints now, but preliminary work suggests they're yours."

"But I didn't do it!" Owen shouted, standing up. "I saw the guy who did it! He admitted that he was framing us! *And* he kidnapped my friend!"

"Can you describe this person?" the detective said, his hands still folded.

"Yes! He's wearing some kind of weird white mask with a question mark on it." Owen paused, realizing how this sounded. "I know it's hard to believe, but it's true. And a Sherlock Holmes hat and coat."

"A deerstalker hat," the inspector said.

"What?"

"It's called a deerstalker hat, the hat that Sherlock Holmes was rumored to have worn. Not that he ever appeared in photos that way." His hands still hadn't moved, not even to jot down a note. This didn't seem to be going that great.

"You don't believe me," Owen said, falling back into his chair hard.

"Oh, I know who you're referring to," the inspector said. "But considering his history with the force and me in particular, I'd find it pretty hard to believe that he's been setting any fires."

What? History with the force? How would a fictional character have—

"Yo, Wikipedia," said a police officer, opening the door. "No sign of the other suspect. We think he got away."

The inspector flinched. "I've asked you all not to call me that," he said, and the police officer just smirked, then shrugged and shut the door. The inspector shook his head, turning back

60

to Owen. "Sorry. They think it's funny because of my child-hood nickname. Owen, do you know where your friend, this Gnomenfoot boy, might have gone? Things might go easier for you if you cooperate."

"He didn't do it either!" Owen shouted. "Don't you get it? We're being framed! I don't even know why, because none of it makes sense, but I saw this masked guy with my own eyes. He set the fire, not us. Kiel and I almost blew up! Why would we do that to ourselves?"

The detective stared at Owen for a moment, then sighed. "I've spoken to your mother, Owen. Would you like to know what she told me?"

Owen flinched. "Probably not?"

"She claims you're home in bed right now, at this moment. Said she was looking right at you." The inspector raised an eye-brow. "Now, I don't know what to make of that. Do you?"

She'd said *what*? Why would his mother lie like that? Or was there some way Kiel had cast a magic spell to make it look like Owen was still in his bed? What was *happening*?

Owen concentrated as hard as he could, trying to remember anything from earlier that night. Fighting through the fog in his brain to get to an actual memory was like trying to punch

JAMES RILEY

actual fog, though: it wasn't accomplishing anything, and probably made him look really stupid.

"Tell me about this Kiel Gnomenfoot boy," the inspector said. "We don't have any record of him, either. Did he put you up to this in some way?"

"No, he's a *good* guy," Owen said, his mind racing. Why couldn't he remember leaving that night? Kiel's magic was so annoying sometimes! "He'd never do anything like this either. We both just want to find our friend."

"Bethany Sanderson," the detective said. "You're right that there's no record of her, either. No one in your school by that name. No one in this city, even." He raised an eyebrow. "Not even a library card."

How was that possible? Owen's mind raced, launching through all kinds of different explanations. Was he going insane? Had he dreamed Bethany this entire time? Was this all a dream now?!

He pinched himself hard and jumped at the pain. Well, at least he was awake. But how could there be no record of Bethany? "That can't be true," Owen said, almost pleading with the inspector. "She's my friend! I've known her for . . . well, for just a couple of months. I think. But I've seen her for longer, in class, in school. She *exists*!"

62

The inspector sighed. "I don't know why you're lying, kid, but this is getting us nowhere," he said. "Tell me what's going on. Tell me how this all started. From the beginning."

"I don't know!" Owen said, dropping his head into his hands. "I don't—"

But just like that, a memory hit him like a hammer, and he *did* know.

MISSING CHAPTER 2

One month ago . . .

The library was silent, with just one light left on in the back by the study tables, which were all covered in books. As if by itself, one of the books opened, and a cartoon hand pushed its way out, followed by two lines for an arm and a doodle of a head.

"So weird!" Bethany said as she emerged, her mouth in the shape of a large O, while her ponytail lines bounced behind her. She used her cartoon hands to pull herself all the way out of the book, then reached in to pull out two more life-size doodles.

"But *so fun*!" Owen said, a smile line stretching from one side of his round head to the other. "Look at this!" He yanked on the lines that made his body, then released them, letting them twang back into place. "It's like they're rubber bands!"

"I know I agreed to this," said Kiel, "but when you said 'diary,' I can't say I was expecting *that*." He held one cartoon hand up to his circle mouth as if he might vomit.

"Turn us back already, will you?" Bethany told Kiel, gesturing with her four pudgy fingers for him to hurry. "The last thing I want to do is figure out how to go to the bathroom like this."

"Wait!" Owen said as Kiel raised his cartoon hands into the air, holding two straight lines that were his wands. "Just give me, like, five more minutes. I want to see how far I can pull my arms out before they snap back."

Bethany sighed and shook her head. "That is the last time we go into an Owen book," she whispered to Kiel. *The last time.*

Kiel waved his wands, and he and Bethany both immediately turned back into their normal selves, Bethany in jeans and a T-shirt, her red hair in a ponytail, Kiel wearing all black, with his cape and wand-knife holsters.

Owen, still a cartoon, grinned widely as he began tying one arm to the table leg.

"So?" Kiel said to Bethany as he took deep breaths, thankfully not looking quite so sick anymore. "Are you ready now? You said we should all pick one adventure to have before we do this, and we've done that. Some were . . . *odder* than others, but . . ."

Bethany couldn't help smiling at Owen slowly pulling his body away from the table, grunting as the arm tied to the table began stretching. "Everyone has their own idea of fun."

"At least mine didn't almost get us eaten," Owen said, then returned to his pulling.

"By fake dragons, no less," Kiel pointed out.

"They're called *dinosaurs*," Bethany said with a sigh. "And unlike dragons, they actually were real here. But now they only exist in stories, so I wanted to see them. I still feel like you two missed the entire point of that."

"My arm's taller than I am!" Owen said, and turned to show them, only to have his arm snap back, yanking him with it right into the table. Owen hit hard enough for little stars to pop out above his head as his pupils turned around and around in his eye circles. "Owwww," he moaned as Bethany and Kiel just lost it.

It took a few minutes before Bethany could even speak, and even then she had to wipe tears from her eyes. "Please do that again?" she said, her voice still high-pitched from all her laughing. "I vote you stay in cartoon form for the rest of the night, and just do that over and over."

"Mean," Owen said, his frown filling up his face. "*Fine*, turn me back."

"You don't want to try using your body as a bow and arrow first?" Bethany asked.

"I mean, *yes*, but not if you're going to make fun of me for it," Owen said, and nodded at Kiel. The magician, still laughing, mumbled the spell and Owen instantly turned back to his normal self. He pushed himself to his feet, then held out both arms in front of him, frowning. "Does the right one still look longer?"

"Definitely," Bethany said, wiping the smile from her face. "Like, by at least a few inches."

"Are you serious?" Owen said, frantically trying to measure them. "Kiel, turn me back, *quick*. I need to fix this!"

"So are you ready?" Kiel asked Bethany, ignoring Owen. "You promised we'd do the spell tonight. We can't keep putting it off forever."

Bethany's joy faded, and a chill went through her body. "Are you sure you don't want to jump in another story? We could each pick another one. . . ."

Kiel grabbed Bethany's shoulders and turned her around, giving her a comforting smile. "Don't worry," he told her quietly. "Your father is fine, wherever he is. I'll use the location spell, we'll jump into whichever book he's in, and that'll be that. You'll have your dad back home by morning."

"It might even be *more* than a few inches," Owen said, squinting at his arms.

Bethany winced. "*If* my father's okay. And if he even *wants* to come back."

"Of course he will," Kiel told her, giving her a confused look. "How could he ever not want to see his daughter?"

Bethany swallowed hard, not wanting to think of all the reasons. She'd come up with a long list over the last few days, ever since she'd jumped Kiel back into his series to retrieve his old practice spell book. Owen and Kiel had wanted to use the location spell that same night to find her father, but she'd convinced them that they should all pick one last story, since bringing her father back would definitely put an end to their adventures. It was hard enough to hide what she'd been doing from her mother. Her father showing up would pretty much get her grounded for a few hundred years.

But that wasn't the real reason. There were too many bad ways this could go, and now that it was finally here, she half expected the worst. Maybe even three-fourths.

"We can still wait if you're truly not ready," Kiel said, but Bethany could see him practically dancing from foot to foot, anxious to finally get on with it.

"No, let's just do it. I'm ready enough." Kiel seemed to believe her lie, so she turned to Owen, who was trying to shove his arm toward his shoulder. "Can you be serious for a second? We're doing this."

Owen flashed a look at her, then straightened up immediately and nodded. "Totally serious. Not that my arm being longer isn't serious too, but that can wait. Though really, not for much longer." Still holding one arm, he led the other two to the center of the library, where Bethany turned to look at Owen and Kiel.

"I've used this spell before," Bethany told them. "When I cast it in the Magister's tower to find Jonathan Porterhouse, the spell created a little ball of light that floated off to the right book. So just be ready to follow it, okay?"

Kiel looked hurt. "I *have* used my magic before, you know."

Bethany glared at him, and he shrugged. "But sure, we'll do what you say." He then winked at Owen, who giggled, which managed to make her more irritated.

Kiel pulled a wand from its sheath and began to speak the words for the location spell, as Bethany's hands and feet both turned to ice. What if her father wasn't alive? Or what if he was, but he'd moved on and had a new family? Or what if he'd been trapped this entire time, tortured by some evil villain, all because of her? Her heart beat so quickly she almost couldn't think straight.

But then a small ball of light appeared right in front of Kiel's wand, and Bethany stopped breathing completely.

All three of them leaned forward, waiting to see where it'd go. The ball hung in place for just a moment, then jumped toward the mysteries section.

Bethany's heart leaped into her throat, and she took a step to follow it, only to stop as the light paused in midair. It seemed to shake just a bit, then move toward the romance books.

Then it paused again and just quivered in midair, like it wasn't sure where to go.

"What's it doing?" Owen whispered.

"I don't know, I've never seen this before," Kiel whispered back.

The ball trembled harder and harder and began to glow brighter as it did, the light soon becoming hard to look at. As it shook, smaller balls of light exploded out of the original, flying off in every direction. First dozens, then hundreds, maybe even thousands of balls filled the air, so bright that Bethany could barely see anything, as if the sun had just appeared in the middle of the room.

"Turn it off!" Owen shouted. "Someone's going to see!"

Kiel shouted some magic words, but the balls of light kept popping out of the first one, then flying off into every corner of the library. Finally, the original ball flew off as well, and the three kids covered their eyes as best they could to see where the light balls had gone.

They didn't have to look far.

Each and every book in the library had a ball of light directly in front of it.

Every single book.

Bethany's mouth opened and closed, but no sound came out. Somewhere in the distance a siren began blaring, and Owen grabbed her hand, pulling her toward the door of the library. She stumbled after him as Kiel followed, behind them the location spells fading away into nothing.

None of them said another word as they quietly made their way into the bushes beside the library while a police car slowly pulled up. The police officer shined his light into the now-dark building, then shrugged and got back into his car. A moment later he pulled away, and Kiel and Owen both turned to Bethany, their eyes filled with questions.

"I knew it," she whispered, her voice trembling. "*I knew it*. It never works. Nothing does. This is my fault, and he's never coming back."

"Bethany," Kiel started to say, but she shoved him away.

"NO!" she shouted. "I'm done, do you hear me? I give up! I can't do this anymore! I just . . . I can't take this. He's gone and he's never coming back. And I'm done! Leave me alone!"

And with that, she turned and ran, the cold wind whipping her face so hard she found it covered in tears by the time she got home. Once there, she snuck up to her room, locked the door, and screamed as loudly as she could right into her pillow, until her throat hurt and she saw spots in front of her eyes.

Finally, she reached under her bed, grabbed a specific book, and dove right in, not wanting to spend another minute in the real world.

CHAPTER 16

01:29:56

With water reaching almost to her knees, Bethany rocked the chair left and right as hard as she could. Finally, momentum sent her over the edge, crashing the chair onto its side and spraying water in every direction.

"AH!" she shouted as the cold water splashed over her from head to toe. Why did it have to be cold? Couldn't this stupid death trap at least have had warm water?

She bent forward in the chair, trying to see where the ropes were attached from her ankles to the chair. As far as she could tell, it looked like the ropes had been tied to the chair's feet. She managed to slip the knots down off the chair legs, then pulled her legs up to her and untied the ropes, freeing her ankles.

Unfortunately, the chains around her wrists were a different story. They looked to be bolted to the chair legs somehow.

She groaned, then took a deep breath, trying to stay calm. There had to be a way out of this. She pulled on the chains, but the chain links bit into her wrists painfully the harder she pulled, and when she tried grabbing the chain itself, she found it was far too slippery to hold on to. Wrapping the chain around her hand was even more painful than just pulling with her wrists.

After a few minutes of experimenting, she pushed her head into the arm of the chair and screamed as loud as she could.

"You seem to be having some difficulty," said a strange voice from somewhere behind her. Bethany instantly looked up, but saw no one.

"Who's there?" she said, not liking how vulnerable she felt, chained up and about to drown.

"Nobody important," the voice said. "I do think it's time we had a little chat, if you don't mind."

Bethany wanted to laugh. A little chat? Who *was* this? "Did Doyle send you?"

"No," the voice said. "He has no idea that I'm here."

"He does now," Bethany said. "He's got cameras all over this place."

"He won't see *me*," the voice said. "I'm here to speak to you. Alone."

That sounded promising. Either that, or he was going to kill her. "Could you help me, then? Get these chains off of me?"

"You can get out yourself. We both know you can."

Bethany eyes widened in surprise, and again, she tried to turn to look at whoever was speaking to her. She caught the briefest glimpse of what looked like the top of a bald head before whoever it was pulled back out of sight. "Who *are* you?" she said, not entirely sure she wanted to know.

"I already told you. Nobody of consequence. But I'm not here to talk about me. We need to discuss your trips into the fictional world, Bethany."

Even with the freezing water, somehow that statement made Bethany feel even colder. "I don't know what you're talking about," she lied, trying not to show how terrified she was.

"Yes, you do," the voice said. "And the trips need to stop. You're never going to find what you're looking for."

"And what's that?" she asked slowly, her heart racing. "What am I looking for?"

"Your father," the voice said, and Bethany almost stopped breathing. "What you're doing is dangerous, girl. Far more dangerous than you realize. There are people in the fictional world who'd do anything to find you, if they learned of your existence. For now, they're unaware, but every time you enter a story, every time something like *this* happens, you create ripples." She heard the person dip what she imagined was a hand into the water, then watched as small waves passed by the chair. "Too many ripples, and people start to notice."

"Who?" Bethany said quietly. "Who are these people?"

"The less you know, the better," the voice said. "For now, just believe me when I tell you that you need to stop."

"No!" she shouted, jerking around in the chair and trying to get a better look, even though the chains bit painfully into her skin. "Tell me who they are. Tell me who *you* are! How do you know me? Do you know where my father is? *I need to know!* Please!"

"Stop trying to find him," the voice said, almost sounding sympathetic. "Looking will only lead to darkness and pain for both worlds. Let him go, and take solace in what you still have: a mother who loves you."

Bethany growled in frustration. "I'm not going to stop!" she screamed. "I *will* find him, I don't care what it takes!"

"And that attitude is what got you here."

Her eyes widened. "How do you know any of this?"

"Oh, I know far more than you think," the voice said. "I

know about you and your friends . . . even your father. So believe me when I tell you that you must *never* find him. That is all I can say."

"No, please!" Bethany shouted. "Help me get out of these chains. Let me see who you are!"

"You know how to free yourself," the voice said, getting farther away.

"No, I *can't*," she said, not sure if there was water on her face or if she was crying. "I can't do it again. Not to *them*, too. I can't!"

"It's the only way," the voice said, even farther now. "You must leave and save yourself."

"Please, help me!" she shouted. *"Please!"*

"I saw what you did on Argon VI," the voice said, and this time she could barely hear it. "I know how you feel, and what this means to you. That is why I *cannot* release you. Escape, Bethany. Leave all of this behind, and forget about it. The worlds will both be safer if you do."

Argon VI?! How could this person have seen her there? "What do you mean?" she shouted. "How would they be safer?"

But this time there was no response.

Bethany shouted again, and flailed around in the chair so

hard that she splashed water all over herself. Crying in frustration, she yanked on the chains over and over, but all she did was make her hands bleed from the hard metal.

Argon VI. How could anyone have seen her there? She hadn't told Owen or Kiel. Doyle didn't know. *No one* knew, other than EarthGirl.

The memory of her time on the other planet filled her mind, and somehow, it actually managed to calm her down. She stared at the chains, then at her red, scratched hands, and finally at the chair she was laying on.

She'd been going about this the wrong way. Too much doing, not enough thinking.

She dropped the chains, and instead reached behind her for the soaking wet cushion on the chair, which she pulled out as best she could. Once she'd managed to get it off the chair, she unzipped the cover and yanked out the cushion. That she tossed aside, then took the cushion cover and wrapped it around her hands for protection.

Then she grabbed the chains again.

The cover protected her skin enough for her to pull as hard as she could. First one chair leg, then the other pulled free, and instantly she jumped to her feet, pulling against the heavy weight of the unattached chains on her wrists, searching for whoever had been talking to her.

Except nobody was there, and there was no way out of the room, other than the door Doyle had used. And that had been in her sight the entire time.

Who was her visitor? And how had he managed to see her on a completely different planet?!

MISSING CHAPTER 3

One month ago, the same night . . .

The green sun of Argon VI beat down on Bethany as she punched a hole straight through a mountain, screaming at the top of her lungs until her throat hurt. She leaped into the air, flying hundreds of feet into the yellow sky, then turned her laser vision on the desert floor beneath her, burning the sand into glass. She then dove back down to the surface, splintering the glass into dust so fine it felt like snow.

"WHERE ARE YOU?" she screamed into the empty sky as she sank to her knees, her voice like thunder. She punched the ground a few more times, tears falling and mixing with the dirt on her face. "WHY CAN'T I FIND YOU?"

She leaped back into the air and rocketed off toward the ocean, a sonic boom exploding behind her. She hit the water with a sound like a bomb going off, tunneling through it so quickly that she left only steam behind her, then aimed straight down. She hit the sea floor hard enough to send tremors in all directions, then spun around in a circle as fast as she could, twisting the water into a funnel all the way to the surface, an enormous whirlpool a mile deep.

She stopped, and as the ocean water began to collapse in on her, she clenched her fists and exploded up through it, leaving behind another cloud of steam as she flew off—

Only to be hit in the face by something that felt hard as a rock. Everything went dark as Bethany spun around, crashing back to the ground in the middle of a field, sending corn flying. She looked up in surprise and found someone floating in the air in front of her: a girl in jeans and a white T-shirt with a blue ball on it and a black hoodie that covered her face. Beneath the hood two red eyes glowed like lasers, and Bethany could feel the heat from where she stood.

No. *No, no, no!* What had she done?!

"Good morning!" EarthGirl said, her burning eyes staring straight into Bethany's. "Now, I'm not sure who you are or why you're being all crazy. But please stop destroying things, if you don't mind. Wouldn't you rather just discuss your problem, so I can help you fix it?" The glow in her eyes began to fade, and she gave Bethany an embarrassed look. "I'm really sorry I punched you, by the way. I *hate* punching. It always feels so ridiculous."

"I . . . I can't talk to you," Bethany said, frantically trying to figure out what page in EarthGirl: *Doomsday on Argon VI* she'd jumped into. Was she interrupting the plot? Had she just pulled EarthGirl away from something important? "I'm sorry, for . . . for all of this. I need to go." And with that, Bethany took off into the air, another sonic boom exploding behind her.

"Thank you!" EarthGirl said from right beside her, her voice somehow reaching Bethany despite them both flying faster than the speed of sound. "Apologies are a good place to start. But I've never met anyone who could do what *I* do before. What's your name?"

"It's not important," Bethany said, abruptly skidding to a halt in midair. The green sun gave anyone from Earth super-powers here, which meant that anywhere Bethany could go, EarthGirl could easily follow.

"I'm Gwen," EarthGirl said, pulling her hoodie off to reveal a dark-skinned girl about Bethany's age with long brown hair. She stuck out her hand, then wrinkled her nose at it. "I hope

I'm not offending you. I've read that people from my home planet used to greet each other this way, with their hands. I'm from a place named Ay-arth."

"Earth," Bethany corrected, then winced.

"So you *do* know it," Gwen said, a small smile playing over her face.

Bethany turned bright red. "You tricked me?" How many rules could she break here at once? Talking to a main character was bad enough, but EarthGirl knew that there were other people who knew about Earth now too!

Gwen shrugged. "Not tricking so much as just skipping some steps. What's your name?"

Ugh. "Bethany," she said, taking Gwen's hand. "I really, really hope you weren't busy just now. Because if I'm interrupting anything—"

"Nah," Gwen said, waving a hand. "I just finished disassembling this robot thing that was trying to destroy the world. A girl at school built it. We're actually good friends." She sighed. "Well, she's friends with Gwen. She kind of hates EarthGirl." She pointed at the T-shirt she wore. "It's a whole thing, and I keep wanting to fix it, but, honestly, I have no idea how."

"Sounds complicated," Bethany said, inwardly sighing with

relief. If Gwen had completed the book's story, at least Bethany might not be changing much, assuming she got away without making things worse. "Listen, I really shouldn't take up more of your time. I was just in the, uh, solar system, and—"

"So you're from Earth too?" Gwen said, pulling Bethany gently by the hand back to the ground. "How did you survive it blowing up? How did you get here? *I have so many questions!*"

"I know you do," Bethany told her, inwardly screaming. "And I promise, someday you're going to find out everything you want to know." Like, two books from now, even. "But I'm not the one to tell you, okay? Trust me. I'm . . . I'm just like you, I have no idea how I survived, or where I am."

Gwen's face fell, and Bethany felt even worse. "Listen, I'm sorry," Gwen said. "I didn't mean to be so pushy. Of course you don't have to tell me anything you don't want to."

"It's not that, really!" Bethany said quickly.

"I hope I'm not weirding you out," Gwen said. "It's so hard to know anything about Earth culture. All I have are some old books my parents put in my rocket, but most of those were about these people called detectives, who are always solving crimes." She sighed. "I'm trying to be a good detective *here*, on Argon VI, but I never know if I'm doing a good job, or if I'd just be embarrassing my real parents, you know?" She paused, her eyes lighting up again. "Wait. Do *you* know anything about detectives?"

She had to get away. This conversation could only lead to bad, bad things. But how? Could she burrow into the ground fast enough to hide before Gwen caught up, so she could jump out of the book? "Sure," Bethany answered, glancing around for a likely spot. "You're doing a great job. Detectives solve crimes, help the police, that kind of thing. Just like what you're doing."

"The police, yeah!" Gwen said, getting excited. "They show up a lot! Only they're usually not very smart, and the detectives have to figure things out for them."

Bethany half smiled in spite of herself. "Don't believe everything you read."

"Bethany, please, talk to me," Gwen said, sitting down on the ground and locking her arms around her knees. "Who are you? Where do you come from? I'll take whatever I can get. I just . . . I just really want to know about my parents and my world."

Bethany gritted her teeth. Maybe she could run fast enough to disappear into the distance before Gwen was back on her feet? She started to turn, then looked down at her hand, which Gwen had grabbed. *"Please,"* Gwen said, her expression one

Bethany had seen far too often on her own face. "Please, I just need to *know*."

And suddenly, the rules just didn't seem that important. "I'm . . . from the future," Bethany said, thinking of the plot of an upcoming EarthGirl book. "I've come back to your time to . . . to look for *my* father. He's lost here somewhere, but I have no idea how to find him."

"The future?" Gwen said, her eyes widening. "There are Earth people in the future? How?"

"I can't tell you that," Bethany said, hating herself for lying to this poor girl. "It'd mess up the entire time line. You know how it is."

Gwen nodded, but her face fell. "Oh. Sure, I guess. Well, at least I can help you find your father. Let's get started. Where have you looked?"

Bethany just stared at her. "You can't . . . I mean, I appreciate the help, but—"

"Detectives help *find* people, Bethany," Gwen said, leaping to her feet. "If I'm going to be one, then this is the least I can do. Besides, you seem nice, when you're not breaking up my mountains." She grinned, and for a moment Bethany almost considered letting her help.

Then something she had said sank in.

"Detectives help find people," Bethany whispered, and all the frustration and horribleness of the night faded away, just like that. "Gwen," she said quietly, "you have no idea how amazing you are. Spectacular. Incredible. All the adjectives."

Gwen blushed, then shoved Bethany's shoulder, a hit that would have sent Bethany flying if she hadn't dug her feet into the ground. "*Stop* it," Gwen said, smiling shyly. "I'm sure all Earth people are like this."

Bethany started to laugh, then stopped and nodded instead. "Yes. They are. All Earth people are incredibly nice and helpful." She hugged Gwen, then stepped back. "*Thank you*, seriously. So much." And then she said something she never, ever thought she'd say. Part of her screamed at the idea, but the rest of her didn't care. "Maybe I can come back and hang out a little more, when I'm done?"

"That'd be great!" Gwen said, giving her a grin as she pulled her hoodie over her head. "By the way, I hope you think this costume of our people is respectful toward them?"

"Very," Bethany said, and laughed. "I love it!" She waved good-bye, then clicked a nonexistent communicator on her wrist. "Bethany, ready to beam back to the future!" she said to no one, then jumped back out of the book, figuring her "time travel" would account for her just disappearing.

As soon as she hit her bed, she got on her computer and searched the online catalog at the library. The first few books she found, she dismissed. It couldn't be anything too obvious, or too big. Nothing that was still going. Had to be a series that was over, and one that as few people as possible had read.

There. Perfect. She clicked the reserve button, just to make sure it was there tomorrow.

Detective books. Why hadn't she thought of this before? When someone went missing, of *course* you went to a detective.

And thanks to the library, she had just reserved one of the greatest detectives of all time.

CHAPTER 17

01:28:49

Kiel rubbed his aching head as he pushed himself off the alleyway's wall, where he'd been leaning after the last memory hit. That one had come out of nowhere (and wasn't the most useful for the current situation) but at least his memories were returning, if slowly.

Still, sometimes magic really *did* create headaches.

But there was no time to waste feeling sorry for himself. Bethany had a little less than ninety minutes before he'd never see her again, and Kiel was no closer now than he'd been twenty minutes ago.

Why couldn't he have his magic? This would be done in seconds! Or even Charm? She always knew what to do in these situations. Sure, Kiel liked to give her a hard time, but only because she enjoyed it so much. And without Charm, he'd never have found so much as the First Key to the Source of Magic, let alone any of the others.

But Charm was far away in Quanterium, and he was stuck in the nonfictional world. Here, he needed an expert on the boring and normal. Here, he needed *Owen*.

With a groan, Kiel started back out toward the police station, each extra minute weighing heavily on his mind. What if he ran out of time and was too late to rescue Bethany? Sure, he couldn't remember the past month or so of their time together, but what Kiel could remember made him smile. And not the smile he flashed for other people, the one designed to put them at ease, to make them think Kiel had a plan and knew what he was doing. Not even the smile he gave Charm to make her secretly enjoy herself in spite of everything.

No, this smile was just for *himself*, and that . . . that was something Kiel had never really felt before.

Bethany was just so unlike anyone he'd ever known. All her rules, all her worries made him want to grab her hand and jump off a cliff with her, just to see her excitement break through. The times when she had just let go and gone fictional, she'd seemed so happy, and the memory gave Kiel a warm feeling throughout his chest.

The sight of the police station, though, killed that feeling. He paused a block away, watching the police cars skidding to a stop outside of it and the steady flow of criminals in and police officers out. Busy night, apparently.

Kiel wiped his hands on his pants, not sure why his palms were so sweaty. He'd done this before, been in police stations dozens of times. The Science Police had picked him up constantly when he was just a thief on the streets.

So why was he so nervous? Kiel Gnomenfoot didn't do nervous . . . at least not so anyone could tell. What would his fans all think if they knew that he was terrified half the time? They'd be let down, and that was something Kiel wasn't ever going to let happen.

He wiped his hands again, pasted a smug grin on his face, and stepped confidently toward the police station. He'd find Owen, they'd escape, and together they'd find Bethany in minutes. Owen would know what to do. This was his world, and he knew this Doyle guy.

It'd all be okay. It'd definitely all be okay.

So why wasn't he moving?

Kiel looked down at his traitorous lower limbs. *Hmm.* Apparently his feet were making this more difficult than it needed to be. He gave them an annoyed look and forced his leg to step forward.

It refused, staying put exactly where he'd had it.

What was happening? Kiel Gnomenfoot, boy magician and savior of all Magisteria, was scared of being caught by the police? Just because he had no magic and no idea what he was doing in this world? Just because for the first time in his life, he honestly wasn't sure he'd be able to get back out once he stepped inside the police station?

Maybe his feet knew more than he did.

Kiel backed away into the shadows, realizing his heart was racing. This was ridiculous! He was Kiel Gnomenfoot! He'd faced down dragons, fought crazy clones of himself, and even gone past the edge of existence. Just because he was completely powerless now, that didn't mean that he couldn't handle himself.

And yet, somehow his palms were sweaty again.

"You made it!" said a voice to his side, and Kiel quickly turned to find a girl about his age with light-brown skin, her long black hair held down with a tight black hat, which matched the rest of her dark clothes. She was also grinning hugely.

Kiel instantly flashed a smile at her in return, letting himself fall back into old habits. It felt good, actually. "I did," he said, unsure what she was talking about.

Before he could ask, the girl threw her arms around him and hugged him quickly. "I thought you'd *never* show up," the girl continued, pushing him away. "This is so exciting, isn't it?"

Ah, a fan. "You must think I look like the dashing hero of the Kiel Gnomenfoot series," he said, using his smug grin.

The girl laughed. "*Nothing* you say makes sense. *Love it.* Never change! Where've you been? I've been waiting forever for you!"

"I get that a lot," Kiel told the girl, then winked.

The girl laughed, then winked back immediately.

Kiel paused, not entirely sure what to do with that. He winked again, and she did too.

"What's happening here?" he said.

"Like *I* know?" the girl said, grinning widely as she shook her head. "I followed that other guy here, like, a half hour ago, but I thought you got lost or something. But you're here now, so we can get moving, my handsome little koala! Time to set this plan into motion, am I right?" She winked again.

This was *not* how these things usually went. "Can we step back a bit?" Kiel asked. "I'm honestly not one hundred percent sure who you are."

The girl nodded. "You're so right. Who are *any* of us? Let's seriously get moving, though." With that, she shoved Kiel forward, out into the road leading to the police station.

Kiel immediately jumped back into the shadows. "Wait a second. *I don't know who you are.*"

The girl gave him an odd look. "You don't?" She looked down at herself. "I mean, I'm in my work clothes, but I don't look that different. Are you just messing with me?" She slowly grinned at him. "You're *totally* messing with me. *I love this.* You guys are so fun!"

Kiel just looked at her helplessly for a moment, then put up his hands in apology. "No, I mean . . . I've had some problems with my memory. It's a whole thing. Magic and all."

"Oh, *totally*," the girl said, and winked. "Magic. Of course."

"Stop that!" Kiel shouted, then put his hands back up as the girl's smile faded into a more dangerous look. "Look, sorry, it's just hard to concentrate when you keep doing that."

The girl gave him a careful look, then shrugged, the smile exploding back over her face. "No need to apologize. Let's just get going!" She grabbed his arm and pulled him back toward the police station.

This was clearly another missing memory, so all he had to do was trigger it. Kiel pulled the girl to a stop, then when she turned around, stared her right in the face for a good ten seconds. Then he closed his eyes, focusing on her face, willing the memory to come. Anticipating the pain, he gritted his teeth and waited for the memory to smack him across the face.

Instead of the memory, though, he got an actual slap.

"Wake up!" the girl said. "I think I lost you there. Did you faint? You fainted, didn't you. You stared at me for a second, then looked like you had to go to the bathroom. Kind of like a koala, weirdly. Is this normal for you?"

Kiel put a hand up to his cheek, which throbbed where she'd slapped him. "Not even a little bit."

"Then follow the plan, my magical koala." She laughed, then grabbed his arm and pulled him toward the police station again.

"Um, we're going to get caught if we get any closer," Kiel told her.

"Uh, *yeah*?" she said. "That's the idea!" Then she turned toward the station and raised her voice. "Hey, cops! Aren't you looking for this guy? I found him. Kiel Gnomenfoot. Come and get him!"

And with that, every police officer around the station glanced up. Kiel's eyes widened and he turned to run, only to feel a jolt like lightning hit his side, and he dropped to the ground, twitching.

The girl in black stood over him, a small sparking device in her hand shooting little blue bolts. "Wow, that was *fun*," she said. "Hope it didn't hurt much. Did it? A lot? Sorry. But still, *how much do I love my Taser*? Anyway, enjoy!"

And with that, she ran off, laughing as Kiel twitched on the ground, police officers surrounding him on all sides.

CHAPTER 18

01:18:12

Owen sat in a different room in the police station, this one a bit more comfortable than the interrogation room, but with the door no less locked. It didn't escape him that there wasn't even a window. Apparently, the police were taking no chances.

After the last memory attack, Inspector Brown had given him some aspirin and said that his mother was on her way now, which almost made Owen's head ache even more. Beyond having to explain exactly what he'd been doing in the library (um, *not lighting it on fire!*), there was the fact that she'd told the police he was still in bed. What did that mean? Was she trying to cover for him, somehow? He snorted. *His* mom? But what else could it be?

All of this would be so much easier if he could just remember what had happened before he'd woken up in the library!

Owen growled in frustration and smacked his head over and over, hoping to jar out some more memories. All of this was beginning to feel like one of those terrible stories, where half of it took place in the present, and the rest was told in flashbacks. So irritating. You knew the characters would be okay during the flashbacks because you were seeing them in the present too, so the flashbacks were always boring. Why couldn't those writers just tell the story the *normal* way?

Again, a tiny part of Owen's brain began trying to tell him something, but he couldn't quite get ahold of it, like it was a slippery water balloon covered in oil. Whatever it was could wait, though. Right now, he needed to remember.

Maybe the flashback thing could help? Sure, it was more of a fictional thing. You didn't flash back in the real world, you just remembered things. But it's not like anything was happening like it was supposed to tonight. There was no record of Bethany anywhere, a second Owen was home asleep, and his library had just been burned down by a fictional character.

At this point thinking a little fictionally might help. Besides, what else did he have to do here in the police station? Wait to either be thrown in jail by the cops or grounded until he was a million by his mom?

Owen took a deep breath and focused on flashing backward, trying to mentally push himself into the past. He brought up the first memory that'd hit him, the day when Kiel had gone back into his series to recover his spell book. That'd been a quick memory, just Kiel and Bethany as Charm (sigh . . .) jumping out of the book. But the next flashback had been much longer, when Kiel had used the finder spell to find Bethany's dad.

But what had happened next? Bethany had told them she didn't want to go into any more books, and . . . and *what*?

"Flash . . . *back*," he whispered, rubbing his temples. "Flashback! Flassssssh baaaaaack." Ugh. Nothing. He swung his head in circles, trying to drag the memories to the surface, but that didn't help either. Finally, out of options, he scrunched his eyes closed, took a deep breath, then banged his head on the table.

"AH!" he shouted, grabbing his poor skull, still entirely memoryless. Clearly, forcing a flashback was just not going to happen.

Not without, maybe, something *bigger*, at least. Owen glanced around the room for something to hit himself over the head with, but other than the table (which he'd just tried), there wasn't anything too promising.

Ugh. This was so frustrating! He glanced at his watch, and realized that in another eighty-five minutes or so, Bethany really *would* disappear. Maybe that's what had happened? Had Doyle somehow removed all record of her from the police database? And maybe he'd been the one to put a fake Owen in Owen's real bed!

But why would he have done those things? Why would he have done *any* of these things? Owen sighed, dropping his head into his hands.

At least Kiel was out there, looking for Bethany. Kiel the hero would actually get the job done, unlike Owen, sitting here uselessly in a police station, powerless, planless, hopeless. Kiel had been right. He should have trusted the magician, and not turned himself in to the police. That's what a nonfictional sidekick did, not a fictional awesome person.

Kiel Gnomenfoot would never be caught dead in a police station. Not *Kiel Gnomenfoot, Magic Thief*.

The door flew open, and Kiel Gnomenfoot, magic thief, stumbled inside, looking shaken and weirdly twitchy. A police officer smirked at Owen, then closed the door behind Kiel and locked it.

"Kiel?!" Owen shouted, standing up just in time to have the

boy magician slump into his arms. "What are you doing here? Did you get caught?"

Kiel gave him a dazed look. "I think? I came to rescue you. But then there was this *odd* girl, and things went downhill from there."

For some reason Owen suddenly wanted to hit the boy magician, and he briefly considered dropping Kiel to the floor. "You're supposed to be finding Bethany, not rescuing me! Get out of here and go find her!"

"Find her where?" Kiel said, using Owen's shoulders to steady himself. "I had no idea where to even look, Owen. I need your help. You're from around here. Where do we start?"

"We don't start *anywhere*, not now!" Owen said, shouting again. "We're both locked up in the police station, meaning neither of us is saving Bethany!"

"I thought you said this was the right thing to do," Kiel said, giving Owen a half-annoyed, half-still-dazed look. "Isn't this what you wanted?"

"No. *Yes*. I thought so, but they won't listen to me. They keep saying she doesn't exist." Owen dropped into his seat in frustration. "They think *we* did it. I have no idea what else to say. How could Bethany not be in their records? I don't get it!"

"Forget about the police," Kiel said, sitting down thankfully in the seat across from Owen. "Focus on the *enemy*. If we find Doyle, we find Bethany. Have you figured out his clues?"

"Clues?" Owen said. "You mean how he said he did this by the book? All that means is he did things the official way, according to the rules. What does that even mean? There aren't any rules for kidnapping someone and setting fire to a library. And if there are, then I feel like that's really messed up!"

"He also said we'd understand if we knew where we were," Kiel pointed out.

Owen's eyes widened. "I think I've made it pretty clear! We're in the police station, and we're not getting out!"

"Calm down," Kiel said, forcing a shaky grin. "You're with *Kiel Gnomenfoot*, remember? I've got this. I'll get us out of here in no time." He winced. "Assuming I don't have another stupid memory come back."

Owen's eyes widened. "You got those too? I've had two memories, one of you getting your spell book back—"

"And the other of us using the finder spell," Kiel finished, giving him a confused look. "Hmm. I must have modified the forget spell I used on us somehow so our memories would return." He grinned for real this time. "I'm amazing!"

"There has to be a reason Doyle made us forget everything," Owen said. "There has to be something important that we've forgotten. Like how he got out of his book, or where Bethany is. Or how he knows who we are in the first place."

"Well, I'm not just sitting here until I remember," Kiel said. "And neither are you. We're going to escape, and then you and I are going to find Bethany, memories or no."

Owen just shook his head. "Don't you get it? If I leave now, I'll be a fugitive. They won't stop until they find me, and then I'll go to a juvenile detention center or something. For the rest of my *life*, Kiel. I can't leave. You'll have to go."

Kiel frowned. "Bethany's life is in danger, remember? Nothing else matters."

"But *you're* going to save her. That's what you do!"

Kiel shrugged. "Of course I do. And now you will too. You saved Charm, and you basically defeated Dr. Verity—"

"No, *you* did that. I messed everything up." Owen shook his head. "It's okay, you don't need to pep-talk me. I know I'm sort of the sidekick here. You have magic, and Bethany has her half-fictional powers, and all I have is that I've read a lot of books. Not exactly a superpower, you know?"

Kiel gave him a long look, then shook his head. "You're coming. And you're going to be a hero, just like I am. And then I'm going to wink, and it's going to be amazing." And he winked, and Owen couldn't help but smile.

"Kiel, this is something you don't come back from," he said.

Kiel nodded, ignoring Owen as he stood up and moved closer to the door, pulling out a small wire from his cloak. Kiel inserted the wire into the door, and a moment later, something clicked. Kiel grinned at Owen, then quietly opened the door.

"The hall's clear," Kiel whispered. "As soon as I say go, follow me as quickly as you can, okay?"

"Kiel, I *can't*—"

"One," Kiel said, watching the hallway. "Two—"

The door flew open, and Inspector Brown and two police officers stood in it. "Three," Inspector Brown said. "Grab Mr. Gnomenfoot for me, will you boys? It's his turn for questioning."

Kiel tried to duck under their arms, but there was nowhere to go, and a second later they had Kiel's hands cuffed behind his back.

"Bring him to interrogation," Inspector Brown said, gesturing out into the hall with his thumb. "I'll be there in a second."

The two police officers nodded and carried out a still-struggling Kiel Gnomenfoot. "Don't worry, Owen!" Kiel shouted as he left. "I'll be back to rescue you."

Inspector Brown shook his head. "That kid's going to be very disappointed. If there's one thing I've learned in my time with Doyle Holmes, it's that no one escapes him."

Owen's eyes widened as Inspector Brown left, locking the door behind him. Inspector Brown knew Doyle Holmes? How was that possible? How could the nonfictional police know a fictional character, act like they'd known him for years?

And maybe just as important, was Inspector Brown right? Was Doyle that good, like he was everywhere at once?

Holmes . . . everywhere . . .

And just like that, another crystal-clear memory hit Owen, right across the face. Ugh. This was getting a bit ridicul—

MISSING CHAPTER 4

Yesterday . . .

O wen sat at the checkout counter, staring blankly at his math homework. His pencil slowly doodled on his homework, sketching a smiling half-robotic girl.

Sometimes he just felt so useless. It'd been a month since he'd seen Bethany, and Kiel seemed to be getting more and more antsy, being trapped in the nonfictional world and going to school. But what could Owen do? Bethany wouldn't take his calls, and it's not like he really knew what to say anyway. Sorry you didn't find your dad, and that magic thinks he's trapped in every single book in the library?

This was the problem. Owen was just the sidekick, maybe not even that. At least Robin knew how to fight, and he had his own comic sometimes. Owen's comic would be all about Kiel and Bethany rescuing him because he bumbled into some new trap every issue. And it'd be canceled after, like, the third one. Maybe the second.

He sighed, sketching some hair on the half-robot girl. If only there was something he could say to Bethany to cheer her up, make her realize that they were still on her side. Even if they never jumped into another book, Bethany was still his friend, and he wanted to be there for her. To help her.

But how?

Someone placed a pile of books on the counter in front of him, and Owen looked up from his doodling to see a boy a few years younger than him looking annoyed. Owen smiled politely. "Do you have your library card?" he asked.

"Why are there so many Sherlock Holmes books now?" the boy said, glaring at Owen. "He's everywhere. I don't get it."

Owen shrugged. "I think he's just popular. Things go in waves sometimes."

"But look at this," the boy said, sliding a book over to Owen. "Since when is he even in the Bad Time Orphan Bunch series?"

Owen raised an eyebrow and took the book. The Bad Time

Orphan Bunch: *Life Becomes Unbearable*. Fun series, but Owen hadn't read it in a while.

"There's no Sherlock Holmes in this," he said, holding the book out to the boy.

"Open it!" the kid said, pushing it back.

Owen sighed and turned to the first page.

Chapter 1

I hope you're sitting down. I hope you've had your fill of fairy tales and nursery rhymes and stories where good conquers evil, or good sits down with evil over tea and talks out evil's problems, because this is not that. This is an altogether different thing than that. Good does not win. Good doesn't even show up on time for the fight.

Good, my beloved readers, decided to stay home and take a nap instead.

So get a blanket. You're going to need it to hide under. Get a teddy bear or your mother or whatever it takes to keep you reading well past when the fear reaches up your spine and into your brain, teasing out the terror. This is that kind of story. The kind of story I'm shaking just *considering* telling you.

This is the story of fourteen children, each one an orphan, though somehow they formed a family. A bunch, if you will. Like bananas, or a random amount of things. That's what these orphans were. A random amount of things.

Let me introduce them to you. Here we are, their home, the ramshacklest of ramshackle houses, officially called the Sunshine Home for Happy Kids, but known to our orphans as the House of Moldy Porridge.

You don't want to know why. But I'm going to tell you.

Here, I'll open the door for you. Walk on inside, and ... eh?

"I've got this."

This is odd. There's a boy in a mask, a mask adorned with a question mark. And he seems to be wearing an odd sort of hat and coat. He's not one of the orphans though. Who might this—

"Doyle Holmes," the boy says, not sticking out

his hand. "Great-great-great-great-great-grandson of Sherlock Holmes. I solved the mystery of these orphans, missing parents. They've all been returned home, and the missing diamonds were recovered."

But . . . you weren't even supposed to learn of the diamonds for several books yet. This isn't how this tale is supposed to go!

"Don't worry, I know the part you played in this too," this Doyle boy says. "The police are on their way. Don't bother running, I can track you anywhere."

The police? What? Sirens blare in the air behind me, and I turn to find several cars pulling up at once.

Is this truly the end, before any of it began?

Um. This was *not* how the book was supposed to go. Owen turned the page, and his eyes widened.

The next page was blank.

So were the next two hundred and fifty pages.

"It's not the only one like that," the boy said in disgust. "This masked Sherlock Holmes grandson guy shows up in a ton of books. Not fantasy or science fiction, just the regular kind of books. Jason Scout: *International Spy of Pancakes*,

Robin of Sherwood Lakes Subdivision, and a bunch more." He sighed. "Is this some kind of stupid crossover? 'Cause I never liked his first book anyway."

"What first book?" Owen asked, barely able to breathe.

"*The Baker Street* something or other," the boy said. "Anyway, this is all lame. I don't even want them. But you should complain to the companies that make these."

"The writers?" Owen asked absently, not even looking up.

"Whatever," the boy said. "Tell them crossovers are terrible, and no one wants them. I just want the Orphan Bunch."

And with that, he left, still mumbling to himself.

Owen was out of his chair instantly, practically running to the children's section. He scanned the shelves for a moment, then yanked out the book he was looking for.

The Baker Street School for Irregular Children.

He flipped it over and quickly read the back.

The great-great-great-great-great-grandson of Sherlock Holmes has inherited the family school, named after Sherlock's Irregulars, the group of children who used to help the great detective solve his mysteries. But Doyle Holmes wants to do more than just help troubled children learn from their mistakes. He's ready to solve the biggest mysteries, capture the most dangerous crooks, and share his adventures with his trusty computer, W.A.T.S.O.N.!

The cover confirmed it. There was Doyle Holmes, a boy in a Sherlock Holmes coat and hat, wearing a question-mark mask. *The criminals don't know his true identity, so they can never see him coming,* the cover said.

Wow. *Yikes.* That did not sound good.

But somehow, this Doyle Holmes character was getting into other books, other stories, and solving mysteries, apparently before those stories even started. How was that possible? It wasn't like he, Bethany, and Kiel had ever visited this book, so at least it wasn't their fault. But still!

Wait a second. What was he thinking? *This was his chance.* Not only to distract Bethany from what'd been happening with her father, but also to show that he wasn't completely useless! Maybe that'd be Owen's thing—being the research guy! Finding books with characters who were escaping their stories, and he'd send Bethany in to stop them? Maybe give her all the plans and cool gadgets, then make jokes when they came back, maybe every so often a hug, so Bethany knew he cared. Maybe this was his thing all along, to be the one finding important things for her to investigate!

Or maybe this *was* just some stupid marketing attempt to get people reading the Baker Street series, since it looked like only one book in the series ever came out, and that was years ago.

Either way, he'd take it to Bethany, and she'd have to check it out, with him and Kiel, too. And maybe this was the start of them doing some good now, instead of just having cool adventures and enjoying themselves.

That thought made Owen feel just a bit proud of himself as he carried *The Baker Street School for Irregular Children* back to the checkout desk, where he dialed Bethany's number.

Just a bit? No. A *lot* proud.

After all, this was completely Owen. He was going to totally get the credit for this.

"AUGH!" Owen shouted into the empty room in the police station, in spite of his pounding head. "Not again! It can't be all my fault *again*!"

CHAPTER 19

01:11:12

 r. Gnomenfoot," a man in a suit said to Kiel. "I'm Inspector Brown. I'm quite interested in who you are, to be honest. According to our files, you don't actually exist."

"You're not the first person to tell me that," Kiel said, still feeling a bit woozy but giving the detective a wink anyway. "That's a whole other story, but trust me, it was a fun time."

The man didn't seem to notice his wink, which was unusual. "I'm told by a reliable source that you're actually some sort of magician." The man leaned back in his chair. "I love magic, myself. It's like a puzzle, figuring out how the tricks are done. Haven't had one magician fool me yet, though."

Kiel raised an eyebrow. "They're not tricks, Inspector Brown. And I already figured out how magic works. Came from science, it was a whole thing." He shrugged. "Still kind of turns my stomach, but it's probably just time to accept that."

"Not a trick, huh?" Inspector Brown said. "Let's see some. I bet I can tell you how you do it."

Kiel sighed. "I'm currently powerless. No magic." He shook his head sadly. "Otherwise, this conversation would probably be going very differently." He winked again, just to see if maybe it didn't take the first time.

"You seem to have an eye twitch," Inspector Brown said.

"I can see why your parents named you Inspector," Kiel said.

". . . They didn't. It's a title."

Kiel grinned. "I've got seven of those myself. Some are a little more clever than others. I like *Kiel Gnomenfoot and the End of Everything* best, I think. It's got the most appropriate level of importance."

"Enough games, Mr. Gnomenfoot," the inspector said. "We have an eyewitness claiming that you set fire to the local library with your friend, Owen Conners. Owen's already given us everything we need. He claims *you* did it."

Kiel frowned. "That doesn't sound like him. Especially since that's not true."

The inspector smirked. "Really? Because Owen couldn't wait to throw you under the bus. I didn't even need to ask. Volunteered that you covered the library in gasoline, lit the match, the whole deal. Are you saying that *he's* actually the one who did it?"

"Oh," Kiel said, smacking his head. "I get it. You're trying to get me to turn on Owen by lying about what he said. That's fantastic, I didn't realize the police still used that old trick."

Inspector Brown narrowed his eyes. "Why don't you tell me exactly what you were doing in the library, Mr. Gnomenfoot?"

"I'd like to, but I don't remember," Kiel said, tapping his forehead. "Magic spell. You should ask your eyewitness about that. I'm fairly sure he was the one who made me cast it."

"You don't remember." The inspector looked annoyed.

"Not a thing," Kiel said, then caught himself. "That's not entirely true, actually. Every so often I get this flash of memory, usually when something comes along to trigger it. You could maybe try saying different words, that might jog something, but I wouldn't count on it."

"This could go a lot easier on you if you cooperated, Mr. Gnomenfoot," Inspector Brown said.

"Honestly, I don't even have time for it to go easily," Kiel whispered, leaning forward. "If I don't rescue my friend

Bethany before this watch counts down, then something bad happens, and I never see her again. You'd think that the police would be interested in something like that. Doesn't that sort of thing fall into your jurisdiction? Or am I getting things wrong in this world?"

"In this world?" the inspector said, shaking his head. "I'm getting tired of this act, Mr. Gnomenfoot. Maybe let the fantasy stuff rest and just answer the questions?"

"Fantasy stuff?" Kiel said, giving the inspector an indignant look. "You police are the ones working with a kid in a question-mark mask! Why not ask him about Bethany, and see what he says?"

"I can keep you here overnight, Mr. Gnomenfoot," the inspector said. "If your friend really is in danger, I'll be happy to help, but I'm going to need you to be honest with me and tell me exactly what happened at the library. If not, we can talk again in the morning."

"Owen and I woke up in the library with no memory of how we got there. Then a guy named Doyle Holmes told us about Bethany, and burnt the place down," Kiel said, starting to get slightly irritated. "I'm guessing Owen already covered this, didn't he?"

The inspector started to say something, but stopped and hit a button on the wall. "Yes?" he said.

"Inspector, you're needed downstairs," said a voice muffled by a speaker on the wall with the mirror. "We found some sort of incendiary device in the evidence room."

The inspector's eyes widened. "I'm on my way." He jumped to his feet and pointed a finger at Kiel. "You're staying here until I get back, and then we're continuing this discussion."

"Don't worry, I'll have broken out by the time you're back," Kiel said, giving the inspector a broad smile.

The inspector finally smiled back. *"Good luck."* He gave a brief nod, then walked out, locking the door behind him.

"You'll see!" Kiel shouted, jumping up and yelling right through the closed door. "I've broken out of prisons a lot more robotic than this one!"

The door burst open, missing Kiel's face by inches, and the girl in all black from before grabbed him by the wrist and yanked him out the door.

"Hey!" he shouted at her, pulling his hand back. "I was making a point!" His eyes widened and he immediately jumped backward. "You!"

The girl covered his entire face with her hand. "Shh!" she

whispered, giving him an excited look. "You're so right, it *is* me! We'll talk later. We don't want the police hearing you! Though that'd create all sorts of interesting challenges." She giggled quietly. "You'd probably have to pay me more gold, though, if you wanted me to save you from *that*."

Kiel slowly pulled the girl's hand off of his face, just staring at her. Pay her gold? Who *was* she? Why was she helping him escape now, after she'd just helped hand him over?

He paused, waiting for a memory to flash into his head as the girl just grinned at him.

"Weird," he said. "I really thought that this would trigger some kind of memory."

"What an odd thing to say," she said with a shrug. "You crack me up! C'mon, Magical Koala. Can I call you MK? Let's go find that other kid, and then we'll get you out of here."

Without waiting for a response, the girl turned and walked carefully down the hall, moving so silently that even Kiel was impressed. Seriously, who was this girl? Had they really hired her in some way?

And where had they found gold?!

CHAPTER 20

01:08:34

So Doyle Holmes had somehow been invading other people's stories, and it'd been Owen's idea to investigate. Which meant that all of this was his fault, just like when he'd messed everything up with Kiel and the Magister. Perfect! Was there anything that Owen didn't ruin?!

Owen lay with his face on the table, his head still aching from the flashback, which, granted, had told him a lot about why he was here now. But what had happened when Owen had gone to Bethany about Doyle? Had she listened, or left him to mess it up even further somehow? If Doyle was getting into other stories, did that mean he had found a way out of the fictional world? That'd explain a lot. But not how he knew who Bethany was, or Owen and Kiel, for that matter.

ARGH. Mysteries were so annoying! And this whole

flashback thing really was starting to get on his nerves. Why did he have to remember in pieces? Why couldn't his whole memory just pop back into place at once?

This was feeling more and more like a badly written story, and if there was one thing Owen hated more than mysteries, it was bad writing. At least with mysteries, you could flip to the end and see who the killer was.

If only he could do that here, just flip to the end, and see where Bethany was, or why Doyle was doing all of this. Stupid real world. Not that the real world was acting very real right now. But that had to be Doyle's doing. It *had* to be.

Hadn't it?

Owen knocked his knuckles against his forehead, trying to bring back more memories when the door opened, and a girl dressed in all black pushed Kiel inside the room, then closed the door silently. Owen blinked in surprise. "Um, hello?"

"Owen!" the girl said, grinning widely. "*Boom*, job fulfilled. Well, started. Isn't this exciting? I'm having *such* a good time. Thank you for thinking of me!"

Owen slowly stood up, having no idea how to react to any of that. "Uh, who is this?" he whispered to Kiel.

"I have *no* idea," Kiel whispered back. "Apparently, we know her." He shrugged. "Oh, and she's the one who got me caught by the police. I haven't entirely wrapped my head around all of it yet."

The girl giggled at him. "You're being *so crazy* right now, MK, I love it. It was all part of the plan, Owen! I needed you both together, and that was the easiest way." She shrugged. "Kiel's cape was going to lead to all kinds of interesting questions if I tried sneaking him in. Though I love it. *I love it.* I'm getting one. I have to have one."

"Who are you, again?" Owen asked, completely confused.

The girl laughed, then leaped forward and hugged him. "That gets me every time!" She pushed him away hard, and Owen went falling back into the table as she ran a hand down over her face, making herself serious. "Now, back to business. When I give the signal, you both follow me, doing exactly as I do, okay? Let's keep those mouths of yours clamped shut, boys. Let me do the talking. Good?"

Owen opened his mouth to ask a question, and immediately the girl reached over and pushed it closed. "No talking!" she said, and laughed again. As he stared at her in shock, she went to the door, opened it slightly, and nodded outside.

On the other side of the police station, a loud bang went off, and smoke began to fill the halls. The fire alarm blared, and everyone began running everywhere.

"Quiet faces, you guys!" the girl said, and snuck out of the room. Kiel flashed Owen a huge grin, then took off after her, while Owen sighed and quickly did the same. This was it. He was officially a fugitive and was going to go to jail for the rest of his life. And his mother would show up at the police station only to find him missing. Apart from the him that was home, apparently.

The hallway outside was chaos, with smoke, running people, and irritating sirens. A police officer ran up and grabbed the girl by her hand. "Where are you three going?" he demanded.

"Inspector Brown told us to go to his office until this was over," the girl said, her face a mask of innocence and confusion. "Is that wrong?"

"No, do what he says," the officer said, already starting to run toward the source of the smoke. "Just hurry."

"Yes, sir," the girl said, then stuck out her tongue at him as soon as the officer turned around.

Through the chaos, the girl led them to a door that actually said INSPECTOR BROWN.

"We're *really* going to his office?" Owen asked.

"Quiet faces," she whispered, then tried the handle, which didn't turn. "Hmm."

"I can get this," Kiel said, stepping forward and taking out the small wire he'd used before. "I've got some experience with locked doors."

The girl giggled. "Really, MK?" she said as her hands flew over the doorknob, then turned it. "You'll have to teach me some new tricks!" The door opened and she shoved the two boys inside, then quietly shut it, locking the knob again.

"How did you do that so fast?" Kiel said, his eyes wide with admiration.

"Runs in the family," she told Kiel, shrugging. "Now, get yourself out that window and quit being so crazy." And to Owen, "Let's push this desk against the door. Just for safety."

Kiel ran for the window and yanked it open. "Four floors up," he said, grinning at Owen. "I like your style, Ms. Whoever-You-Are."

The girl sighed as she and Owen pushed the desk against the door. "I still don't get this joke. How could you not remember who I am?"

"It's been an interesting night," Owen told her. She made

a kissy face at him, then raced to the window, where Kiel was stepping out onto the ledge.

Owen frowned, hating his memory right then. Why would they have someone to help them? Where had they found her? And who was she, opening a locked door so quickly and setting off smoke bombs in a police station?

He stared at the girl as hard as he could, willing the flashback to start. GIRL. GIRL. GIRL.

And then a memory hit him right in the face.

"Who can tell me the name of the president of the United States during World War II?" Mr. Barberry asked.

No one raised their hand.

"Really? No one knows?" Mr. Barberry said. "This was home-work, people!"

Owen gasped, but mostly at the boringness of the memory. That one had barely even hurt. What had happened? Had the flashback broken somehow?

"Come *on* already!" the girl said with a huge smile, yanking him forward. "The plan takes exact timing, Owen. Get your silly behind out on that ledge before I kick you off of it!"

Owen stepped out of the window and put a shaking foot out onto the incredibly shallow ledge. Who built ledges like this, anyway? Either they were big enough to walk on or they weren't! Why split the difference?

"This way," Kiel said from one side.

"Uh-uh," the girl said, pushing Owen out of her way to climb out as well. "That way gets us caught, MK. *This* way!"

Owen looked down at the police cars below and the flashing red fire-alarm lights. They were so tiny, and so far away, it made them look almost adorable.

Less adorable was Inspector Brown, who stepped outside, looking in all directions, before turning around and glancing up. Then he smiled like he'd just seen through a magic trick or something.

And that's when another memory hit, which was just terrible timing at that exact mome—

MISSING CHAPTER 5

Yesterday . . .

"Bethany!" her mom shouted from downstairs. "Owen and Kiel are here."

Bethany looked up at her bedroom door from where she was lying on the floor, her feet up on her bed. What were they doing here? She hadn't talked to them since, well, the finding spell night. And with what she'd done since . . .

The last thing she wanted to do was face either one of them.

"Tell them I'm busy!" she yelled down, then covered her head with a pillow. They probably wanted to check on her or something, and their sweetness made it even worse that she couldn't face them.

Her bedroom door opened, and Bethany tore the pillow off her face to find her mother staring down at her. "You realize I'm not your butler, right?" her mother said. "Come on in, boys."

Bethany gave her mom an annoyed look, and her mother threw her one right back as Owen and Kiel stepped into her bedroom. "Don't work too hard on that homework project," her mom said as she left, leaving the door open.

"We won't," Owen said, then began to blush. "I mean, we will!"

"Looking lovely as usual, Mrs. Sanderson," Kiel said, waving as her mom left.

"What are you doing here?" Bethany hissed at them as quietly as she could. "I told you guys I didn't want to talk."

"I know," Owen said, taking some books out of his bag. "But something came up that couldn't wait. Something big."

"What, a real homework project?" Bethany asked, looking at the papers in his hand.

Owen shook his head and handed her the papers. She glared at him, then flipped through them in annoyance. They were all newspaper articles that he'd printed out.

Sherlock Holmes Takes Over the Literary Scene.

The Game Is Afoot: Sherlock Crossovers the New Big Thing?

Sherlock—

She tossed the papers back at Owen, and he fumbled them all, dropping them. "I already said no to jumping into Sherlock Holmes," Bethany told them, shaking her head. "And I *told* you guys. We're done!"

"Did you read them?" Owen said. "Look." He picked up the *Crossovers* article. "Sherlock Holmes is showing up *everywhere* right now. Well, at least his great-great-great-something-grandson. Doyle Holmes is appearing in other people's series, Bethany, and the authors say they didn't even know it was happening. Some are even suing their publishers. People think it's one big publicity stunt."

Bethany's heart almost stopped when Owen said the name Doyle Holmes. "Okay," she said, taking the article and swallowing hard as she pretended to skim it. "So it probably *is* just a publicity thing for this Doyle Holmes book."

No, no, no, *no*. What was Doyle *doing*?

"Have you ever heard of fictional characters crossing over into other series?" Owen asked her.

Every mention of a book in the article made her feel worse. The Orphan Bunch books, really?! "How is this my problem?" Bethany said, not looking Owen in the eye. "*We* didn't do it, right?"

"Not yet!" Kiel said, giving her a grin.

Bethany had to swallow hard to keep from throwing up.

Owen pulled a book out of his backpack and handed it to her. *The Baker Street School for Irregular Children*. The same one she'd checked out two weeks ago. "This is the book Doyle Holmes comes from," he told her. "I think we should go in and investigate. You know, be detectives, kind of."

"Detectives that take this kid down," Kiel said, juggling a wand on her bed. "It's way too long since I've had a good fight. I'm starting to get worried I'm not as impressive as I used to be."

"No fights," Bethany told him, ripping the book from Owen's hands. This was the exact same copy she'd used. If Owen had looked in the computer, he could have seen her name listed as checking it out.

"Maybe we can help," Owen said quietly to her. "Take a quick look and see if it *is* just a publicity thing, or if there's a fictional character who's figured out how to cross into other stories. If it's the second one, don't you think we should do something about it?"

"Why?" Bethany said, realizing how whiny her voice sounded, even to her. "We're not the *story police*, Owen. We don't have to fix every problem." In her head, she begged Owen to just let it go, leave her alone, so that he and Kiel wouldn't find out what she'd done.

"I vote we're not the *anything* police," Kiel said. "Let's be thieves. That's a lot more fun."

"It's up to us because who else can fix it?" Owen said. "I know it's a lot to take in, but I'll handle it all. I'll read up on Doyle today, and have a plan ready for tonight. I'll take care of everything. You just have to jump us in and out."

"I'll handle the fighting," Kiel said, back to juggling. "Hopefully there are monsters. Oooh, or dragons! I *miss* dragons."

"We *can't* do this," Bethany said, almost pleading with them. "This goes against all the rules." The same rules that she'd broken. "It'll be interfering with a story." A story that she'd already *completely* interfered with. "You know I can't do this."

"This isn't about saving the Magister this time, Bethany," Owen said. "I promise. I'm being completely up front. I just want us to take a look and make sure it's not something horrible and world-ending. Think what would happen if a character like that got out into other stories. He's the world's greatest detective—"

"I thought that was the Bat guy you like," Kiel said.

"And there's no end to the stories he could ruin," Owen finished, then nodded at Kiel. "You're right, my mistake. *Batman* is the world's greatest detective. Sherlock Holmes was the world's greatest Victorian detective. Huge difference."

"Thank you," Kiel said, nodding at him.

They weren't going to let this go, and a part of Bethany realized they were right not to. It did look really bad, honestly. The only thing was, she knew something they didn't.

She knew that it was all her fault.

"I'll go alone," she told Owen, trying not to hyperventilate. "There, satisfied? I'll check it out and let you know what I find."

"Never!" Kiel shouted, and jumped up from the bed. "One for all and whatever else that musketeer guy told us. You need our help."

"Don't worry, I'm going to be useful too," Owen said, and his hopefulness almost broke her heart. "I've totally got a plan. I've even got a *backup* plan." He gave her a guilty look. "It's a bit weird, but when you go up against a Sherlock Holmes character, it doesn't hurt to have a little help on your side."

"Just let me just do this," Bethany said, not sure what else to say. "Please?"

"Nope," Kiel said, hugging them both. "We're in this together, until the dragons come, at which point I call the first two. No, first three!"

Owen smiled nervously at her, and Bethany sighed. "All right. Tonight at the library. But you guys have to do *exactly* what I say."

"Deal," Owen said.

"Deal!" Kiel said. "There's no way this can possibly go wrong!"

CHAPTER 21

01:04:23

Bethany sat shivering on the back of the chair, her chains curled up on the seat beneath her as the water slowly rose up toward her neck. Soon she was going to have to move, and there weren't that many more places to go. The shelves nearby rose another few feet higher than the chair did, but even they didn't get close to the ceiling.

Not only that, the water seemed to be flowing in faster now, as if it'd doubled at some point. Perfect.

As the water rocked her back and forth, all she could think about was the day before, when Kiel and Owen had come to her with *The Baker Street School for Irregular Children*. Why hadn't she just called it off? Doyle could do whatever he wanted, as far as she was concerned. And then none of them would be in this mess.

Except she wouldn't have let it go, because it was already too late by then. She'd have gone back into the book anyway, and been caught. Though at least then, it'd have just been her.

Jump, part of herself said. *You're going to by the end anyway. Kiel and Owen are never going to find you. Why put yourself through this?*

Because she deserved it.

You don't *deserve this. You did the only thing you could to find Dad.*

And look what had happened.

MISSING CHAPTER 6

Two weeks ago . . .

"Mr. Holmes will see you now," said a giant bald man wearing a white shirt printed with the words THE BAKER STREET SCHOOL. Despite having arms thicker than her head, his heavy English accent somehow made her feel a bit more comfortable as he held open a thick wooden door. Bethany nodded at him, then stepped inside the headmaster's office.

The entire room was covered in wood and leather. Chairs so deep you could dive into them sat in front of a roaring fireplace, which was topped with a violin hanging above the mantle. A pistol in a glass case labeled THIRD ACT also sat on the mantle, probably some sort of trophy from a previous case. An enormous desk filled the far part of the room, and a tall leather chair was currently turned around, facing a wall of monitors behind it.

Each of the monitors showed either a classroom or what looked like a cellblock, and the images switched so fast that Bethany could barely keep up.

"Yes?" said a voice from behind the chair's tall back. "State your business. I have little enough time as it is."

Bethany frowned. Maybe this hadn't been a good idea. She could have at least found a nicer detective. Still, a Holmes was a Holmes, and there was no one better. Except maybe Batman, but that was something else entirely. "I came to hire you to find a missing person," she said quietly.

"Obviously," said the voice, and the chair swiveled around, revealing a boy wearing a question-mark mask, a Sherlock Holmes hat, and a big brown overcoat. Bethany grimaced in spite of herself. Seriously, a question-mark mask? Who wore that?

Doyle Holmes snapped his fingers, not even looking up from his desk. "Give me whatever information you have."

Bethany stepped closer and laid down a folder full of photos on the table, most from before she was born, a few from after. Doyle ignored the folder, instead glancing up at her.

"I've seen you before," he said quietly. "But not like this. You looked different somehow. And there's something very *off* about you."

"I'm not from around here," Bethany said, taking a step back nervously. This was already breaking all of her rules, *every single one*, about not interacting with fictional characters, let alone the main ones. But this was the end of Doyle's only book, right? It's not like there'd be any more to come. And things seemed to have gone okay with EarthGirl, so maybe it'd all be fine!

But honestly? Even if this messed up Doyle's entire story, she was just beyond caring. If he helped find her dad, it'd all be worth it. *Be more fictional,* Kiel had said. Well, here she was, throwing out all of her responsible rules and careful plans.

And if even after all this, she *still* couldn't find her father . . . no. She wouldn't even think about that. This boy would find him. He was a Holmes.

Doyle stared at her for another moment, then opened the file and flipped through the pictures before pushing them aside and turning back to her. "Missing father. Mother has same odd quality that you do, something off about her, as well. Just more so. Something I've never seen before." He glanced up at Bethany. "And that's not something I say lightly."

"I've heard you're very good at what you do," she said, trying to change the subject. "Do you think you can find him?"

"Of course," Doyle said, sitting back in his chair and

steepling his fingers. "That is, if he's still alive." He paused. "I'm sure I've seen your face before. Not a photograph, though. A drawing. A book." Another pause, then he abruptly sat straight up in his chair, his hands slapping the desk. "*Story Thieves!*"

"I'm sorry?" Bethany said, taking another step backward.

Doyle stood up slowly, his masked face giving no indication of what he was thinking. "Do you know the story of my great-great-great-great-great-grandfather's supposed death?" he asked Bethany quietly. "What am I saying, of *course* you do. Everyone's seen the news articles. *Sherlock Holmes dies in fall over Reichenbach Falls. A Nation Mourns.*"

"Sure, I know it," Bethany said nervously, stepping back again. "Who doesn't?"

"Later it was all revealed to be a hoax, so he could take down Professor Moriarty's criminal network," Doyle said, getting closer. "Moriarty being his greatest enemy. But do you know that he actually *should* have died that day? That he did go over the falls, but somehow lived?"

Bethany took another step backward. *Of course* she knew that. She'd been there, taunting the Magister about it, since the wizard had broken Sherlock Holmes's fall with his own magically flying body. "I . . . I didn't know that," she said, her voice cracking.

"My family has kept it a secret," Doyle said, stepping closer. "No one was to know. We couldn't let the world find out that the great rationalist Sherlock Holmes believed he was saved by a flying man, of all things."

Bethany swallowed hard. "I should be going."

Doyle crossed his arms, and for some reason she thought he was smiling behind the mask. "Of course. I'll start the investigation. But we haven't spoken about my payment."

Relief flooded Bethany's body, and she almost felt weak. "Of course! Payment. I've got gold, if that works."

"Gold?" Doyle said. "That's unique. Most offer a more standard currency. But that can wait. I'll let you know what the information I find will cost once I know your father's whereabouts. I shall contact you when I'm finished."

Bethany shook her head. "I'm usually not very contactable. Can I just come back in a few weeks or something?"

"Why?" Doyle asked, taking another step toward her. "Going somewhere?"

She tried to shrug nonchalantly. "It's just much easier if I come to you. Thank you. And please, don't tell anyone about this. It's between us. I can pay extra for that."

Doyle slowly nodded, then gestured toward the door. "Interesting to meet you, Ms. Sanderson," he said.

"Same to you," Bethany said, then stepped outside and closed the door behind her.

And for the first time since the finding spell had failed, Bethany actually felt hope again. Doyle Holmes *had* to be able to find her father. Part of her mind was screaming at her that this was wrong, that she was changing Doyle's story, that even if Doyle found her father, what else would that tell Doyle? Her father might come from any story, after all. Could Doyle even cross into different stories? Was that possible?

But that part of her mind got shouted down by one simple thought: *I am finding my father! I don't care what it takes, I am making this right!*

It wasn't until the enormous guard led her back to the front gate of the Baker Street School that she realized she'd never told Doyle that her last name was Sanderson.

CHAPTER 22

01:03:29

Owen grabbed his head from the pain of the flashback and unconsciously took a step forward . . . into nothingness.

His eyes flew open, and he realized he was falling straight off the ledge, forty feet above the police parking lot below. Suddenly the pain in his head was replaced by a shrieking terror.

Something grabbed him from behind and yanked him backward. "Whoa there, killer," the girl in black said. "Going somewhere? You're not an owl, Owen. Mostly you look more like an adorable panda who's always sad. Sad Panda."

Owen tried to answer, but he couldn't get a word out, or catch his breath even. "I . . . I . . ."

"Don't worry, I've got you, SP," the girl said, putting an arm around him. A noise behind them made her twirl around, almost sweeping Owen off the ledge again. Someone was banging on the door in Inspector Brown's office. "Whoops, time to go!"

But Owen couldn't move any more than he could speak. His heart wouldn't stop racing, and all he could think about was how far down it was. One step and he'd be falling into nothingness, and then . . . *splat*.

"You've done scarier things than this, Owen," Kiel said. "Think of what you did with Charm. That was *far* more dangerous than this is!"

"That was . . . a book," Owen said between breaths. "This is . . . real. No . . . happy . . . endings if . . . I fall."

The girl in black stepped in front of Owen, barely still on the ledge, and gave him a sympathetic look. "I get it, SP," she said. "You're freezing, but I'm here to help. You just need a little incentive. Get moving, okay, or *I'll throw you off this ledge*."

Owen's eyes widened and he took an unconscious step to the right, trying to get away from her. "See?" she said. "That got you moving. Look at you go!" And with that, she pushed him onward. "Yay, SP! You're killing the game!"

"You two go on, I'll take care of them," Kiel said from the other side of the window. His hands went down to his belt and he sighed. "It would have been a lot more fun with magic, but oh well." He started to climb back inside the window, but the girl yanked him back out onto the ledge.

"No one gets left *behind*!" she said in a singsong voice. "Including people trying to be heroes."

"You three, stop this instant and go back inside!" Inspector Brown shouted in a bullhorn from the parking lot. "There's nowhere for you to run. We don't want you to get hurt."

Owen paused at this, but the girl gave him a not-so-small push, and he continued moving along the ledge. He picked up speed and slid carefully farther toward the edge of the building.

Unfortunately, there wasn't much farther to go. The ledge ran out just past a few more windows. "So when you say you know what you're doing . . . ," he whispered to the girl.

"Oh, I've *so* got this," she said, patting him on the shoulder.

"So I'm guessing you just had a memory return too?" Kiel called to him.

"Yup," Owen said. "I convinced Bethany to look into Doyle, Kiel. This is all my fault."

"We both went to her," Kiel said. "Don't blame yourself."

"It was my idea," Owen said. "But I said I had a backup plan. Did you get that memory yet?"

"Nope," Kiel said, sounding a bit frustrated. Not having his magic must be tough for him, Owen realized. He had seemed a bit different ever since he'd arrived at the police station. Not down so much as just . . . less *Kiel.*

"Turn around and go back inside!" Inspector Brown shouted into the bullhorn. "This isn't helping your case. Come in and we'll talk."

"They'd rather die, cop!" the girl shouted back, her voice harsh and threatening. "You'll *never* take them alive!"

"What?!" Owen said.

"I agree with the theory, but let's not go overboard," Kiel said.

"Follow my lead," she whispered to them, grinning. "Trust me, it's more fun that way!"

Owen gave Kiel a look, who shrugged, then smiled his Kiel smile. "Might as well," the smile said. "It could be fun!"

"Who *are* you?" Owen whispered to the girl.

"Just a criminal genius who could probably stand a haircut at this point," she told him. "Why, who are *you*?"

"Stop right there!" a police officer yelled from the ledge, coming out of Inspector Brown's window behind them. They must have broken down his door.

"Oh, they're calling our bluff!" the girl whispered, her eyes lighting up. "Looks like we're jumping to *extreme measures*."

Then she grabbed Owen by the back of his shirt and pushed him off the ledge.

"Aaah!" he screamed, terror exploding through his body as he fell into nothingness. He paused in midair just like last time, only this time the girl didn't yank him back to the wall. Instead, she left him hanging there, her grip on his shirt the only thing keeping him from splatting.

"Let us go or I drop the kid!" the girl shouted at the assembled police. "I swear I'll do it!"

"No dropping!" Owen shouted, his heart trying to break his chest open.

"If he falls," Kiel said, his voice low and scary, "*you* go next."

"Turn off those spotlights!" the girl shouted, then turned to the police officer in the window. "And you, back inside. Now!"

The police officer glared at her, but slowly retreated back into the window, while below the spotlights clicked off one by one.

"Don't you love when plans just go perfectly?" the girl asked quietly, her voice back to normal. She pulled Owen back onto the ledge, and he pushed against the building as hard as he could, so thankful to feel hard concrete.

"Never do that again!" he hissed at her, his voice cracking.

"No promises," she said with a huge smile. "Let's go. Don't fall behind, MK."

"Would you call me Kiel?" Kiel whispered, but started sliding along the ledge again.

"On the side of the building, there's a drainpipe," the girl whispered to them. "We're going to climb up it to the roof."

The roof? Climbing? A *drainpipe*? "Other than that being a great way to die, won't we just be trapped up there?" Owen asked, trying to be as polite as possible to this crazy person.

"You'd *think* so!" she told him. "I guess we'll see!" She pushed his shoulder again, and Owen sidled on down the ledge until he was just out of sight of the police below.

This side of the building was empty, filled mostly with garbage cans, and surrounded on two sides by bushes. The third side was an open alley down the block, and even from this high, Owen could hear running feet. They wouldn't be out of sight for long.

"Up we go," The girl shoved him into the drainpipe, then playfully kicked him in the bottom.

"Stop that!" he whispered as angrily as he could, then began climbing, trying not to look down. The pipe was small, yes, but it was firmly latched into place, which made for convenient footholds. This girl had done her research. Either that, or she had gotten lucky. Owen didn't particularly want to know which.

After a harrowing fight against gravity, Owen pulled his trembling body up and over the edge of the roof and tumbled down onto it. He considered kissing the roof, like he'd seen people do when they landed from crazy plane rides, but honestly, it looked pretty disgusting, so he passed.

A moment later the other two joined him, neither one having any trouble with the climb.

"Now what?" Owen asked, trying to cover the fear in his voice.

"Now you see where some of your money is going," the girl said, looking proud of herself as she pointed back down. Owen groaned, then pushed himself to his feet, and with a tight hold on the edge of the roof, looked down.

On the ground below, a girl and two boys about their size jumped out from between the garbage cans and pushed through the bushes, just as police officers reached the alley.

"Stop!" the officers shouted, and Owen heard one talking into his radio. "They're on the street, on foot, heading for Alexander Road." The officers sprinted past the garbage cans and pushed through the bushes, following the fleeing kids.

Owen stepped back away from the roof and turned slowly toward the girl, staring at her in awe. "You have . . . decoys?"

The girl shrugged. "Minions, really. I've worked with them before. Quality henchpeople. Five stars, would hire again."

"But the police will be able to see that we're not them," Kiel said, then mumbled something about "Not even a disguise spell or anything."

"Not in the *dark*," she said, looking far too excited. "Besides, they won't catch up. My people have done this before. We give them two minutes, then climb down the drainpipe and head in the opposite direction. See? Perfect plan! And it was so easy! Then you just pay me the rest of what you owe me, and we all hug, maybe a few tears, promise to stay in touch, and then we go home!"

". . . Pay you?" Owen said.

The girl's smile slowly faded, and her eyes narrowed. "You don't have the other half of the *gold*?"

"Other half?" Owen said, a second before the memory slammed into him like a freight train to the face, and he fell backward onto the roof. Kiel managed to stay on his feet, but didn't look any happier.

"Are you okay?" the girl said, helping Owen stand up. "What keeps happening to you two?"

"Memories," Kiel said.

"I know who you are," Owen told her quietly. "I *remember* now!"

The girl give him a confused smile. "And who exactly am I, then?"

Owen swallowed hard. "You're my backup plan. You're a *Moriarty*."

MISSING CHAPTER 7

Yesterday . . .

O ur backup plan," Owen whispered from their hiding spot in the bushes, nodding at the girl with long black hair being led out of a police station in handcuffs. A detective unlocked her cuffs, then sighed, putting his keys away as he sat down on the steps of the police station.

For a moment the girl just looked at him sadly, then started to walk away, but the detective called for her. "Moira Gonzalez," he said, "get *back* here."

The girl froze. "You already questioned me. What more do you want?"

"That was the official interrogation," the detective said, patting the stairs next to him. "This is for me."

Moira turned around and slowly walked back, then dropped to the stair beside the detective.

"She's a criminal?" Bethany asked.

"Sort of," Owen said. "She's trying not to be, but she's the great-great-great-great-great-granddaughter of Professor Moriarty, Sherlock Holmes's greatest enemy. So she's got crazy natural talent."

"Do you want to talk about this?" the detective asked the girl.

"Not even a little bit," she said, her chin on her palms as she watched traffic go by.

The detective nodded. "I know you want to find your mother. But she's *gone*, M. And everything you did to find her just led you here."

Bethany seemed to stiffen next to Owen, and he realized too late the similarities. Ugh. Still, the damage was done. And maybe Bethany would be more willing to get Moira's help with so much in common?

"Her mother is Moriarty's descendent," Owen whispered. "Her dad, on the other hand . . ."

"Is that all, Detective Gonzalez?" Moira asked, not looking at her father.

"I miss her too, you know," the detective said, putting his arm around his daughter's shoulders. "Every day. But your mom made terrible choices in life, probably including marrying me. The only good thing that came from it is you, and I'm not going to let even her memory change that. I know you're not like her, M. You're too good a person to keep . . . well . . ."

"Breaking the law?" Moira said. "I'm trying, Dad. I really am. I know it doesn't look like it—"

"You just robbed four banks—"

"They got their money back!" Moira said, then grinned at him. "It was way too easy, by the way. They should *thank* me for highlighting their weaknesses—"

"Moira!"

"I know, okay?" she said, her smile disappearing. "I just thought maybe mom was watching, to see if I had what it took. I thought she might have noticed if I did something big."

Her father sighed. "Your mother loves you, Moira. And let's hope she's staying away because she's trying to do the right thing, which is not bring you into her world. But I need you to stop this. You're lucky none of the charges stuck. You think I want to investigate my own daughter?"

"They'd never have put you on the case, Dad," Moira said, grinning at him. "You know that's a conflict of interest."

The detective stared at her, and she rolled her eyes. "Okay, I'm sorry." She paused. "But just so we're clear, none of the charges stuck because I'm really good. You know that, right?"

Her father glared at her for a second, then smiled. "Yes, fine, you were amazing."

"Woo!" she shouted, and threw her arms around him. "That's all I want. Take pride in what you've got, Dad!"

He laughed and hugged her back, then pulled away. "You know I *am* proud of you, right? You can do so much with your life, and I just don't want you following your mom down the wrong path. Promise me, M. Promise me you'll be good from now on."

Moira sighed loudly. "I mean, what's 'good' exactly?"

"No law breaking, no criminal activity of any kind, and definitely no bank robbing!"

"Fine, I promise," Moira said, shaking her head sadly. "But you're definitely going to need to raise my allowance then. I needed that extra cash from the banks!"

Her father stared at her hard.

"We'll talk about it," she said, then leaned over and kissed his cheek.

"Remember, you promised," her dad told her, standing up.

"I know, I know," she said, standing up too and hugging him. "See you tonight."

"Let's make it at home this time, instead of in jail," the detective said, then tousled her hair and walked back into the police station.

"That's the end of the book right there," Owen whispered, staying hidden in the bushes as Moira came closer.

"This is the girl you want to help us against Doyle?" Bethany hissed as Moira passed by. "She's a criminal!"

"So was I," Kiel said, grinning at her. "Don't you trust *me*?"

"That's different," Bethany told him. "You were stealing to live. She's doing it because it's fun. And because . . . she's trying to find—"

"She's perfect!" Owen lied, trying to avoid the topic of Moira's missing mother. "She's like Doyle's opposite. I'm surprised they're not in the same series. They're both descended from some of the greatest minds who ever lived. Who better to help us?"

"He's right," Moira said from the sidewalk. "You clearly need help if you're trying to be inconspicuous." She turned around and gave them an excited look. "*Please* tell me you're from my mother?"

For a moment, not a proud one, the thought of answering yes passed through Owen's head. It'd get her help, wouldn't it? And maybe Bethany could actually find her mother in the book somewhere.

One look at Bethany's face killed that thought, though. "Uh, no. We were hoping to hire you, actually."

"Owen," Bethany hissed at him, but before she could say anything else, Moira grabbed Owen by his shirt with both hands and kissed his forehead.

"*Thank you!*" she shouted. "Do you have any idea how long it's been since I've done something I shouldn't?! I'm so bored I've been wondering if I'm in a coma!"

"It's not anything criminal," Owen said, blushing hard from her kiss. "We just want you to be ready in case we need your help with anything. We're investigating this guy—"

"You want me to rob him?" Moira said, her eyes widening. "*No*, identify theft?" She gasped, then frowned. "You don't want me to kill him, do you? I've got a line. Though I might be able to recommend someone—"

"Whoa!" Bethany shouted. "Definitely no killing!"

"I can't tell you too much," Owen said. "But we're going to this school, the Baker Street School for Irregular Children, and—"

"I've heard of that," Moira said, shrugging. "You trying to break someone out? That's always fun! I haven't done a break-out in, like, weeks!"

Owen froze. She'd heard of that? How could she have heard of a school in a different book? "Uh, no, no breakouts," he said, trying to stay on track. "Just, like, protection—"

"You want me to make the school pay protection money?" she said, frowning. "I might need a bunch of muscle for this, then. How much can you pay?"

"Owen," Bethany said, yanking him backward, "this is a bad idea!"

"Just backup, not a protection racket," Owen said quickly. "Do you . . . know who runs the Baker Street School?"

Moira shrugged. "I don't know, a principal? Who cares. It's like juvie for big-timers. I've heard some of the older kids talking about it. They're all afraid, so I think the cops use it to scare them." She smirked. "Don't worry, it's not a concern. I *never* get caught."

"You just got caught now," Kiel said, nodding at the police station.

"Ha, good point!" Moira said, and smacked his shoulder. "But I'm free, aren't I? I never get charged. Speaking of charging, this is going to cost a lot. My fee, travel expenses—though I'll probably just steal a car—and incidentals. Let's call it ten grand."

"What?!" Bethany shouted.

"Would you take gold?" Owen asked, taking a step away from Bethany.

"What?!" Bethany shouted, this time at Owen.

He gave her an embarrassed look, then handed her a page from *Kiel Gnomenfoot, Magic Thief*, specifically the page talking about the dragon's lair filled with treasure, within which Kiel and Charm were going to have to find their first key.

"The dragon won't miss it," Owen pointed out.

Bethany just stared at him, her mouth opening and closing. She was never going to go for this, he realized. This was breaking *way* too many rules. But this was all he had. He didn't have Kiel's magic or her power, so all Owen could do was try to be clever and come up with plans. And this one actually made sense, sort of. You fought fire with fire.

"Fine," Bethany whispered, and turned around.

"Gold's good," Moira said, trying to see over Bethany's shoulder. "I'll have to look up the exchange rate . . ."

"Do the math later," Bethany said, passing her a handful of gold coins.

Moira's eyes lit up. "This is probably close to half . . ."

Bethany turned away, then dumped another bunch into Moira's hands. "We'll get you the rest after the job, then."

Moira nodded, not looking at her. "I'm just *so happy* right now. So, so happy. So, so, *so*!"

"Didn't you make your father a promise?" Bethany asked her, and Owen sighed. He knew she'd agreed too easily.

"Sure," Moira said, not looking up from the gold. "And I kept it all the way over to you guys. That's a lot for me!"

"Be at the school tonight," Owen said. "And make sure you don't let anyone see you."

This finally made Moira glance up. "You're just adorable, you silly little man," she said. "I just want to eat you alive for saying something so cute. No one sees me when I don't want them to. Trust me, I'm an expert!"

They exchanged phone numbers, so Owen could call her in case of emergency while they were in the school. Then Moira turned and walked away, murmuring to her gold. "You're so pretty, aren't you?" She held it up to her face. "So pretty and shiny and *worth so much*."

"Thank you for going along with this," Owen told Bethany as she took his and Kiel's hands, ready to jump them out.

Bethany looked at him for a moment like she wanted to say something, then sighed. "I don't even know what to say anymore. Everything's weird and crazy now, Owen. Let's just hope this all works out."

He nodded, inwardly screaming at himself over Moira's mother. Why hadn't he looked closer at her story? The last thing he wanted to do was make Bethany's life *worse*.

CHAPTER 23

00:58:42

"You really weren't kidding about forgetting, were you," Moira said, still looking confused. "But I'm not a Moriarty. My mom was, but I'm a Gonzalez. Come from a long line of law enforcement." She glanced at Owen and Kiel. "Yeah, okay, that wasn't going to hold up. I'm a Moriarty. So?"

"Hold on," Owen said, squinting against the pain in his head. Remembering who Moira was helped, but that wasn't the bigger deal. No, it was something in the memory.

Moira had heard of Doyle's school. Which meant that their stories were taking place in the same world.

"Owen, we should get off the roof," Kiel said.

"One second," Owen said, putting a finger up. "Something's *very* wrong."

He sat down in the middle of the roof, covering his eyes with his palms. Wait. Okay. So if Moira and Doyle's stories took place in the same world, did that mean that *every* story did? At least the ones that took place in a real-world setting?

That would explain how Doyle had shown up in other books. It wasn't about switching stories so much as just finding a main character and getting in their way. But why hadn't it happened before? Why hadn't fictional characters ever crossed over into each other's stories?

Except maybe they *had*, but since there was no reason for one main character to recognize another, why would they? If a boy with a lightning scar on his forehead happened to be sitting next to you and you'd never heard of Harry Potter, why would you even notice?

So was there an entire realistic planet, then, in the fictional world? Right down to the same cities and countries? Right down to the streets? To the buildings?

Right down to the libraries? And even to the people?

Oh, oh *no*.

"Kiel," Owen whispered, dropping his hands from his eyes

and looking up at the boy magician with horror. "I think I know where we are."

"Look at you, you're like a map!" Moira said. "I love it. But are we going to leave, or . . ."

Kiel bent down and helped Owen to his feet. Owen pulled him a few feet away and grabbed Kiel by the shirt. "I think we're in the fictional world," he said, his voice shaking.

Kiel frowned, looking around. "You realize we're in your hometown, right? Did that memory hit you too hard?" He felt around Owen's head. "You seem okay, but maybe it's, like, internal damage."

"No, I'm fine," Owen hissed. "But it all makes sense. Listen." He raised his voice. "Moira, did the three of us and our friend Bethany ever all hold hands and, you know, *jump*? And then you ended up here?"

"Unless that's a funny way of saying 'I stole a car and drove here,' then probably not," Moira said. "Can I use that though? I *jumped* a car to get here. I like it!"

Kiel's eyes widened. "How could she have gotten here, then? Maybe she found a way out, like Bethany's father?"

"This is the fictional world," Owen said. "Listen to me.

We've jumped into stories that take place in a world exactly like ours, right? Well, they all had to exist somewhere, and apparently it's here. Together, in one place. That's how Moira had heard of the Baker Street School." Again to Moira, he said, "And how did you track us down?"

"I watched the school, like you paid me to do," Moira said with a shrug. "You two and that girl came out all tied up, and they threw you in a truck. I followed it to that library, which then blew up. I saw you two get out, but not the girl." She made a face. "Hope they left her in the truck, actually. That pulled away a little bit after dropping you off."

Kiel almost collapsed, but Owen caught him. "No, she wasn't in the library!" he said. "Remember, Doyle said she would disappear in . . . less than an hour from now. She couldn't have died."

"Not unless he was lying," Kiel said, his eyes squeezed shut. "If she's hurt, Owen, I swear to you that Doyle will—"

"We'll find her," Owen told him. "And that's good news. We know she's not at the school anymore, so she's probably somewhere in town. But that explains everything, Kiel. Why there's a second me still in his bed at my house, why the

police acted like they were in a movie, even why . . ." But he stopped. Why *was* there no record of Bethany? If there was an Owen, why no Bethany?

Unless there was a fictional Owen because there was a non-fictional Owen. The worlds must be connected somehow? And maybe there was only one Bethany, because she was from both?

It didn't matter. What mattered is that Owen now understood. Everything made more sense. They were still in a book! That's how Doyle was here, that's how the police had heard of him, and that's why they believed everything he said when Doyle framed them.

"If we're in the fictional world, then why is Bethany trapped?" Kiel said, and this time Owen looked at him in confusion.

"Seriously, my crazy co-caper-comrades, we're going to get caught up here if we stay much longer," Moira said, not looking quite as excited as she usually did. "And we really need to talk about the rest of my gold."

"One second," Owen told her, then turned back to Kiel. "I don't know . . . it doesn't make sense. He said that we'd never see her again, but if she jumped out, she could just come back into the book and find us."

"Except we're not exactly anywhere close to Doyle's story anymore, are we?" Kiel said.

Owen paused, then looked around, his entire body going ice cold. They weren't, were they? And that meant if Bethany jumped out, she might never find them again. She could search Doyle's story for years, and never think to look in her own hometown. She'd probably never even considered that it might be in the book.

Which meant that it wasn't Bethany who needed rescuing. *They* were the ones who needed to be rescued by *her*, before she jumped back out of the book. Otherwise they'd be stuck in this book, maybe forever. After all, she hadn't been able to find her father. Even if she used Kiel's finder spell and it pointed to *The Baker Street School for Irregular Children*, there was a whole world for her to look through before she found them.

"We need to find her," Owen said. "She's going to be fine—we're the ones who might never go home!"

Kiel nodded, and together they turned back to Moira, who was looking less and less thrilled as the minutes passed. "We need your help," Owen told her.

"I think we already covered that," she said, smiling just

slightly. "That's why I'm asking for my money, remember? I rescued you guys. You asked for protection, and I protected."

"We paid you to protect us all," Kiel pointed out. "We never did find Bethany."

Moira narrowed her eyes and didn't say anything, but she was no longer smiling. Suddenly Owen remembered some of the crimes she'd committed, and the happy, excited girl seemed very far away. "We'll pay you double," Owen said quickly. "Triple! Just help us find Bethany, and you can have as much gold as you can carry."

Instantly the smile returned, bigger than ever. "Oh, these arms are *made* for carrying!" she shouted. "I'm in! Yay! Let's go find her. Where is she?"

Kiel and Owen looked at each other. "No idea," Owen said. "But you said you'd worked with people here before. Do you know of anyone in town who we could go to for information?" Detectives always got clues from criminal informants, didn't they? Sounded right, anyway.

Moira sighed. "There's a local crime family, they might know something. But they're not exactly friends with my family. Specifically, they've tried to kill my mother a bunch of times. So not, like, best-best friends."

"Sounds like they're our only option," Kiel said, sounding a bit more excited himself.

"Whoa, wait a second," Owen said. "They're not our only option. There's a world of possibilities out there!"

"Where is this crime family?" Kiel asked.

Moira shrugged. "Not too far. Sweet, let's go!" She stopped abruptly and gave them both a serious look. "But if I say run, you *run*, got it? Because that might be our only chance to escape." She stared at them for a moment, then broke out laughing. "I'm just kidding, once we go in, there'll be no escape. *Let's do it!*"

CHAPTER 24

00:53:01

With the chains hanging over her shoulder, Bethany carefully climbed the metal shelves, which were over half-submerged. Her chair had gone under a few minutes ago, and though she'd tried standing on the back of it, the water moved too much to stand securely.

And falling meant going under, then having to pull the chains back to the surface with her. Given their weight, that was quickly becoming impossible, as cold and tired as she was.

The shelves were a thin metal and not too stable themselves, but she'd pushed the chair over for some extra support. And it's not like she had any choice now. More importantly, the shelves could hold her chains, and she wouldn't have to hold them and tread water as the water filled the room.

Of course, once the water rose three or four feet higher than the top of the shelves, she was going to be holding the chains no matter what. The ceiling was easily fifteen feet high, which was seven or eight feet taller than the shelves. And that meant she was going to hold the chains or drown, or . . .

Or jump out, and abandon Kiel and Owen. Just like she had her father. Not to mention that Doyle's cameras would capture it all, and potentially give Doyle . . . what? What could he possibly do with that? It was *her* power! Could the world's greatest detective really learn how to jump between the fictional and nonfictional worlds just by closely watching *her* do it?

But what if he could?

She'd stay until the very last moment. *The very last.*

"How's the water?" said a voice from above her. Bethany gasped in surprise, then climbed as best she could to the top of the shelves, where she found a computer tablet displaying a mask she recognized, even if the voice was a bit hard to hear over the noise of the water.

"They're going to find me!" Bethany shouted at the tablet. "And after they do, we're going to find *you*. And then—"

"You're quite mistaken, Ms. Sanderson," Doyle said. "As we speak, Kiel and Owen are locked away safely. No, you have only one way out."

No. "If I jump, I'll be back, Doyle," she said, trying to make herself sound intimidating despite her teeth chattering from the cold water. "I'll find them, no matter where you hide them!"

"Like you found your father?" Doyle asked.

Bethany's entire body burned with anger, and she desperately wanted to toss the tablet into the water, but she was half afraid the movement would knock over the shelves, dropping her into the water too.

"I won't leave them," she said, trying to calm herself down.

"Then you'll die," Doyle said. "And we'll all lose. Well, you more than me, of course."

She'd never hated anyone so much in her life. Not even the Magister. But this guy was a Holmes, wasn't he? Wasn't there *some* way to reason with him? "If I jump out, and you learn whatever it is you're trying to get from me, will you give me back my friends?"

"Of course not," Doyle said. "Why would I do such a thing? Contrary to your bravado, you'll soon leave, and I'll get exactly what I want without rewarding you for having humiliated my family."

Bethany started to say something, only to yell in surprise as her chains slid off the shelves, yanking her off as well. Their weight dragged her down below the surface of the water, all the way to the floor.

Her mouth still open as she plunged in, Bethany swallowed water and struggled to kick back up to the surface. The chains held her just below it, though, and she couldn't get her mouth high enough to breathe.

Finally, she dove to the bottom and gathered up all the chains in her arms, then dropped them onto the seat of the chair. Then she climbed up the chair and shot back up to the surface just as everything began to go dark.

She felt air hit her face and coughed up water, then immediately sucked in as much oxygen as she could get, barely an inch above water.

"*That* looked dangerous," she heard Doyle say from the tablet, still on top of the shelves. "I really would jump out, if I were you. But it's your choice. Good luck!"

And with that, the tablet went silent, leaving Bethany gasping for air and wishing she'd left Owen and Kiel behind in the first place, like she'd intended.

MISSING CHAPTER 8

Yesterday . . .

Bethany entered the library an hour ahead of the time she was supposed to meet Owen and Kiel, using the key that Owen had given her. The entire place was dark except for emergency lighting, but she knew where Owen kept the books they planned on jumping into, and she quickly found the one she wanted.

The Baker Street School for Irregular Children.

If she wanted to learn what Doyle had found out about her father, it'd have to be now, before Owen and Kiel arrived and the three went in to investigate Doyle. There was no more time to procrastinate, no more time to worry either way. He'd either found her dad or he hadn't. She took a deep breath, carried the book into Owen's mother's office, then slipped into the last page.

The Baker Street School itself was just as intimidating now as it had been the last time. Thunder cracked above and lightning lit the black iron gates as she hit the intercom button, glad that it at least hadn't started raining.

"Ms. Sanderson," said a voice with an English accent. "He's been expecting you."

Bethany shuddered as the gates squeaked open loudly. *Why are you doing this? Just jump out now and come back with Kiel and Owen. Kiel can take this guy down with magic, and then you can find out what Doyle knows safely.*

But then Owen and Kiel would know what she'd done. After everything she'd told them since day one about following the rules, never speaking to main characters, never messing up stories, how could she possibly face them now if they found out?

Bethany pushed through the gates and walked quickly through the courtyard, trying to shut down the loud, annoying part of her brain that kept telling her to jump out and come back with her friends. Sometimes you had to do something wrong to make things right. That's just the way it was. Wasn't it?

It'd all be worth it in the end, when she was hugging her father. It would. It *had* to be.

The same enormous bald guard from the last time waited for her at the entrance, holding one of the gigantic wooden doors open for her. "Right this way," the guard said, and led her through the candlelit entry hall and up the double staircase at the back. She passed by classrooms filled with children, but she barely noticed them as she went. All she could think about was what Doyle might have found.

The guard led her to the doors labeled HEADMASTER'S OFFICE again and knocked gently.

"Let her in," said a voice, and the guard opened the door, waving formally for her to enter. As she did, the guard closed the door softly behind her.

And then she heard the lock turn.

That hadn't happened last time.

This was bad. She shouldn't have come alone. This was way too dangerous. Doyle was obviously up to something, if he was visiting other stories somehow, and she shouldn't be here, not without Kiel and his magic. Even having Owen here would have been more of a comfort than standing alone, shivering in the flickering candlelight.

Just like last time, the tall leather chair at the enormous wooden desk was turned to face away from the door. This time, however, the monitors showed the empty cellblocks, as all the students were in class. In fact, it looked like only one of the cells even had a light on.

"I expected you sooner," said a voice from the other side of the chair. Just as it had last time, the chair slowly twisted around, revealing Doyle in his mask and Sherlock Holmes hat and coat, his fingers steepled in front of him.

"I've been busy," Bethany said, trying not to sound nervous and failing completely.

"I suppose you'd like to know what I found concerning your father's whereabouts?" Doyle asked.

Bethany started to speak, but her mouth was so dry, she could barely move her tongue. She swallowed hard, then again, and finally was able to form a word. "Yes."

Doyle stood up from the chair, then slowly walked around to the front of the desk and leaned back against it, his arms crossed behind him, not saying a word. A moment passed, then another, and Bethany could feel sweat dripping down her neck, despite the room being chilly and the lack of fire in the fireplace.

"We haven't discussed the matter of payment," Doyle said finally.

Bethany let out a huge breath, wiping her hands on her pants. "Of course," she said. "I can pay you however you'd like. Would gold be okay?" She'd given some to a Moriarty now, after all. Why not a Holmes?

Doyle, though, slowly shook his head. "It will *not* be okay, actually. I require something more rare."

"What?" Bethany asked, getting a bit impatient. Were they really going to haggle over the price? "Diamonds? Platinum? What do you want?"

"I want *books*," Doyle said simply.

Books? Bethany's mind began screaming at her to jump out, to come back with Kiel and Owen. "What books?"

Doyle reached behind him and took a book off his desk. "All of the books in your friend Owen's library."

It took Bethany a second to accept that she'd really heard what she thought she had. "*Whose* library?" she whispered.

"If you want to find your father," Doyle said, stepping closer to her with the book in his hands, "then you will get me a digital copy of every single book in Owen's library. You can ignore the nonfiction. That means nothing to me. I want the *fiction*."

"Who . . . who's Owen?" Bethany said, stepping back away from Doyle. "I don't know anyone by that name."

"Oh, but you *do*," Doyle said, and he held the book in his hand out to her.

Bethany shook her head, taking another step back, only to run into the door. *Jump!* her mind shouted. *Jump now!* But if she did, Doyle would see it all.

He stepped closer, holding the book out to her. "Take it," he said. "This one you can have for free."

Bethany reached out a trembling hand and took the book from him, then brought it close enough to read the title in the flickering candlelight.

"*Story Thieves*?" she said, then glanced down at the drawing of two kids leaping into a book. The girl had red hair, and the boy wore all black and carried wand-knives.

"Oh, didn't you know?" Doyle said, his voice sounding like it was a million miles away as Bethany stared at the cover, not believing what she was seeing. "The fictional world's been enjoying your exploits for a few months now. None realized it was a true story, of course. Not even me. Though I did wonder how exactly this author, James Riley, knew of my great-great-great-great-great-grandfather's claim of being saved by a flying man." He paused. "Turns out, my family's embarrassment was all thanks to you."

Bethany couldn't speak, could barely breathe. This book was about her? How was that possible? She wasn't fictional! Half, maybe, but she wasn't living in the fictional world. How could someone see what she was doing? People were reading about her? People knew her secrets?

"I know where your father is, Bethany Sanderson," Doyle continued. "I know what you and your friends are doing. And I know what you *are*. So now you're going to provide me with all the books in your library. That is the payment I require. You'll pay it, or you'll never see your father again. Now, please: Jump out of my book. I'd rather not look at you a moment longer than I have to."

And with that, he turned his back, and Bethany immediately jumped straight out of the book, screaming at the top of her lungs.

CHAPTER 25

00:46:02

"I come here all the time!" Owen said, pointing at the Napoleon Bakery storefront. "You're telling me this is just a front for the mob?"

"Nah, they're not mob, SP," Moira said, crinkling her nose. "Your town isn't really that big, so they're unaffiliated. But they're trying, so you have to give them that! They've made a few big moves, just enough to get on the radar."

"Like trying to kill your mother," Owen said, giving Kiel a glance. The boy magician, though, barely seemed to notice where they were, and just kept looking at the countdown watch. Owen nudged him with his shoulder, and Kiel looked up and winked, but then he got the same faraway look in his eye.

"On the bright side, they would have had to know where

she was in order to off her!" Moira said, pushing the door open. "So let's see what they know, shall we?"

"The sign says 'closed,'" Owen pointed out. It was after midnight, after all.

"That's for the regular people," Moira said, sticking out her tongue at him. "You're with me now, you adorable little monkey. And besides, the door's open. They *want* us to come in!"

The inside of the fictional Napoleon Bakery looked exactly like the nonfictional version that Owen had been to so many times, just darker, considering that most of the lights were off. Small white metal tables filled the front of the bakery, each with two or three chairs around them, while a large display case filled the back, empty now, but usually complete with every possible sweet or baked goodie you could ever want.

Lights shone in from behind the case, and fun smells drifted in from the kitchen. They were probably up baking already for the next day.

Was his version a front for a crime boss too? Did his hometown actually *have* a crime family, or was this just the fictional world? So much of this was confusing!

"I'm going to do the talking, okay?" Moira told Owen and Kiel. "Usually I love hearing what you two crazies come up with, but in the hopes of at least one of us getting out alive, let me handle things."

"This is such a bad idea," Owen told her, wondering if he'd ever have been willing to go along with this in the real world. Did it feel less dangerous just because it was fictional, and things tended to work out in this world? Or was he just so tired and headachy that following Moira just seemed easier?

She blinked at him and Kiel. "A wink for each of you!" she said, then shoved them forward through the door to the kitchen. "Pretend you're my bodyguards!"

As Owen passed through the door, all action in the kitchen stopped, and ten different bakers, all in white, immediately stopped what they were doing and pulled out guns, each one aimed at them.

Owen swallowed harder than he had in his life, struggling to not just collapse in a heap. "Bodyguard," Kiel whispered, and Owen fought through the terror to try to look tough and bodyguard-like, then just as quickly realized he had no idea how to do that.

"Tell the Piemaker that Moira Gonzalez is here to see him," said a dangerous voice behind Owen, and he turned to find Moira, a deadly calm look on her face, staring the kitchen down. The excited girl from a minute ago had completely disappeared, and again Owen remembered that in spite of her demeanor, this girl was a criminal.

No one moved in the kitchen for a moment, then Moira snapped her fingers, and Kiel shoved a cart full of pans over. The clatter made Owen almost jump out of his shirt, but he wasn't sure which was more surprising . . . the noise, or that Kiel had embraced his role so quickly.

"The lady said to move!" Kiel shouted, then turned to wink at Owen, his face still filled with anger. At least he was having some fun.

From a room toward the back, an enormously fat man in a chef's hat and a business suit emerged, drying his hands on a towel. He glanced in their direction, then snorted. "Back to work!" he shouted, and immediately the kitchen jumped to it, the bakers putting their guns away and returning to whatever it was they were doing. One baker even started picking up the pans that Kiel had just knocked over.

"Sorry about that," Owen whispered, and Moira smacked him.

"Moira Gonzalez," said the man in the suit. "This is a surprise. And what might you be doing here?"

"I'm here for information, Piemaker," Moira said. "I hear you're the one to talk to in this pathetic little town."

Hey! Owen wanted to yell, but kept his mouth shut to avoid getting smacked again.

"And why exactly would I help you?" the Piemaker said, walking toward them slowly while glancing over the shoulders of his bakers. "Seems to me I ought to bake you and your little guards there into a pie and send it to your mother as a warning, instead."

"She lets you operate because you're not a threat," Moira said, dipping her finger into one of the baker's chocolaty bowls and tasting it. "Not bad. No, you're not going to touch me *or* my friends. And you're going to give me exactly what I want. Or you and this bakery will disappear in twenty-four hours like you never existed."

The Piemaker laughed. "Not a threat? Tell your mother that next time we sink her boat, she'll be chained to it."

Moira paused, then turned to the Piemaker, her eyes burning. "*Enough.* I was going to let you bluster to impress your people here, but that's all over now." She pulled out her phone and began dialing.

The Piemaker's eyes widened, and he leaped forward, only to

stop short as Kiel grabbed a knife from the counter and held it almost casually between them. Behind them, Moira began to murmur into her phone. "Yup, he's not cooperating. I think his bakery's about to go bankrupt."

"No!" the Piemaker shouted. "I'm cooperating! This was all just a big misunderstanding!"

Moira paused, then said, "Hold on," into the phone. She turned to the Piemaker. "Apologize."

The large man looked around at his bakers, who were staring at him. "I can't—"

"Apologize."

The Piemaker swallowed hard, then nodded. "I'm deeply sorry if—"

"On your knees."

The man started to protest, but Moira just put the phone back to her ear, and he immediately sank to his knees. "I'm deeply, *truly* sorry if I offended you. I am happy to help in any way I can."

Moira nodded, then put the phone to her ear. "Okay," she said, then hung up. "My mother says that she's now bored of this game where you try to disappear her. One more attempt and *you* go away. Am I clear?"

The Piemaker nodded vigorously. "*Crystal* clear, Ms. Gonzalez."

"Good," Moira said. "Now, get me a croissant or something. You've got two minutes."

Exactly two minutes later, the three of them all had pastries and coffee, while the Piemaker sat across from them at one of the small metal tables, visibly sweating. "Of course I've heard of Doyle Holmes," he said, after Owen filled him in on their questions. "The families are watching him, just to make sure he doesn't get too far in his family business. But he's mostly stuck to little stuff. He was here a few weeks ago, but that's the last I heard of him."

Doyle was here a few weeks ago? That was news!

"Oh, he's back," Moira said. "And he's got a friend of mine. What was he doing here before? Give me something, Piemaker, or my mother's going to be *very* disappointed."

The man started breathing hard, and despite the fact that the Piemaker was a criminal, Owen still felt bad about all of this. "Nothing, I swear! All he did was go to the local library. That's it!"

The library? Why would he have gone there? Maybe to get it ready to burn down? But that was ridiculous, Owen's mother, or her fictional version at least, would have noticed something.

"What did he do there?" Owen asked.

"Just talked to some kid, that was it," the Piemaker said. "They left together. Guess he's the son of the librarian or something. We looked into him but didn't find anything. And Doyle left soon after. So I'm sure it was nothing."

Owen's hands began to shake, and he had to grab the table to stop them. Doyle Holmes had spoken to his fictional self a few weeks earlier? What was *happening*?

CHAPTER 26

00:35:12

Are you sure meeting yourself is a good idea?" Kiel asked for the fourth time as they hid in the bushes outside of the fictional Owen's house.

"Nope," Owen said. "But if Doyle spoke to this Owen, then he's involved somehow. His mom's library just got burned down, and he and I are being blamed. If Inspector Brown is right, Doyle even got our fingerprints on the gas cans. Doyle must have put us in the library for a reason. Maybe it was just to throw us off and make us think we were in the nonfictional world, but maybe not. Either way, right now this is the only clue we have."

"I just feel like we're losing time and are no closer to finding Bethany," Kiel said, shifting from foot to foot. Owen glanced at him, not sure how well the magician was holding up. His books had always given Kiel a clear goal, with the Magister telling him what to do, and then Charm helping him get there. Now, though, everything was so nebulous, and nothing was certain. That and not having his magic must be making the magician crazy.

At least Kiel *had* power when he had his wands and spells. The best Owen could do was let a criminal genius get the clues for him, and then question a version of himself.

Like he didn't question himself enough already.

"What do *you* think?" Owen whispered to Moira.

"I love this plan, Sad Panda!" she said, patting him on the shoulder. "I suggest we hang this kid outside his window by his ankles until he talks. If that's uncomfortable for you, I'm happy to do it."

Very helpful, as always.

"Follow me," Owen said, and crept toward the back door. His . . . fictional Owen's mother *should* be down at the police station by now, but who knew when she'd be back. For all he knew, there'd be police cars on their way to the house, too.

Fortunately, there was no need to break in, as Owen had a key. Assuming his nonfictional key worked in the fictional lock.

He pulled his keys out quietly and began to slip the key into the door, before Moira excitedly shoved him out of the way and unlocked it herself, then pushed the door open.

"Sorry, I *love* picking locks," she said, grinning at him. "There's just something so satisfying about it."

Owen stared at her for a moment, desperately missing Charm, then slipped inside a very familiar-looking kitchen.

Everything looked exactly the same as the house he'd left just . . . well, who knew how many hours earlier. The same stove, the same report cards and photos up on the refrigerator, the same nicks in the countertop where he'd learned to slice potatoes years ago. How could it all be so similar, but so different? How connected *were* these worlds?

"I should be upstairs," Owen whispered, then grabbed Moira's arm and yanked her backward before she could take the lead. After the ankle comment, there was no way he was letting her take charge, not with his fictional self. Kiel brought up the rear, seeming more and more uncomfortable with this whole thing.

In the living room something small, furry, and extremely unexpected rubbed up against Owen's leg, and he almost shrieked before leaping backward. He quickly looked down to find a black cat with a white fur spike in the middle of its face staring back at him, purring.

His fictional self had a cat?! Owen didn't have a cat! When did *this* happen?

"Aw, kitty!" Moira whispered, and the cat immediately trotted away, then stopped a few feet away, blinking at Owen. "Hmm," she said, her eyes narrowing. "*Not* cool."

Kiel absently scratched the cat on its head as they passed, Owen giving the animal one last look. A cat? Really? But he'd always wanted a dog.

On his way up to his own bedroom, Owen avoided the creaky stair just by habit, and Moira followed his lead, but Kiel stepped directly on it, which at least confirmed that not everything changed. The noise didn't seem to wake anyone up, so Owen continued the climb, and after quickly confirming that his mother's room was empty, he walked quietly down the hallway toward his own bedroom.

That was an odd feeling, walking toward your own room but knowing that it wasn't yours.

"Let me talk to him," Owen whispered to the other two. "Out of all of us, I'm probably going to freak him out the least." He paused. "And that's saying something."

Moira silently clapped her hands excitedly. "And *then* we hang him out the window!"

"No hanging anyone out windows!" he whispered to her. "Kiel, you okay?"

Kiel just nodded quietly, so Owen slowly turned the doorknob to his bedroom.

Just like his own room, Fictional Owen's bedroom was a bit of a book graveyard. All the library books too beaten up to last on the shelves inevitably were either given to Owen or sold at fundraising sales, so his bedroom tended to look like the night of the living dead books.

The curtains let in just a bit of light, enough to show someone sleeping in Owen's bed (which sent an unpleasant chill down his spine), but not enough to see the titles of the books on the floor. Owen considered stopping for a moment just to see what kind of books Fictional Owen would have, but sighed, figuring that was probably not going to help things right now.

Instead, Owen crept toward the bed, trying not to make a sound, and took a deep breath.

Then he turned on the light.

There, sleeping in his bed, was Fictional Owen, looking

exactly like the Owen that Owen saw in the mirror every morning. As soon as the light hit them, Fictional Owen's eyes flew open, and he proceeded to lose it.

"AH! What's going on?" he shouted, shoving himself away from the intruders until he hit the wall.

"It's okay!" Owen shouted at his fictional self. "Don't freak out! It's just me! It's you! I'm you, I mean!"

"AH!" Fictional Owen shouted again, his eyes frantically switching from Kiel to Moira to Owen and back. "Who are you? What do you want?" And with that, Owen saw his fictional self reaching for a nearby bat.

The same bat that Owen had used to knock out Dr. Verity, actually.

"This is *amazing*!" Moira said, starting forward with her Taser. "He looks *just* like you! I'm so in love with this I want to marry it. How'd you do this, anyway?"

Owen caught her by her shirt and yanked her backward. "No!" he shouted. "Let me *handle* this."

She gave him a sad look, then sighed and put the Taser away. "You're starting to sound like my dad."

"Good!" he told her, then turned back to his fictional self. "Owen, it really is me, so, *you*. You know how you've always thought there was more to the world than school and home-work and chores? Well, you're right, and I'm the proof! I come from a different world, and I need your help."

Fictional Owen paused, looking closely at Owen. Then his eyes widened, and he jumped to his feet. "You're *real*. He said you were real, but I didn't believe it. I *couldn't* believe it. You're here, you're really here!" He turned toward the boy magician. "And *you* must be Kiel!"

Uh-oh. "You know Kiel?" Owen asked, his stomach dropping into his shoes.

Fictional Owen nodded. "And is that Bethany?" He leaned forward and squinted. "You don't look like the version of you on the cover."

"Nope!" Moira said. "I'm *Moira*!" She stuck out her hand, but Owen noticed the Taser behind her back, so he quickly pulled her away from his other self.

"Bethany?" Owen said to the other Owen, his mind racing. "Where did you hear that name? How do you know Kiel?"

"He told me you would come," Fictional Owen said, shaking his head. "I can't believe it. You're actually here! All this time, I thought this was just a weird joke by that James Riley writer. I couldn't believe that he used my name and my mom's library in his book. But you're real! You actually exist!"

With that, his other self began rooting around on the books on the ground. Finally, he found what he was looking for and handed it to Owen.

"See?" Fictional Owen said. "*Story Thieves*. And you're really here! He was right! Doyle said you'd come, and you did!"

Owen reached out a trembling hand and took the book from his fictional self. *Story Thieves*, by James Riley.

And on the cover was a drawing of Bethany holding Kiel's hand and jumping with him into a book.

"Ah, congratulations!" Kiel said, leaning over his shoulder. "Looks like we're both in a series of books!" He clapped Owen on the back. "Think about all those people who've read all about you, Owen. Just think about it!"

Owen did. And then he threw up right on the floor of his fictional self's room.

CHAPTER 27

00:30:56

Bethany's face was the only thing that could still reach above the water. Her chains were on the highest of the shelves, and her arms were so tired of holding them that she wasn't sure she could keep swimming even if the chains weren't there at this point.

There was nothing else to it. What help would she be to Owen and Kiel if she drowned? None. She'd just have to go find them in whatever book Doyle hid them in. She could do it. It wasn't like what happened with her father, because this time . . .

This time, she'd brought them in on purpose. That made it even *worse*.

Bethany gasped for breath, slowly kicking as she pulled the chains up just a bit more, trying to keep her face above water.

Could she just jump a little ways out? Just enough to keep breathing, then slip back in it? But the chains would still be there, dragging her back in.

But maybe she could leave the chains behind?

She'd never actually tried that. Every time she'd been carrying something or touching someone's hand, she'd *wanted* to pull them in or out with her. What if she tried to leave the chains behind, in spite of them being on her wrists?

She focused hard on just one hand, then took a deep breath and dropped back into the water to stare at it. Instead of thinking about jumping, she concentrated on just that one hand, up to her forearm, rising up out of the pages of *The Baker Street School for Irregular Children*.

Her hand began to transform into letters and words, then disappear as it shifted to the nonfictional world, and she could feel the pages of the book on her fingers. She grabbed the pages and held on.

But the chain was changing into words too, and disappearing along with her hand. NO!

She yanked her hand back inside the book and, with her lungs burning, pushed back up to the surface, barely able to reach it this time. She gasped for air, kicking desperately to keep her head above water. The water had finally risen high enough that she'd have to hold the chains with her if she wanted to breathe.

It was now or never.

She dropped back into the water, let the chain hit the shelves again, and concentrated harder. Only her hand. Only the words "skin, bone, fingers, fingernails, thumb, veins, blood, wrist," everything that made up her hand, and nothing else. Her hand began transforming again, and disappearing, but this time, before the chain itself could follow, she grabbed the chain and pulled it up and over her wrist, right where her missing hand had been.

The chain briefly turned into the word "chain" as it passed her missing hand, then solidified back into metal and tumbled down to the bottom of the floor.

She wanted to scream in happiness, but she didn't have enough air left. Quickly she brought her missing hand back to the fictional world, then concentrated on slowly pushing her other hand out, her lungs screaming for air.

Her left hand disappeared, and she immediately tried to yank the chain off her wrist, but it disappeared too.

Her vision started to blacken at the edges as she panicked,

bringing both hand and chain back for another try.

All she wanted to do was breathe. If she didn't leave now, she'd pass out and drown. *Jump!* her brain screamed at her. *Jump out! You can't stay, you'll die!*

She shook her head and concentrated on her hand. It disappeared more quickly this time, and Bethany frantically tried slipping the chain off her wrist.

It felt like the chain disappeared, but everything was turning numb, and she couldn't fight the impulse to just breathe in. Instead, she kicked as hard as she could, barely sure which way was even up, her legs burning with exhaustion, her lungs about to explode.

Then she felt cool air on her face, and she opened her mouth to gasp for air. She drank it in, sweet breath filling her lungs, and realized there was nothing pulling on her arms anymore.

The chains were both gone, coiled up at the bottom of the room.

Bethany let herself float for a moment, her face gently swaying in the water as she breathed in over and over, her body rising with each inhale, falling a bit with each exhale.

For a moment she let the water buoy her, just feeling what it was like to not be chained down. Her wrists still felt like they'd been torn up, but they'd heal.

And then she caught sight of the countdown on her watch: 00:27:18.

In twenty-seven minutes, she'd have to leave Owen and Kiel behind forever.

CHAPTER 28

00:26:11

This couldn't be real. There was no way. Owen opened the copy of *Story Thieves* and flipped through it. It had to be a joke, some kind of prank.

Owen thought back to all the books he knew, and what he could remember about the ends of chapters. Most seemed to stop on some kind of ironic one-liner, or a cliffhanger. Cliffhangers would be a bit tough in here, with no cliffs to hang off of, but maybe he could trick the book into chaptering by saying something horribly ironic, and then waiting for it to (*surprise!*) happen.

That . . . that had *happened*. He'd thought those things, when he'd been trapped by the Magister between pages. How could this author have known that? Was someone seeing his thoughts right now? Was he a made-up character too?

Was someone reading about him right at this very moment?!

"Cool, huh?" Fictional Owen said, grinning widely. "You're *so* lucky. I mean, you're not on the cover, and basically Bethany and Kiel do all the cool stuff and are the heroes of the book, and you're just the jerky guy who messes everything up, but other than that, it's pure awesome!"

Owen just stared at his fictional self, his mouth hanging open but nothing coming out. He barely even noticed as Kiel grabbed the book from his hands and gave the cover a quick glance. "A bit stylized, but it does look like me. Glad to see I didn't stop with just the first series." He grinned, almost looking like his old self. "These readers just can't get enough of me, can they?"

"Someone wrote a book about you?" Moira asked, trying to grab the book out of his hands, but Kiel moved it out of her way too quickly.

"Wait your turn," Kiel told her with a smile.

Fictional Owen gave Moira a strange look. "I don't remember a Moira in the book, so you must be new. A lot's probably changed since the first book, I guess. Hey, what's the title of this one?"

"Title?" Owen asked, still barely able to follow the conversation.

"Yeah, I mean, the first one was just *Story Thieves*, but the second one must have a title, right?" Fictional Owen said. "The book you're living out now. What's it called?" He frowned. "Though honestly, I wasn't altogether clear on who the story thieves were. *You* obviously were stealing Kiel's story, but it's almost like the nonfictional authors are the real thieves, since they're the ones saying they made up stories, when really they're just somehow watching fictional people's lives. There's no way someone made us up. That's just ridiculous. The Magister should have realized that." He shrugged. "Guy needed to relax, honestly. Even if he *was* made-up, who cares? That's, like, the first step to breaking out of the story and becoming real anyway."

"You're not . . . we're *not* made-up," Owen said, slowly shaking his head. They weren't, right? Owen wasn't, that was for sure. . . . Was he?

"We've been through this," Kiel said. "Probably in that book right there, actually. How about we hold off on the life-changing revelations until we find Bethany? Then we can all come to terms with whether we're real or just made-up by someone named Jonathan Porterhouse, of all things. Who'd you get?" He glanced at the book and made a face. "James Riley. Okay, not much better."

"Oh, that Riley guy isn't real," Fictional Owen said. "That's what Doyle said, at least. He looked for him for days and found nothing. Said it's a fake name to hide the real person. Probably some nobody."

This finally pulled Owen out of his fog. "So you do know Doyle?" he asked his fictional self. "Did he say anything about us? About Bethany?"

"Well, *yeah*," Fictional Owen said. "That's why he came to me. I guess she showed up a few weeks ago hiring him to find her father. Doyle realized he recognized her from the book, which of course he didn't think was real. He just figured someone wrote about her, or she was a big fan and was pretending to be the book's Bethany. But when he started investigating, and it turned out the author didn't exist but that an Owen Conners did, he came to me." He grinned. "It's a whole story, actually."

"Let's hear it!" Moira shouted.

"I'm not sure we have the time to waste," Kiel pointed out.

"This is important," Owen said to the magician. "Owen . . . can I call you Fictional Owen?"

Owen paused, tilting his head as if considering it. "Um, no?"

"*Fowen,*" Moira declared. "There you go."

Fowen gave her an annoyed look, but she just jumped onto the bed and bounced excitedly, waiting for him to start his story.

"Doyle has Bethany somewhere," Owen told Fowen. "We need to find her in the next . . . twenty-three minutes, or we're going to be stuck in your world forever. We could really use your help. Honestly, we have no idea where to find either Doyle *or* Bethany. If you know anything about where he might have put her—"

"That's not much time," Fowen said, glancing at his watch. "And I really don't want to get in trouble if my mom catches me." He paused, trying not to smile, then laughed loudly. "Ha, don't worry. I'm *kidding*, I've waited my whole life for this. Let's go!"

"Go?" Owen said. "We don't need to go anywhere. You just need to tell us everything you know about Doyle."

Fowen frowned. "Don't you think that getting out of here would be smarter? Aren't they after you?"

Before Owen could respond, sirens began blaring from down the street. How did Doyle know everything they were doing?!

"Oooh, this Doyle guy is *good*," Moira said, glancing out

the blinds. "How does he always know where we are?"

"That's his whole thing," Fowen said, pulling on pants over his pajamas and then throwing on a sweatshirt. "He's the greatest detective that ever lived. He can see what you're going to do before you do it. Knows everything about you, from what you ate for breakfast to which movies make you cry."

"Wait till you see the movie of *Kiel Gnomenfoot, Magic Thief*," Kiel said. "There will *definitely* be tears. That's what Jonathan Porterhouse told me, at least. He said he was crying the whole time he was signing the contracts."

Fowen gave Kiel a weird look, then leaned in close to Owen. "I get that you like him for some reason, but you should *really* read your book. He's kind of annoying, and totally steals all the credit for everything you did. You should have been on the cover, Owen." He slowly grinned, his eyes widening. "Hey, I bet we're *both* on the cover of this next one!"

"There *isn't* a next one!" Owen shouted, running to the window to peek past the curtains at the cop cars outside. "We're not in a book, *that* book isn't real, and none of this is happening!"

Two squad cars parked in front of Owen's house, while another two sped down the street, then hit the brakes two houses away to both skid perfectly into place right next to the first two. Of course they did.

"We need to go out the back," Owen whispered.

"Way ahead of you," Fowen said, handing him a rope that led out his bedroom window. "I've been preparing for this day ever since Doyle told me you guys were real!"

The Amazing (But True!) Adventures of
Owen Conners, the Unknown Chosen One

CHAPTER 1

Owen wanted to scream at the horror before him. But the sound wouldn't come and the nightmare only continued, forcing Owen to ask himself, deep down, one question:

"Can anyone tell me what year the Declaration of Independence was signed?"

Mr. Barberry stood at the board at the front of Owen's classroom, his arms folded, waiting for a hand to raise.

No, not *that* question. The real question was this: Was there anything in the world that could possibly be more boring than history? Owen frowned as Mr. Barberry gave up on volunteers and just picked someone. "Huck? What year?"

Waiting in a two-week-long line for the chance to wait in another line? That'd be pretty boring. But not *history* boring—

Something hit Owen on the shoulder, and he glanced down to find a folded-up note on the floor next to him.

"1776," Huck said, then covered a huge yawn.

"That one was easy," Mr. Barberry said. "Who can tell me *where* it was signed?"

Owen slowly reached down and picked up the note between two fingers, than carefully brought it up to his lap, making sure Mr. Barberry didn't see him.

"Emma?" the teacher said, turning away, so Owen unfolded the note.

Have lunch with me? I have so many questions! —B

Well. *That* was new.

Class went on for another thirteen or fourteen hours before the bell rang, finally releasing them to lunch. Owen stood up slowly to hide his excitement, then walked to the cafeteria with his most confident strut. There, he quickly grabbed some food and sat down at a table, waiting.

Less than a minute later, a girl with long bronze hair sat down across from him.

"So?" Brianne said, smiling at him for probably the first time ever. "Do you *know* him? Are you two friends?"

For some reason, her smile made Owen's mouth dry up, and

he had to swallow a few times. "Do I—" he croaked, then took a quick drink of water. "Do I know him? Him *who* him? I mean, who him?"

Brianne's smile faded momentarily, only to reappear as she slammed a book down on the table. "The author of *Story Thieves*!"

Hmm. *That's* something he'd never been asked before. In his daydreams, when girls admitted they'd always had a secret crush on him, the conversation went very differently.

Still, he could work with this. "Huh?" Owen said, trying to sound smart.

This time the smile disappeared completely as Brianne gave him a suspicious look. *"Story Thieves,"* she said, pointing at the cover. "You've never heard of it? The book's all about *you*!"

Owen glanced at the cover showing a redheaded girl and a black-haired boy in some kind of costume jumping into a book. "Um, which one am I supposed to be?" he asked, really hoping it was the black-haired boy.

Brianne narrowed her eyes. "I don't get this. I thought you knew the author or something. I wanted to know what's going to happen in the second book."

Owen fought hard against his instincts to keep asking questions or just look confused, so instead he nodded. "Right," he
said. "Of course. The second book." He paused. "Is . . . *this* the
second book?"

Brianne growled, and opened the book to the first chapter.
"How have you not heard about this? It's about a boy named
Owen Conners whose mother works at a library, and—"

"Um, *I'm* Owen Conners," Owen said. "And *my* mother—"

"I *know*, I'm the one telling you about this," Brianne said,
looking much more irritated now. "There's this half-fictional
girl named Bethany, and Owen catches her popping out of a
book in the library—"

"A half-what now?"

"That part's all made-up, obviously," Brianne said. "There's
never been a girl named Bethany in our class, but Mr. Barberry's
in here too! I thought you had to have known about this." She
paused. "Shouldn't they have gotten your permission? You
know, to use your name like this?"

Owen picked up the book and read the back. Apparently the
half-fictional girl took him into some book, and then things got
clearly *awesome*. "How . . . how is this real?" he asked, though
inside he knew the answer. This was *The Sign*. The Sign that

said Owen Conners was never meant to live such a boring life, that all along he'd just been waiting for Fate to come along and Choose Him. There was no way someone boring and ordinary would ever have a book series about him. This was it!

"I'm a *hero*," Owen whispered, staring at the book in awe.

"Uh, not really," Brianne said. "It's just a book."

"But I'm the hero of the book!"

"More like the sidekick, honestly," she said, making a face. "Bethany's the real hero. Her and Kiel. You just mess things up. Listen, Mari's father is a lawyer, maybe you should talk to her about suing this author? He's probably got tons of money. I hear authors are all rich."

Suing? Because the author had made Owen the not-actually-the-sidekick hero in a book? The *last* thing he'd ever do was sue! "*Story Thieves*," he said, running a hand over the cover. Why wasn't the Owen character on the cover, anyway? Was that Owen too busy being amazing and doing all kinds of cool things? "Can I borrow this?"

Brianne smiled, and he smiled back. "Nope," she said. "But let me know if you track the author down. I want to know who Bethany's father is. I think the whole thing with Nobody is too obvious, and it's kind of annoying that she didn't find him in the first book. Way to leave things on a cliffhanger, right?"

"Totally," Owen breathed as Brianne grabbed the book and walked away.

He had to get a copy, of course.

He had to get a copy *now*.

The school library didn't have one, and a quick phone call to his mother from the payphone outside the school's office told him that neither did her library. That explained why he hadn't seen it. He asked his mother to order a copy, and she said she'd look it up, but why was it so urgent?

"Because I've been waiting for this my entire life," he told her.

"Owen," she said, sighing. "What did I say about you being the chosen one, destined to save the world?"

He rolled his eyes. "That the real world is exciting enough, and that I can find plenty of fun things here."

"Without . . ."

"Without being the long-lost son of a king or a secret wizard."

"Or . . ."

"Mom, I have to go!"

"Or . . . ?"

"Or an orphan who grows up to fight crime."

214

"That one was always a bit insulting, honestly," his mom said. "I'll look into this book. Get back to class."

Owen put down the phone with a sigh. She could say those things all she wanted (or, well, make *him* say them), but it didn't matter. He knew the truth, and right now the truth was that some author had made Owen Conners the hero of a book called *Story Thieves*, and that meant . . .

Well, that meant *something* amazing. Now all he had to do was find out what!

"Bethany," he whispered out into the school hall. "If you're actually out there, and if you're really real, *come get me*, okay? That's all I ask. Come get me and bring me into your world. Deal?"

No one answered, so Owen quietly whispered in a girl's voice, "Deal. I can't wait to meet you, Owen!"

"You too, Bethany," he whispered back with a smile. *"You too."*

Later that night Owen sat at the checkout counter of the library, trying to research this James Riley author. There was weirdly very little on the Internet about him, and even his author photo was apparently just an actor or something. That was odd . . . why bother? Who even *looked* at author photos?

"I'm going to start closing up," Owen's mother said, tapping him on the shoulder. "Start putting those books away." She pointed at an enormous pile next to Owen, which he'd been ignoring all night.

He started to object, but he saw her face and sighed, then nodded. She smiled at him, and headed into her office, while Owen carefully picked up the pile of books and walked it toward the children's section.

Carefully balancing the pile, Owen had walked it slowly to the back of the library, trying to make sure he didn't trip over anything. The pile was so large, though, it wasn't easy to see around.

"Owen Conners?" said a deep voice from just inches in front of him, and Owen shrieked, dropping every single book.

"You scared me—" Owen started to say, then lost his train of thought when he saw who he'd almost walked into. There, standing in front of him, was a boy in an overcoat, wearing a hunter's hat and a mask with a question mark on it.

"WHOA!" Owen shouted. "You're—"

"Doyle Holmes," the boy said, extending his hand. "World's greatest detective. And you're clearly Owen."

Owen's mouth dropped. The incredibly famous detective *Doyle Holmes* knew *his* name! "I . . . I am!" he said, much too loudly, and took Doyle's hand.

"Everything all right in there?" Owen's mom yelled from her office.

"Tell her it's fine," Doyle said softly, taking a step backward. "What I have to say is for your ears only."

"It's fine, Mom!" Owen yelled, then whispered to Doyle, "I'm your biggest fan! I knew you were real. The Internet says you're just an urban legend, but I knew you had to be real. Things couldn't be as boring as they look!"

"I encourage those rumors to keep from being overrun by idiots," Doyle said, sounding bored. "But apparently, now I need one's help. I'm investigating someone, and you are sadly my only lead."

"You want my help?" Owen said, his eyes widening in awesomeness. "Of course! Who are you investigating?"

"The man who wrote *this*," Doyle said, and handed Owen a copy of *Story Thieves*.

This. Was. The. Greatest. Day. EVER.

CHAPTER 29

00:21:42

A nd that's how I met Doyle," Fowen finished, then sighed heavily. "Only, after he found out that I'd never heard of the *Story Thieves* author either, he left, and I never saw him again."

Owen peeked above some bushes at the police cars still outside his house. *Fowen's* house. He kept forgetting. Either way, how was Doyle able to track them this fast? Even the greatest detective in the world shouldn't have been able to know where they'd be headed, right when they got there. How had he found them so quickly? Had someone seen them sneaking around in the backyards?

And seriously, even his fictional self was having flashbacks now? More importantly, why hadn't *Owen* had one in a while?

"Why did you tell us what happened like it was a chapter in a book?" he asked Fowen quietly.

"Because obviously someone's going to want to make a book about *me* someday," Fowen told him. "I've been trying to decide where it should start, and that seemed like a good place, since that's when my life finally got interesting. Your authors can't write about *everyone* here, since it'd be too boring most of the time. But look what Doyle's done. This is totally exciting enough for a book!"

"None of this helps us find Bethany," Kiel said, his joy at finding out he was in a second series of books apparently wearing off. "We can't keep wasting time. We're down to twenty minutes!"

"Doyle must have given you some clue," Fowen said. "He wouldn't have been able to resist. It's just how he thinks. Maybe I can help?"

"Aren't you on the wrong side here?" Moira said. "I mean, don't get me wrong, you seem absolutely delightful as a human being, and I'm sure we're going to be best friends until we're being chased and I end up tripping you so the cops get you instead of me. But you just said you were helping Doyle."

"I didn't realize he was trying to hurt you guys!" Fowen said. "Of course I'm on your side. Your side *is* my side."

Moira laughed. "I still don't at all get this. You guys are twins or something? No, don't tell me, I like the mystery. Shh, *no*, don't explain!"

"If he can help, then we're all on the same side," Kiel said, throwing an arm around Fowen's shoulders.

Fowen glanced over at Owen and rolled his eyes.

"All Doyle said was that we didn't even know where we were, which was true. We knew we were in the library—" He froze, realizing that Fowen didn't know. "But we were confused about other things. We got that part. The only other thing he said was that he was doing it by the book. Whatever that means." Owen sighed. Why did mysteries have to involve so many things to solve? No wonder Owen hated them.

"Hmm," Fowen said, his eyes lighting up. "I just love mysteries. See? It's all about noticing the things that don't seem important. Like what Doyle said. It sounds almost like a riddle to me."

"I love riddles!" Moira said. "Have you heard of the sphinx that ate people who answered his riddle wrong? That sphinx definitely had it *all* figured out."

"What do you mean, a riddle?" Owen asked Fowen, trying to ignore Moira.

"Think about it," Fowen said. "Doyle said he was doing things by the book, right? What if that didn't mean doing things the official way? Maybe it was a clue to where Bethany actually is."

Owen started to respond but instantly went quiet as he heard a familiar voice. "Check the surrounding areas," Inspector Brown said from less than ten yards away. "Doyle said they were here not ten minutes ago, so they can't have gotten far."

Moira's smile disappeared, and Kiel jumped to his feet.

"What are you doing?" Owen hissed at him.

"Running isn't getting us anywhere," Kiel said, forcing a grin. "It's time to *fight*."

"Fight the police?" Fowen said. "With what? You said you don't have magic, and isn't that all you can do?"

Kiel's eyes widened, and he paused for a moment. "There's more to me than magic," he said quietly, then began silently moving through the bushes toward Inspector Brown.

What was he doing? They needed to run! There was no time for this. Kiel was acting like he was still in a fantasy series instead of a mystery book. Mysteries involved thinking, not fighting!

"Over there!" a policeman yelled, and Owen pushed out of the bushes to see what was happening, only to fall backward a second later, as a police car almost ran him over.

"Get in!" Kiel yelled from the driver's seat as police officers ran at them from every direction.

"Oh, you did *not* steal a police car!" Moira shouted, and tried to push Kiel out of the front seat. "I'm officially completely in love with you, Magical Koala!"

Kiel pushed her back to the passenger's side as Owen considered what he was about to get into. This was probably the *worst* way possible to avoid getting caught.

But weren't they basically caught already? He sighed, pulled open the back door, and jumped in. A moment later Fowen followed, his eyes gleaming with excitement.

Well, at least *one* of them was having fun.

"Hold on," Kiel said, turning around to flash a real, honest smile at Owen. "I'm not entirely sure how to work this thing."

Okay, maybe two of them, then.

As Kiel looked out the back window to reverse, the car jumped forward, taking out a mailbox first, then a stop sign, and narrowly missing two police officers, who had to leap out of the way.

"Stop!" someone shouted from behind them, and Owen heard the squeal of tires as two other cars raced after them.

"Never!" Moira shouted out the window, then slammed her foot over Kiel's on the gas pedal.

And three of them. Fantastic.

The car's acceleration sent Owen crashing against the backseat, then straight into Fowen as Kiel skidded around a corner, jumping the curb before crashing back onto the street.

"He's going to get us caught for sure!" Fowen shouted at Owen as the two banged against each other when Kiel took another corner hard. "If not *killed*."

"Kiel, we have to stop!" Owen said, trying to sit upright. "You've got the sirens on. They're going to follow us everywhere!"

"Good point," Kiel said, taking his eyes off the road as they spun out onto a major street with oncoming traffic. "How do I turn them off? We need to be stealthy."

"Here, I've got it," Moira said, reaching past Kiel to turn off not only the sirens but also the car's headlights as a truck barreled toward them.

Maybe if this really is *a book, then we won't die,* Owen thought to himself. Then he remembered how that had worked out for him in *Kiel Gnomenfoot and the Source of Magic,* and how his heart was now robotic, and decided that maybe it wasn't a good idea to take the chance. Not to mention that this was potentially *his* book, and given his luck, he should probably be expecting bad things.

"Watch out!" Fowen shouted as the truck's headlights blinded them, its horn blaring.

"Wow, someone has no idea how to drive," Kiel said, turning the wheel hard. The car jerked almost ninety degrees to the right, and the truck passed within inches of them.

The two cop cars behind them weren't so lucky. One managed to follow them, but the other went careening off the road and crashed right into a huge pile of trash.

"Good thing that garbage was there," Fowen shouted from next to Owen.

It's how things work in fiction, Owen wanted to say, but he just sighed in relief before falling straight into his fictional self as Kiel took another hard turn.

"Where should we go?" the boy magician said, turning back to Owen.

"Who cares?" Moira shouted, grabbing the wheel from Kiel momentarily, a wild look in her eyes as she aimed them toward an empty newsstand on the side of the road. Newspapers went flying, smacking into the windshield of the police car right behind them, which caused the car to turn widely and skid to a stop against some nearby parked cars.

"How'd you know that would happen?" Owen asked in awe.

Moira looked confused, then glanced behind them. "Oh, perfect! I'd just wanted to hit the newsstand."

"Okay, *we're stopping right now*!" Owen declared. "Kiel, pull over!"

Kiel slammed on the brakes, despite Moira's loud groan, and Owen and Fowen both crashed against the seat in front of them. Through the pain, Owen tried hard to be thankful that at least they weren't dead. "Everyone out!" Owen shouted, then went to push open his door, only there was no handle.

"Police car back doors don't open from the inside," Fowen told him. "It's to keep criminals in."

Criminals. *That* was appropriate. Even if they hadn't set the library on fire, now they'd stolen a police car. Oh, and resisted arrest, broken out of a police station, and about a dozen other things. Could Owen really argue now with Inspector Brown that he was innocent?

Kiel opened Owen's door from the outside, and Owen spilled out onto the sidewalk, then crawled away from the car before standing, Fowen just behind him. "We're doing this all wrong," Owen said as more sirens began sounding in the distance. "We keep running from place to place instead of *thinking*. That's not how you win mysteries!"

"You don't really win mysteries," Fowen said.

"Fine, you solve them, or whatever," Owen said, wondering

if *he* was ever that annoying. "Which means investigating, and finding clues, then putting those together in the only way that makes sense."

"Enough thinking!" Kiel said. "Sometimes it's good to just take action."

"That's not the kind of story we're in, Kiel," Owen said. "We need to use our heads!"

"Think about the clue Doyle gave you!" Fowen said as the sirens got closer.

Owen sighed. "It's not a clue. It doesn't mean anything! By the book? All that means is . . ." And then he stopped. By the book. As in *by* the *book*.

It *had* been a clue all along, and Owen hadn't even noticed. Doyle had practically told them exactly where Bethany was, and it took Fowen to point it out.

"I know where we're going," Owen said. "Come on!" And with that, he took off at a sprint.

Fowen ran after him, a big grin on his face, followed by Kiel and finally Moira, who looked longingly at the police car they left behind. "I'll come back for you, my love!" she said. "Don't forget me, or our all-too-short time together. You'll always be in my heart!"

CHAPTER 30

00:10:34

"Um, we've been here already," Kiel said, staring at the still-smoking library. A second fire engine had arrived at some point, and even after this long, the firemen still had hoses turned on the smoldering building.

Owen almost couldn't look at the library, even knowing it wasn't exactly his version. Did that really make a difference? Sure, it was fictional, but this was still a place that people could visit and find doorways to other worlds. All those books, gone. What would his fictional mother be thinking right now? How much had her entire life been torn apart?

He turned to Fowen, not sure what to say. If his fictional self felt a fraction of the sadness and horror he felt, then Fowen was going to be devastated.

"I should have told you," Owen told him.

But Fowen didn't seem to hear him, and just stared at the library. "Doyle really is evil, and must be stopped," he said quietly. "This is going to take a true hero, nothing less."

Owen paused, then touched Fowen's shoulder. "Are you okay?"

Fowen jumped as if he were surprised that Owen was there. "So what's the plan?" Fowen asked, his eyes burning with excitement. "Where do you think Bethany is?"

"Aw, I hope she didn't burn up," Moira said, looking sadly at the remains of the library. "I'm *so* going to miss my gold. . . ."

Owen just stared at her for a moment, then sighed and glanced around, no idea what he was looking for. There *had* to be a reason that Doyle had left them in the library. And the "by the book" line seemed almost like bragging, now that Owen realized what it meant. Or might mean.

It *better* mean what he hoped it did, because they were down to ten minutes.

But if Bethany *had* been in the library, it was way too late to find her now. She'd for sure have jumped back to the non-fictional world, which meant Owen and Kiel were stuck here in the fictional world, probably for good.

And not only did that make one too many Owens, but he, Kiel, and Moira were all wanted by the police. Not to mention he'd never see his mother again, or the outside of a jail cell, probably.

"She's here," Owen said, faking confidence, trying to be more like Kiel. Just to prove it, he glanced at the boy magician and gave him an awkward wink.

Kiel gave him an odd look back. "Are you sure?" he said. "I don't feel my spell book anywhere close. If Doyle has them and he's with her, then she's not here, Owen." He glanced around, his hands opening and closing anxiously.

"I'm *not* wrong," Owen said, hoping he was telling the truth. "Doyle put us here to taunt us. We were here all along, and she was right under our noses! We just have to find her. Split up, but don't let anyone see you."

"I've got *all* the faith in you guys!" Moira said, leaning back on the ground and closing her eyes. "Let me know if you find her and need to get rid of the body or something."

Owen glared at her, which she didn't see, then set off with Kiel and Fowen, Kiel moving one way, Owen the other, with Fowen following Owen.

"*I* think you're right," Fowen said, his eyes on Owen. "She's got to be here. That's exactly how villains work, you know?"

"That's the weird thing," Owen said, picking his way slowly through the bushes around the side of the library, trying to stay out of the lights of the fire engines. "Since when is the great-something-grandson of Sherlock Holmes a villain? Why is he doing all of this? What could he possibly get out of locking me and Kiel away and making Bethany leave us behind? I think he wants something."

Fowen shrugged. "All he ever said to me was that he was looking for Bethany's father, and that your author—"

"He's not *my* author," Owen said, far more angrily then he expected. "I'm *real*."

"That your author isn't real," Fowen finished, then raised an eyebrow. "So wait, you don't think *I'm* real?"

Whoops. "Of course you are," Owen said, glancing at his watch. "That's not what I meant. I just . . ." He groaned. There was no time for this right now. "Look, *you* don't have an author either. You and me, we're just extras, background characters for important people. No one's writing stories about us, you know?"

Fowen shook his head. "You're *wrong*. Look at you right now. *You're* the one saving the supposedly important people. Where's Kiel? Bumbling around, useless without his magic. Bethany's captured and needs saving—"

"Actually, I think she's the one who's going to save *us*," Owen said quietly.

"And you're the hero of *Story Thieves*," Fowen finished. "The book doesn't make you out to be, but you are. Or you *should* have been! You're a bigger hero than either Bethany or Kiel were, for sure. You saved the Magister, Charm, *and* Kiel, even if they didn't all deserve it."

For a moment Owen let himself imagine it was Charm standing next to him instead of his fictional double. "He's not wrong," Imaginary Charm told him. "But why are you wasting time with doubting yourself? Bethany needs you."

"I'm looking for her, but I feel like I'm missing something," he told Charm in his mind.

"Of course you're missing something," Charm said, her robotic eye shining on him. "Why would Doyle put her here, then light it on fire? What happens when something burns down?"

"The fire department comes," Owen said, glancing at the trucks.

"And what do *they* do?"

"Put out the fire?"

"With?"

Owen's eyes flashed to the hoses still spraying water on the various small fires around the building. Most of the library was now soaked down, with excess water running down the sidewalks and into the sewer.

Oh!

Ohhhhhh.

Oh *no.*

"You've got it," Imaginary Charm said, and gave him a half smile.

"I miss you," Owen said as she faded out.

"You do?" Fowen said, giving him an odd look.

Owen started to blush, but grabbed Fowen's hand and pulled him back to where Moira waited. He whistled softly, then waved when Kiel turned back. The boy magician quickly returned too, and Owen gathered them all in a huddle.

"I think I know where Bethany is," he said. "I—"

And then police sirens sounded down the street, and Owen shook his head. "Just follow me, okay?"

With that, Owen took off, following the flow of excess water from the library.

"Where is she?" Kiel asked. "Owen, we're almost out of time, and—"

"Doyle burnt down the library with us in it and started the clock when he heard the fire engines," Owen said, wincing as the sirens got closer. "If the two are related, then Bethany's danger had something to do with the fire. What if the clock had to do with the fire department putting out the fire?"

"Nothing like a ticking clock to make things more exciting," Moira said, yawning.

"I'm not following," Kiel said, as Fowen began nodding vigorously. "What would that have to do with Bethany?"

The water flowed down the sidewalk and into a sewer grate, and from within, Owen could hear a deep splashing. *There.* "What if it's not the fire that's the danger," he said, "but the water?"

CHAPTER 31

00:04:17

Bethany had never felt so tired in her life. Every muscle in her body ached, and all she wanted to do was slip below the surface of the water for a minute, maybe two, and just . . . relax. Close her eyes and stop kicking, stop treading water. It was just so tempting to let the water hold her up, do all the work. Not for too long . . .

Her lungs began to burn, and her eyes burst open. She *was* underwater!

Her legs were so tired they refused to respond, so she frantically pumped her barely functioning arms until her face broke the surface, less than a foot from the ceiling now, and rising.

This was it. She'd failed them. Kiel and Owen were going to be trapped in the fictional world, but she just couldn't hold out any longer.

The guilt felt like a truck parked on her back between her shoulders, but alongside that was a feeling almost like relief. She'd hung on until the very last moment, hadn't she? She'd almost drowned a few hundred times over the past two hours, and now . . . now she could just let go, and jump back to reality.

. . . Where she'd have explain to Owen's mother why her son had gone missing, and probably was never coming back.

She forced her dead legs to slowly kick, switching up between her numb, dead limbs as the water rose and her face got closer and closer to the ceiling.

Of course they hadn't found her. How could they? Doyle had hidden her away somewhere secret, and neither Owen nor Kiel was a detective. Not that Moira would have been a help either, if she'd even shown up. That girl was the opposite of a detective. She should have made Owen find someone better. Or just left them both behind and come alone.

Bethany sank below the water level again, this time letting herself drop deeper until she was suspended weightlessly, her legs and arms crying out in thanks. She closed her eyes and tried to ignore the fact that soon there'd be nowhere in the room for her to breathe, and she'd have no choice.

She'd look for them. Of *course* she would. Every bit as long and hard as she had for her father. And maybe it'd even be easier. After all, she knew they'd have to be in some sort of realistic world. Doyle had crossed into other stories somehow, but they'd all been set in the real world.

Unless he figured out how to do whatever it was she did when she jumped out in a minute. Then he could take them wherever he wanted, and Kiel and Owen were both going to be just as lost as her father. Lost in a book, or worse, lost in an unwritten book, stuck somewhere she could *never* find them.

Her lungs began burning again, but she didn't bother kicking back up to the surface. There was no point. They weren't going to find her. It was all impossible.

Be more fictional, Kiel had said before she faced the Magister. And she had been. She'd taken the advice, and when his finder spell hadn't worked, she'd broken her own rules, broken *all* the rules when she'd hired Doyle.

And for that, she was paying the price. Doyle had won.

Something inside of her screamed in rage and anger at that thought, and in spite of everything, her legs began kicking again. Part of her tried to quiet the screams, just wanting to stay underwater where everything was silent, but the screaming part was too wild, too angry. It forced her to the surface, forced her to push her mouth up just inches from the ceiling, and breathe in, even as the air tasted far too stale and made her light-headed.

She stayed there, windmilling her arms behind her, practically kissing the ceiling for a minute.

Then another.

And another.

And then, finally, her watch blinked 00:00:00 and the water rose above her face.

Everything felt weird and sleepy as she sank back into the water. She'd stopped noticing the cold a long time ago, but her arms and legs began feeling weirdly warm now, like she was floating in a warm bathtub, completely comfortable.

Some part of her was still screaming about her friends, about Kiel and Owen, but that part needed to shush. It was really too loud. And the water was so warm, and everything was just nice and relaxing.

Jump, something in her head said. *You* need *to jump.*

But that was the last thing she needed to do. Not when she could just float effortlessly, letting the current of the water do all the work.

Sorry, guys, she thought, but had to struggle to remember what she was apologizing for. Had she done something wrong? And to who?

And why was she holding her mouth closed? Her lungs were saying they needed air, so why not open her mouth and just breathe in?

She parted her lips, and the cold water hit her tongue, just enough to jolt her back to awareness. *JUMP!* her mind screamed. *JUMP OUT NOW!*

Bethany began to jump, pushing her aching, nonresponsive muscles to cross from the fictional world to the nonfictional one before she drowned.

Weirdly, though, instead of pushing up and out of the book, she felt like she was being pulled down instead. Down toward the bottom of the room, where she could hear a roaring even under the water.

Jump! her mind screamed again, and she tried, pushing her arms and legs as hard as she could.

But the water pulled her down toward the roaring, and between the fog in her mind and the ache in her lungs and muscles, she just couldn't make herself fight it.

Kiel, Owen! she screamed soundlessly. *I'm so sorry. I deserve this! I deserve what's happening! It's all my fault. I'm so, so sorry.*

And then the water pulled her down to the floor, and her eyes closed, her breath completely gone as everything went black.

CHAPTER 32

0:00:00

"You're putting two worlds in danger just by being here," the stranger behind her said.

"You brought this on yourself," Doyle Holmes said from behind his mask.

"You *promised* you wouldn't go to the fictional world," Bethany's mom said. "You've broken my heart!"

"You left us behind, Bethany," Kiel said.

"Just like you did your father," Owen said.

"Give her mouth to mouth," said a second Owen.

. . . Wait. *Two* Owens?

"I'm not sure how!" said the first Owen, just above her.

"Oh, *you guys*," said a girl's voice. "What would you ever do without me?"

Then silence.

Abruptly, Bethany began choking, coughing up water, and her eyes slowly opened.

Moira, criminal genius and great-great-great-great-great-granddaughter of Professor Moriarty, Sherlock Holmes's greatest enemy, was bent over her, giving her a disgusted look. "I get that you were almost dead and all," she said, wiping water off of her face, "but basically you just puked on me. You're honestly not my favorite person in the world right now."

"Bethany!" Owen shouted, and pushed Moira out of the way. Bethany weakly let Owen hug her, relief and confusion fighting for dominance in her brain. They'd found her? She hadn't left them behind? But *how* had they found her? And were those sirens in the distance?

She looked around over Owen's shoulder, and saw they were at the bottom of a ladder leading up to a manhole, letting in the only light around them. The smell confirmed what the slippery walls and dank floor hinted at: They were in the sewer.

"I'm so sorry," she whispered to Owen, her throat raw from coughing. "I waited for you two as long as I could. It's all my fault."

"It's *my* fault," Owen whispered back. "I never should have told you about Doyle in the first place."

241

"No, she's right," said a *second* Owen, and Bethany's eyes widened. She hadn't been imagining it . . . there really were two Owens. What exactly had she missed? "She came to Doyle before you even knew about him, Owen," the other Owen continued. "She's the whole reason you're in this mess."

The first Owen let her lie back down, and Bethany turned from one Owen to another, having trouble finding the words. Finally, she pointed at the Owen closer to her. "Who?" she said.

Mercifully, Kiel swooped in for a hug at that point and held her close. "The one farther away is the fictional version of Owen," he whispered in her ear. "We didn't really have a choice. Turns out he's met Doyle." Kiel squeezed her hard then, and for a moment she couldn't breathe again but didn't really care. Instead, she just hugged him back and didn't let go, trying not to worry about anything else.

Then Kiel pulled away, and reality came flooding back. A *fictional* version of Owen? And they'd gotten him involved? He must know everything by now! What had they been thinking? How *could* they—

No. She wasn't going to blame them for breaking the rules, not after she'd done it herself. And it sounded like involving this Owen was her fault too, if Doyle had spoken to him.

"How did you find me?" she whispered, her throat still raw.

"Owen figured it out," Kiel said, and Bethany caught a slight bit of disappointment in his voice. "After Doyle set his mother's library on fire—"

"WHAT?"

"The fictional version of her library," Owen said quickly.

"He's a *monster*," said the other Owen, the fictional version. The one who's mother's library had just burned down. "You need to take him down, or who knows what he'll do next!"

"What did Doyle want with you?" the real Owen asked her. She gave him a confused look. "You were there when he took us."

Kiel and regular Owen looked at each other. "We, uh, haven't really remembered everything," Owen said.

"Doyle made me use the forget spell on the two of us," Kiel said, looking embarrassed now. "I modified it when I cast it so we'd gradually get our memories back, but it's taking longer than I'd like. I was never that great at changing spells, honestly."

"So?" Fictional Owen said. "What did Doyle want?"

"Books," Bethany whispered. "He wanted books."

"That's it?" Kiel said, raising an eyebrow. "All of this over a few books?"

"Not a few books," Bethany said. "*Every* book. He wanted me to bring him an electronic copy of every book in the library. *Our* library. All the fiction books it had."

Owen gasped, but Kiel looked confused. "Why would he want those?"

"He'd have known every secret in the fictional world," Owen said quietly. "He'd know what people were thinking, what they planned on doing, and when. What more could a detective want? He could solve every mystery before it even started."

Moira waved a hand at Bethany. "I love this craziness, I really do, but I kinda need to get home soon. Don't want my father finding out I've been gone. Want to pay me now, or . . ."

"I'm still not seeing why the books thing is so bad," Kiel said. "Granted, he's evil, but solving mysteries isn't the worst thing."

"It is if you see everyone as a criminal," Fictional Owen said. "Look what he did to you two, and you're not exactly hardened criminals."

"Wait, hold up," Moira said, raising an eyebrow. "What's this, now, about hardened criminals? Tell me you didn't give Doyle this information."

Bethany looked away, not saying anything.

There was silence for a moment, other than the sound of people shouting above them somewhere.

"So that's it, then," Fictional Owen said finally. "You've unleashed a monster on us. *Great job*, Bethany."

"It's not her fault," Kiel said, stepping between Bethany and the fictional Owen.

"We'll fix this, don't worry," regular Owen said. "She just needs a chance to rest."

"So what, we just sit here while Doyle begins his reign of terror?" Fictional Owen said. "You guys can do that if you want. I'm not going to let this happen, though."

"Hey, just wait for a second," regular Owen said to, well, himself. "We'll figure something out, and—"

"He's right," Bethany said, then went silent as the sirens stopped and red and blue lights flashed down through the manhole. That couldn't be good.

She started to get to her feet, and Kiel moved to help, but she pushed him away gently. "Look at what Doyle's done," she said. "And that was just to punish us. We can't let him have those books. We need to fix this. *I* need to fix this."

"Even if we get the books back, he'll still know all about you, about the real world," Owen whispered to her.

"Nonfictional world," Fictional Owen said.

"Then we use Kiel's forget spell on *him*," Bethany said.

"Small problem with that," Kiel said, pointing at his waist. "Doyle has my wands and spell book."

"Then we get you replacements first," she said, getting irritated. "Not like we haven't visited the Magister once already."

"The wands I can re-create," Kiel said. "But that was my last spell book. The only other one would be my master's, and that's the one Owen ended up using. We can't take that away from him, he'll die."

"Then we get your spell book back from Doyle," Bethany shouted, not sure why everyone had to argue. "I'm sure it's in that school of his!"

"That school is the most heavily guarded place on earth," Fictional Owen told her. "And ignoring the surveillance cameras, the guards, and the electrified fences and doors, *Doyle* is there. He knows what you'll do before you do it. You'd need a miracle to even get close to him."

"We've got her," Bethany said, nodding at Moira.

Moira laughed. "Do you? You already owe me more gold than you can possibly pay. Oh, *don't worry*, that's just an expression, you'll totally find a way to pay it. But after that, I'm done.

This has been a hugely fun time for me, but I can't be caught doing this. My father finds out, I'm done for."

"Really?" Bethany said. "A chance to steal something from the descendant of Sherlock Holmes, right out from under his nose? You don't want in?"

Moira snorted. "You'd think I'd care about that, wouldn't you! But that's my mom's thing, not mine."

"Then it'd be the kind of thing she might notice," Bethany said quietly, feeling terrible for even mentioning it.

Moira went silent, just staring at her. Finally, she sighed. "I'm in." There was no excitement or joy in her voice, just resignation.

"I hear voices!" someone shouted from above. "Inspector Brown, I think they're in the sewers!"

They all looked up, but Fictional Owen was the first to move. "Go," he hissed. "I'll distract the police."

"What?" Owen said. "You can't, they'll think you're me and throw you in jail!"

Fictional Owen paused for a second, then shook his head and smiled. "They'll have to catch me first. Now go! Go beat Doyle, and get him to admit to everything he's done. The police won't be able to hold me if you win. And you *will* win,

Owen. I have faith in you. Be the hero you're meant to be. You can do it. I *know* you can!" And with that, he ran to the ladder and began scampering up it as they saw flashlights approaching through the manhole.

"NO!" Owen shouted, and tried to catch his other self, but Bethany grabbed his hand and stopped him.

"We have to go," she said, pulling him toward Moira and Kiel. "We'll fix this, and get him out. I promise."

Owen just looked at her, and she'd never seen so much doubt in his eyes. But finally he nodded, and Bethany grabbed the hands of the other two and jumped them out of the book.

She was so weak, they barely made it past the cover of the book, slipping out in a pile to land on the floor of the library.

One by one, they all stood up, and Bethany faced them each in turn. Kiel, the magicless magician, who still managed to wink at her, though somehow it seemed more forced than usual. Moira, who looked around with wide eyes, then turned back to the book they'd just left in amazement. They'd need Kiel's forget spell for her, too.

And finally, Owen, who met her gaze for just a moment, then turned away, shaking his head.

UGH. She deserved that. But she'd make it up to him. She'd

make it up to his fictional self too, and the entire fictional world. She'd fix this, she'd fix *all* of it. She had to.

"Hold up," Moira said, pointing at *The Baker Street School for Irregular Children* on the floor with a shaking finger. "Did anyone else just see us pop out of that book?" She began to laugh nervously.

Bethany nodded, too tired to talk.

Her visitor had been right. Jumping into books was just too dangerous. As soon as she fixed things with Doyle, that'd be it.

She'd never step foot in the fictional world again.

CHAPTER 33

Owen wandered through the library's bookshelves, partly to pick out books that Bethany might be able to use as weapons if she needed to, and partly just to reassure himself that the library was still standing. In spite of the craziness of the night, he found himself yawning every few minutes and realized how late it must be. *Wow*, had it been a long night.

And it was only going to get longer for Fowen now.

Why had his other self done it? Bethany could have taken Fowen out too. But instead, he'd done the heroic thing, and now he was probably locked up in jail. Or *worse*, facing his horrified mother.

And in spite of all that, Fowen still believed in him. In both of them. Why? All Owen had done was mess things up. He wasn't the hero that Kiel was. He wasn't even the hero that his fictional self was!

Through the shelves, Owen saw Moira reading *The Baker Street School for Irregular Children*, preparing for the break-in. He and Kiel had managed to calm her down a bit since they'd jumped out. They'd even shown her a copy of her own book. She refused to look at it, though, and only had one question: Did it say anything about where her mother was?

Owen had shaken his head, and since then, she'd just jumped into planning. She'd even come up with a list of tools she'd need, but they'd all been easy to find. In fact, he'd simply had Bethany reach into Moira's book for most of them. Not that he'd told Moira that.

"This is all so crazy, isn't it?" he said to Moira. "That there's a world where people read about you? I just found out the same thing about me today, so I know what it's like."

"It doesn't matter," Moira said, not looking up.

"It doesn't bother you at all?" Owen asked.

"*You're* bothering me." There wasn't a trace of her excited energy now, just annoyance.

"Think about it. Someone can see into your head," Owen said. Abruptly, he glanced around, wondering if he could see any readers. And then the worst thing in the world occurred to him. "Wait! What about the bathroom? They don't read about you going to the bathroom, do they?"

Moira sighed loudly, but Owen barely heard her. "Maybe that's why they never show people going to the bathroom in books?" He had to go now, in fact, but like *that* was going to happen. If necessary, he'd just hold it for the rest of his life. . . .

"Are you not busy?" Moira said, looking up at the ceiling. "Do you need more to do? Because I can give you a job, or I can shut you up permanently. Those are your two options."

Owen paused for a moment. "What's bothering you, Moira?"

The Baker Street School for Irregular Children slammed shut, and Moira's face appeared on the other side of the shelves an instant later. "Permanently it is!" she said, and a hand shot through an empty space to grab for him.

Owen leaped back out of reach. "Just think of this as more rule breaking," he said. "Because you're totally breaking all kinds of laws of physics just being here!"

Moira didn't reply, and instead tried to shove her arm farther through the shelves.

"Isn't that your whole thing? You love being bad?" Owen asked, stepping back again.

"That's not what this is!" Moira shouted. "Don't you get it?"

"No?" Owen asked. Moira's hand disappeared, and he realized she was coming around the shelves at him, so he quickly circled around, keeping the shelves between them.

"Before, when I was helping you and my Magical Koala escape, that was fun! I love that kind of thing because it doesn't matter. If you two got caught again, it's not like I'd be in trouble."

"Hey!" Owen said, moving quicker now as she continued following him around the shelves.

"But this?" she said. "This is *important*. I've been trying to get my mother's attention all my life, and nothing I do works." She stopped abruptly, then switched directions, causing Owen to do the same. "And now we're trying to break into a place that, if I'm reading it right, has some of the best security I've ever heard of. So excuse me if I'm taking this a bit more seriously!"

Owen gave her a confused look. "So it's not because there's a book about you?"

"Who cares!" Moira shouted at him. "What does it matter if people read about me? They should, I'm brilliant! There should be classes taught in how I commit crimes!" She slowed down and sighed. "I'm sorry, Sad Panda. I shouldn't be taking this out on you. I always get a little more stressed out when I'm trying something big. And it doesn't get bigger than this."

"But you're a criminal genius," Owen told her. "If anyone can do this, you can."

"Obviously," she said, cracking a smile. "But what if *no one* can? That's the part that worries me, Owen. And failing on this kind of stage not only is embarrassing, but will get back to my dad. More importantly, it'll get back to my *mom*. She might not want anything to do with me after that."

"Your mom loves you," Owen said, coming around to her side of the shelves, still ready to run if necessary. "Your father said so, and he hates her, so why would he lie?"

Moira snorted. "I don't need a pep talk. All I want is a way to bypass a security system designed to counter every break-in tool that exists."

Owen paused for a moment, then walked over to the science-fiction shelf, grabbed a book, and tossed it to her. "Then it's good that we can get you things that *don't* exist."

Moira started to say something, then stopped, staring at the cover. "Huh," she said.

"What?" he asked, suddenly nervous.

She looked up at him, a huge grin on her face. "So Bethany can just reach in and grab stuff for us, right? Anything we might need?"

"As long as it doesn't interrupt the story somehow, she can."

Moira smiled even wider, then started pulling book after book off the shelf. "This might actually be fun after all," she whispered, then switched shelves.

Owen moved with her. "So you have a plan now?"

"Always!" She threw some books on the floor, and Owen winced.

"Try to not beat them up?"

"Eesh, you're right," she said, glancing down at the books. "What if by dropping them, I'm causing earthquakes or something in all those stories?" She kicked one, then bent down and put her ear to the cover.

"I don't think that's how it works," he told her. "It's just that the better you take care of a book, the longer you get to read it."

She laughed. "You're *adorable*, SP. You sound like someone's mom! I love it!"

That was fair. He *did* sound exactly like his mother, he realized. "So what?"

"Sew buttons!" she said, then dropped a pile of books in his arms. "This is going to be *so much fun*!"

CHAPTER 34

Kiel slid down the wall next to where Bethany had collapsed earlier and handed her a copy of *What's to Come in the Future*, a book of made-up futuristic inventions. He'd opened to the page about Recovery Pills, which claimed, *You'll feel like you've had a week of sleep with just one pill!* She reached into the page and grabbed one, trying not to look out the nearby windows at the rising sun.

There wasn't much time before Owen's mother would be showing up to open the library. If they hadn't made it back by then, they'd get caught for sure.

Right now that seemed like it wouldn't be the worst thing.

"This can wait, you know," Kiel said. "We don't have to go back in just yet."

"He's too dangerous," Bethany said, not looking up. "The longer he has the books, the more damage he can do. And we need your magic back as soon as possible. Besides, I'm feeling fine." She swallowed the Recovery Pill, then started to push herself up the wall to a standing position, but Kiel gently put his hand on her shoulder.

"Just relax," he said. "Rest for a minute. And don't worry, we'll beat him." He gave her a Kiel smile.

"Will we?" Bethany said, still looking at the ground. "He's a Holmes. You think he doesn't know we're coming? He's probably prepared for everything we do before we even do it." She shivered.

"You're afraid," Kiel said, and he wasn't asking.

She nodded slowly. "Our only real way to fix this is to make Doyle forget it all, Kiel. What happens if we can't get your spell book back? Think of what someone like him could do."

Kiel nodded. "I have been. It's . . . unpleasant. But what made you think you had to go to him in the first place?"

She dropped her head into her arms. "I just . . . *there was no other way*. Once your spell failed, what else could I do? It was either this, or just give up completely."

"But why hide it?" Kiel asked. "Why not tell Owen and me?"

Bethany raised her head. "And what would you have said?"

Kiel grinned. "I'm in?"

"No, you wouldn't have," Bethany said. "You'd have said it was a bad idea. And Owen would have been even more against it. And you'd have both been *right*. But I had to try one last time. And the worst thing?" She sighed. "I think he might know where my father is."

Kiel paused. "Then we'll get that from him."

"He won't tell us," Bethany said. "Don't you get it? Say we outwit him, which we won't. How do we force him to tell us anything?"

"There's magic for that."

"Magic that he knows about," Bethany said, then pushed to her feet. "We need to get going."

"We still have time," Kiel said from the floor, staring up at her. "You're not telling me something, Bethany. What are you still hiding?"

Bethany turned away, not looking at him. There was *so* much she wasn't telling him at this point. That some stranger had seen her in Argon VI and claimed it was dangerous for her to be in the fictional world. That the stranger knew her father. That she wasn't sure what she'd do if Doyle offered her the location of her father in exchange for letting him keep his memory.

That after all of this, she'd decided enough was enough,

and she was done jumping into books. Which meant that she'd need to bring Kiel back into his books and say good-bye for good.

"I'm just exhausted," she said, forcing a smile at him and giving him her hand to help him up.

Kiel took the offered hand and slowly stood. "Don't worry. We'll get my magic back, wipe Doyle's memory, and be back before breakfast."

"Oooh, pancakes," Bethany said, her stomach rumbling maniacally. When had she even eaten last? Dinner last night? It felt like weeks ago.

She led Kiel back to the checkout counter, where Owen was waiting with an enormous pile of books. Moira appeared a minute later from Owen's mother's office and tossed *The Baker Street School for Irregular Children* onto the counter. "*That* was poorly written!" she said, grinning.

"What were you doing in there?" Bethany asked her.

"Research," Moira said. "I've got a plan now. An *unbeatable* plan!"

"Before we start, can I make a suggestion?" Owen said, not looking at Bethany. "Whenever people go over plans in books or movies, they always fail. It's the plans that stay secret that work. So maybe we should just let Moira fill us in as we go."

"You're such an adorable panda, aren't you," Moira said.

"That's just so the readers can get a twist," Bethany said, giving Owen a tired smile. "It's not like we've got that problem here. It's just us. We're not in the fictional world."

"Bethany," Owen said, still not looking at her. "There's a chance that someone's writing about us."

"*Story Thieves*, I know," she said. "I've been trying not to think about that. Maybe fictional authors can see us like our authors can see fictional people?"

"So what if we're in a sequel?" Owen asked. "I'm just saying, we have to be careful, especially giving plans away. If someone's writing this up, then that means anyone could find out about our plan. Just think of it as not jinxing ourselves."

"Like a baby panda holding a teddy bear!" Moira said.

Owen sighed. "Maybe if we *are* in the *Story Thieves* sequel, it'll change chapters right now and skip over the plan. If that happens, at least we'll still have a chance."

CHAPTER 35

"Okay, here's the plan," Moira said, grabbing some paper. She quickly sketched out a box with big, intimidating lines in front of it. "This is what I like to call the Baker Street School," she said.

Owen raised one eyebrow. "Seriously?"

"I really do call it that, yes," Moira said, nodding at him.

He sighed. "And that's the fence?"

"You have an eye for detail, my little panda!" Moira said, and quickly started marking spots around the box. "There are cameras every five feet surrounding the courtyard, as well as inside the school. The gate is ten feet tall and electrified. The walls are *eleven* feet tall, just to be different, and topped with barbed wire, which is *also* electrified. But that's the easy stuff."

"Which part of that is easy?" Bethany asked.

Moira laughed. "The challenging part is the computer

system. It sounds like it handles security for the school *and* helps Doyle solve his cases. It's got some weird acronym that doesn't mean anything."

"W.A.T.S.O.N.," Owen pointed out. "Because that was the name of Sherlock Holmes's best friend and assistant, Dr. Watson."

Bethany groaned and smiled at Owen. He forced a smile back, then looked away.

"In spite of W.A.T.S.O.N.'s adorable lineage," Moira continued, "it sounds like the computer is basically our worst nightmare. It monitors all the cameras as well as a whole suite of motion and thermal detectors. So basically if anything moves or even just exists at a higher temperature than seventy-two degrees, then W.A.T.S.O.N. knows it's there."

"How are we going to get past it, then?" Bethany asked.

Moira winked at her, then patted the pile of books. "You can thank my Sad Panda over there for the idea. We've got it covered."

"Thanks, Sad Panda," Bethany told Owen, and smiled at him again. This time he didn't return it.

"What does W.A.T.S.O.N. do if it detects you?" Owen asked, still trying not to look at Bethany.

"All *kinds* of fun things!" Moira told him. "Every door in the school can be electrified. Even some floors, it sounds like. The book was a little vague. It can also release sleeping gas in any room in the school, alert the guards, call the police, anticipate your next move, wake you up in the morning, and I think do the laundry. That part was vague too."

"You mentioned guards," Kiel said. "How many?"

"You don't remember them yet?" Bethany asked.

Kiel shook his head. "Should I?"

"They're enormous," Bethany said, shuddering. "They're all big and bald and look exactly the same."

"They're ex–British Special Air Service, the SAS," Moira said. "Like our navy seals. Top of their field, the toughest of the worst. And Doyle has about thirty of them, all armed to the teeth."

Owen swallowed hard. This had sounded good when Doyle had been describing it in the book as a way to keep the hardened criminal kids he caught locked away in his rehabilitation school, but from this side it felt a lot less comforting and a lot more impossible.

"Why don't we just jump into a page already inside the school?" Kiel asked, flipping through the book.

"Because those scenes all take place before Bethany went

in the first time," Owen told him. "If we're going to get your magic back and erase Doyle's memory, we need to go in after she hired him."

"Can we talk about this whole wiping his memory thing?" Moira said, giving them a suspicious glance. "Don't think I haven't noticed how it keeps coming up. You don't plan on doing that to *me*, do you?"

Bethany, Kiel, and Owen all stared at the floor.

"What?!" Moira shouted. "How *could* you! I thought we were all friends!"

"You're charging us all the gold you can carry," Bethany said, giving her a guilty look.

"Right, I'm charging my *friends*. You're going to wipe my memory?" She shook her head. "No way. I'm out. Keep your gold. Or better yet, don't wipe my memory and give me all the gold."

"You know," Owen said, shrugging a bit, "if you did have your memory wiped, you'd be able to deny doing anything wrong this whole time. If your father asked, you'd be able to tell him you lived up to your promise."

Moira stared at Owen for a second, then burst into a huge grin. "My silly, sad little panda," she said. "I love when you get underhanded. Okay, you can wipe my memory too, but you better still pay me. Memory or not, I know when I've been cheated, and I'm giving you guys a *great* plan here."

"Which part of this has been your plan?" Bethany said. "All I'm hearing so far is how impossible it's going to be to break in there."

"That's what *I* thought too," Moira yelled excitedly. "But we'll get to that! So it sounds like Doyle keeps all of his important treasures in a safe in his office. The book doesn't say where the safe is, only that it's hidden, and he's the sole keeper of the combination. Supposedly even W.A.T.S.O.N. doesn't know it." She beamed. "So *that* will be a fun challenge. If it takes me any more than two minutes to crack it, I'll give back every gold coin you're going to pay me."

"So what are these books for?" Bethany said, taking the top one off the pile. *"Alpha Predator?"*

"Invisibility suits that also hide our heat," Owen pointed out. "The book's about this race of aliens that hunt down humanity, and the only survivors have to wear these suits to go about their lives. And if the suit gets ripped even a little—"

"I get it," Bethany said, frowning. "I hope there's a less scary place to jump in and grab some of those suits."

"This one has hover shoes, in case the floors get electrified,"

Owen said, handing Bethany a book called *RoboJones*. "Then there's *Boxing Day 2150* with its knockout gloves. They use them in these crazy fighting tournaments. It's actually a terrible book."

"I'm not hearing how that'll help us against W.A.T.S.O.N.," Bethany said, taking the books from Owen.

"That's the best one!" Moira said, and knocked over the rest of the books in her excitement to grab the bottom one. "Take a look!" She shoved the book into Bethany's hands, then stepped back, giving Owen a smug look. "Nailed this one. I'm *so* proud of us."

"Do Computers Worry About Electric Cooties?" Bethany said, then slowly looked up at Owen and Moira. "Are you kidding me?"

"It's about a virus that teaches computers how to love," Owen pointed out, blushing. "It ends up creating this whole dystopian world because every computer stops working, and humanity loses all of its technology."

"Electric cooties," Bethany repeated, still holding the book.

"We can just grab a drive with the virus on it, then plug it into W.A.T.S.O.N.," Owen told her. "It should only take a few seconds after that."

"Before W.A.T.S.O.N. falls in love."

"Isn't it sweet?" Moira said.

Bethany tossed the book onto the table. "You guys seem to have done a lot of work here, and I think it all makes sense. Sort of."

Owen glanced from the books to Moira grinning proudly, and back. It *could* work. It was elaborate enough. But the edges of an idea tickled his brain just enough to make him pause. "You know, there might be another way," he said quietly.

Moira and Bethany looked at each other. "Set the place on fire?" Moira asked.

"It's a school!" Bethany said, her eyes widening in horror.

Moira shrugged. "Yeah, but it'd get us in pretty quick. I'm not *suggesting* it, I just thought maybe that's what he had in mind!"

"Not exactly," Owen said, frowning as the idea formed. "It'd be dangerous, but it doesn't involve actually hurting anyone or making computers fall in love."

"It's fire, got to be," Moira said, grinning widely.

Owen looked down at the table. "Nope. No fire. Just me surrendering to Doyle."

CHAPTER 36

Though it was early morning, the Baker Street School for Irregular Children was covered in a dreary, almost sticky fog that clung to streetlamps and the front gate as if it were alive.

Owen slowly approached the front gate, wishing the others hadn't let him go through with this idiotic plan. Why had he even mentioned it? Moira was the criminal genius. Why hadn't he just followed her lead?

I believe in you, Fowen said in his head, and Owen nodded. That was why.

It was time to prove once and for all that the Owens of the world weren't just sidekicks, weren't just someone to be rescued. No, the Owens might be comic relief, but they could also come up with a pretty clever plan, if he did say so himself.

His breath quickening, Owen reached a trembling finger out to push the intercom button.

It beeped, then a voice with an English accent answered. "Yes?"

"My name is Owen Conners," Owen said, leaning forward to talk into the speaker. "I'm here to turn myself in to Mr. Holmes."

The line went silent for a moment, and Owen wondered if the plan was over before it started. Maybe it wasn't too late to go with the computer love virus after all?

But then the front gates clicked and ponderously swung inward as an enormous bald man opened the double doors at the opposite end of the courtyard.

"Mr. Holmes has been expecting you," the guard said, and held the door open for Owen.

Doyle was expecting him? No way. That had to be a bluff. "Thank you," Owen said, and forced himself to step into the courtyard, remembering the cameras that Moira had mentioned. All were probably aimed at him right now, which didn't exactly help his confidence.

He held the envelope in his hand tighter, took a deep breath, and hurried across the empty courtyard to the doors. The guard looked twice as big up close and seemed to know something was up, given his suspicious look.

Or was that just his face? It was hard to tell.

"This way, please," the guard said, and led Owen inside to the foyer, with its huge staircase that split halfway up, turning on both sides to lead to the second floor. Owen followed the guard up the stairs and past a bunch of classrooms, all empty at this time of morning.

Good. That'd make things easier.

Owen glanced at his watch, the same one Doyle had placed on his wrist: 00:04:23. Four more minutes until the plan kicked into Phase Two, as he called it. Things were going right on schedule.

The guard led Owen to another set of double doors, this time labeled HEADMASTER'S OFFICE. The guard knocked quietly, then turned the knob, opening the door for Owen without entering. Owen nodded at the guard, then stepped into Doyle's darkened office, lit only by flickering electrical candles and a fire in the fireplace, which was close to going out.

As soon as he was inside, the guard closed the door and Owen heard the lock click. Great. There was no turning back now.

At the opposite end of the room behind an enormous desk, a bank of monitors showed various cellblocks, all quiet with no movement. The desk's tall chair was turned toward the monitors, so Owen couldn't even tell if Doyle was there.

"Hello?" he said, then rolled his eyes at his own nervousness.

He cleared his throat and tried again. "Mr. Holmes, I'd like a word with you."

That was better. And would have been even more impressive if his voice hadn't cracked.

The chair slowly rotated around, and Owen almost stopped breathing when he saw the question-mark mask and the Sherlock Holmes hat.

"Mr. Conners," said the same deep, fake-sounding voice he'd heard in the library. "Right on time."

Owen's heart stopped. It was a bluff. There was no way Doyle knew his plan. *No way.*

"I'm here to give you a message from Bethany," Owen told Doyle, and stepped closer to the desk. "We're surrendering, but only under our terms."

Doyle didn't say anything, so Owen quickly laid the envelope he'd been carrying down on the desk and took a few steps back. He knew better than to look at his watch, but the time must be getting close.

"And these are your terms?" Doyle said, picking up the envelope without opening it. "Why send only you? Where are Kiel and Bethany?"

"I'm the messenger," Owen said. "Bethany is ready to pull

me out at any moment, if you don't agree to our terms."

Doyle slammed his hand down on the desk. "You're *not* just the messenger, Owen. What is wrong with you? You need to Owen what you're doing!"

Owen gasped. "You mean own it?"

Doyle paused. "That's what I said." He stood up and carried the envelope over to the fire. While his back was turned, Owen glanced down at his watch: 00:00:59.

Just one more minute.

"I don't think these are surrender terms," Doyle said, looking at Owen over his shoulder. "No, I think this is a trick."

Owen could almost hear his own heartbeat, it was beating so hard. "I don't know what you're talking about. Bethany agrees not to trespass in anyone's story ever again, as long as you tell the police that Kiel and I didn't set the fire. Agree to that, and you'll never have to worry about us again. And you can keep the books. That'll be the end of it."

"No, I don't believe it will be," Doyle said, then absently tossed the envelope into the fire.

"NO!" Owen screamed, and leaped forward, but Doyle swept a leg out, knocking Owen to the ground. Before Owen could move, Doyle had Owen's arms behind his back and a knee to

Owen's neck. "I am the greatest detective who ever lived," Doyle said, his fake voice sounding even more eerie up close. "Did you really think you could trick me like this?"

Owen watched as the envelope slowly caught fire, burning away to reveal a page from a book, before that too went up in flame. "No," he said again, quieter this time, as behind him his watch began to beep.

"So let me see if I have the plan correct," Doyle said. "You come in, ostensibly surrendering, but carrying a page from a book that Bethany and friends are hiding within. At a designated time, right now, it sounds like, Bethany jumps out of that page to take me by surprise, bypassing all of my security in one swoop. Do I have it correct?"

Owen groaned and tried to free himself, but Doyle just yanked Owen's arms up painfully, and Owen stopped moving.

"Shall we see if they're coming?" Doyle said as the book page shriveled up in the fire, blackening into ash.

Finally, the page disappeared entirely into the flames, and Owen dropped his head to the floor, unable to even look anymore.

"Ah," Doyle said, releasing Owen's hands and standing up. "*Now* I will accept your surrender."

CHAPTER 37

"Don't be so melodramatic," Doyle said, using a poker to stir up the ashes from the book page. "It's not like they're trapped in that story. If they jump out now, they'll just end up back with the rest of the book."

"How can you know that?" Owen said quietly.

Doyle turned and looked at him in what Owen assumed was a sarcastic way. "I'm Doyle Holmes. I've cataloged Bethany's powers multiple times, and know exactly how she does it. But that's for later."

Owen's eyes widened. Could he be telling the truth? Had Doyle really figured out how Bethany's powers worked? The Magister had used magic to re-create her abilities, after all. Maybe Doyle's science had done the same thing.

"So was this it?" Doyle asked, pulling Owen to his feet. "Was this your entire plan? Sneak a page of a book into my office, and then what? Pull me out of the book with you?"

Owen wouldn't look him in the eyes, or, well, question-mark mask. "Thought we'd get Kiel's wands and spell book off of you and then make you forget any of this ever happened."

Doyle snorted beneath the mask. "You never had a chance, Mr. Conners. None of you did. I was two steps ahead of you this entire time. Three or four, for most of it." He moved over to his mantle, lifted a glass case off a pistol labeled THIRD ACT, and pulled on the gun.

It raised just an inch, and something behind the desk began to rumble. Owen turned to find the bank of monitors pulling aside to reveal a safe with fourteen different combination locks. "No peeking," Doyle said, and started working his way through each one.

For a moment Owen considered just jumping Doyle and trying to knock him out. All he'd need was a weapon. His thoughts turned back to the pistol on the mantle, wondering if it came off, or was just part of the safe mechanism. The rest of the office was strangely empty of anything weapony, unfortunately. The chairs were far too big to pick up, and the desk was completely out.

"Just another minute, if you don't mind," Doyle said, almost taunting Owen by not bothering to turn around. Owen nodded to himself and crouched down, ready to simply tackle Doyle right into the wall.

"And before you move, you might want to consider that countdown band on your wrist," Doyle said, still not looking. "Every student at the Baker Street School wears one. Most of the time it's just a watch, but within the school grounds it also works as a deterrent. Try to leave the school or act up in any way, and you'll be twitching on the ground in seconds."

Owen's eyes widened, and he immediately went to take the band off, only to get a shock that sent him to his knees.

"Oh, and I wouldn't try taking it off," Doyle said, finally turning around as he pulled the safe door open. "Sorry, probably should have mentioned." He shrugged, then reached into the safe and pulled out Kiel's wands and spell book. "Beautiful, aren't they? I know they shouldn't exist, and that as a man of science I should reject them outright, but I simply can't put them down." The spell book tried to bite his head, but Doyle smacked it hard against the desk, and the book started whimpering.

"What are you going to do with those?" Owen asked quietly.

"What do you think?" Doyle said. "Come, let me show you something." He gestured for Owen to follow, then led the way out of his office.

Owen paused, then followed slowly, glancing behind him at the still-open safe. Was there anything else in there that—

And then the safe door slammed closed, and all fourteen combination locks whirled around.

Maybe not, then.

"Put the school on lockdown," Doyle was telling the guard outside of his office. "I want a total quarantine. No one in or out. I'm expecting some visitors will be arriving in a matter of minutes, and they may be using technology you've never seen. Just ensure that all doors and windows are electronically sealed."

The guard nodded and jogged off, barking orders into a tiny device on the neck of his T-shirt while Doyle gestured for Owen to follow him. "I'd really like to go over my plan now, if you don't mind? There won't be time once Bethany and Kiel show."

"Maybe they're not the only ones," Owen said. If Doyle didn't know they had a Moriarty on their side—

"What, Moira Gonzalez?" Doyle said. "I've been watching her for years, waiting until she might present a bit of a challenge. Didn't want to just cut her legs out from under her before she could hold her own at the game. She has potential, but nothing like the original."

And that was that. Doyle knew every last bit of advantage they had.

"Was that what you've been hiding?" the detective asked, throwing a look Owen's way. "Your body language has been virtually screaming that you were keeping something from me."

Owen nodded sadly. "I thought she'd be our secret weapon. What better way to fight a Holmes?"

"That's just it, Mr. Conners," Doyle said, sliding his hand down a portion of the wall near the stairway. "You can't."

The wall next to him split apart, revealing an elevator filled with newspaper articles framed in gold. Owen looked at the first few and realized they were about the actual Sherlock Holmes. *Consulting Detective Solves Murder; Doctor to Publish Account.* That was their first case. *Holmes Uncovers Hound Hoax. Holmes Not Charmed By Murderous Snake.* All of the famous cases of Sherlock Holmes, here in actual newspaper articles. Some even had drawings.

"All we had was his reputation," Doyle said quietly, staring into one of the mirrors as the elevator shook, then began to descend. "That's all the family had. We were of the house of *Holmes.* And that meant something until your little book arrived on the scene and gave away our family secret, even if it was in what everyone thought was a made-up story."

"What secret?" Owen asked quietly.

"That my great-great-great-great-great-grandfather was saved from his death at Reichenbach Falls by a flying man," Doyle said, practically spitting. "Sherlock Holmes then spent the next *three years* looking for that man, tracking down magicians and yogis of various sorts, trying to learn the secret of flight. Do you understand how humiliating that'd be if it got out? That this great man of science and deduction was taken in by magic, of all things?"

Owen just shook his head as the elevator rumbled to a stop, and the doors opened into a dark, dank hallway.

"Bethany will pay for what she put my family through," Doyle said, then stepped out of the elevator. "And she's given me the tools to do just that."

"Where are you taking me?" Owen asked, wondering if Doyle was going to leave him down here to starve. Or worse, make Owen start attending his school.

"Thanks to Bethany, I now have copies of every single fictional story in your library," Doyle said, ignoring Owen's question as he walked farther down the dark hall, forcing Owen to jog to catch up. "And since I have Kiel's magic, I can follow the Magister's example and re-create Bethany's powers with a simple spell. All I need now is the girl herself, and I'll have access to every fictional world ever."

No. This couldn't happen! Owen stopped dead in the hall as Doyle reached his destination, a lone cell door, too shadowed to see inside.

"You don't have to do this," Owen told him, backing away. "You're supposed to be a good guy. You're supposed to be a Holmes! You just said that your reputation was everything. Well, taking over the fictional world and becoming a tyrant is the last thing a Holmes should do! You're better than that. You're better than this!"

Doyle raised a finger and beckoned Owen to come closer.

"No," Owen said quietly. "I won't let you hide me away down here."

"I need you to see this," Doyle said. "I need you to understand what I've done." He beckoned again with his finger, and Owen swallowed hard.

What choice did he have, though? Doyle could just electrocute him again through the band on his wrist if he didn't do what the detective said. So Owen stepped forward slowly, dreading what he was about to find. The bones of Sherlock

Holmes? A jar for Bethany's essence? A robot W.A.T.S.O.N. with a mustache like the real Watson?

Owen passed Doyle and put his face up to the bars, peering into the darkness.

Two eyes filled with hatred glared right back.

Owen gasped and stepped away as the boy stood up and moved to the front of the cage. A gag covered his mouth, so he couldn't speak, but the boy's eyes were filled with rage as well as something else. A cold, dead, calculating stare. A stare that looked right through Owen, that took in every detail and spit out secrets.

"This can't be," Owen said, barely able to breathe.

"Meet Doyle Holmes, Mr. Conners," said the boy in the mask. "I'm sure he'd like to introduce himself, but he's far too smart for me to take off that gag while I'm not wearing earplugs. I hate when he deduces strange things about me. It's creepy."

Owen turned around and stared at the question-mark mask. "If he's Doyle . . ."

The boy reached up and took off his mask, revealing a very familiar face.

"I'm so disappointed in you," Fowen said, shaking his head. "How did you not figure this out?"

CHAPTER 38

ow are you here?" Owen asked, backing away from his fictional self. "I thought you gave yourself up to the police?"

Fowen snorted, holding up the question-mark mask. "I had the mask on the second I was out of the manhole, Owen. Catch up here. How are you this slow?"

No. *No.* "Did you . . . did you beat Doyle? Is that how you have his mask?"

"Are you kidding?" Fowen shouted. "I've *been* Doyle. At least, the only Doyle you ever met. I was the one who found what I figured were other stories and messed them up, just to bait you guys in. The real Doyle's been down here since a few days after he came by the library."

Owen turned around to look at the ordinary boy in the jail cell, who now was glaring at both of them, his eyes burning, his nostrils flaring as he breathed hard over his gag. "You were Doyle . . . this whole time?"

"Try to follow along, Owen," Fowen said. "You're making me embarrassed for us both. Don't you get it? This was all me. I set this up. I told Bethany I wanted to be paid in fictional books. I framed you and Kiel for the library burning down, which *I did*." He snorted. "How did you not see through me? You think the real Doyle is actually smart enough to know where you are at all times? I was alerting the police because I was standing next to you! I even told you that your own fingerprints were on the gas cans. How did you not suspect me when you found out that I existed?" He shook his head. "They're right about you. You *are* useless, aren't you. I'm doing you a favor with all of this, I really am. I'm doing *us* a favor."

Owen tried to breathe, but it felt like an anvil was sitting on his chest. He backed into a wall and slid down, not looking at his fictional self. This couldn't be true. He was dreaming. "Why . . . why would you do this?" he said, his heart pounding in his ears.

"Why?" Fowen's eyes widened. "Have you *seen* everything I did? I was amazing, Owen! You stole Kiel's story to live it out, but I *built* you a story. I created this for you, and gave you the chance to fight a really great villain! Sure, it happened to be you in disguise, but you didn't know that. I gave you that! I gave you one of the greatest adventures of all time, and you sit there asking me why? If you'd done this for me, I'd be thanking you!"

"You burned down your library!" Owen said, finally able to look at Fowen. "You almost drowned Bethany. You stole Kiel's magic. All just to give me an adventure?"

"Oh, not at all," Fowen said. "I just thought you'd be a little more grateful. No, I did all of this because I wanted to be the hero, and to do that, I needed a big, awesome adventure to hero in. And when Doyle showed up, I realized I'd found one."

Fowen slowly walked toward the bars, where Doyle stood, giving him a look of death. "Only, Doyle gave up," Fowen said softly. "Doyle, boy genius and famous detective, up and quit. He recognized Bethany from *Story Thieves* and was all offended by the whole family-secret thing getting out. But once he realized that James Riley, the author, didn't exist, and he couldn't find any trace of who'd actually written the book . . . well, he just decided that this was all a waste of time. He just wasn't smart enough to see the whole story."

Abruptly, Doyle launched his arms through the bars of the

cell, but Fowen leaped backward, grinning. "Nice try, smart guy," he said, then gave Owen an almost embarrassed look. "He tries that every time I bring him his food. See, Doyle was all lonely up in this school and wanted a friend. A Watson to his Holmes, someone who'd tell him how great he was and how smart his deductions were. So I played that for him, I became his Watson. And he told me *everything*, all of this school's secrets. Even how to access the camera system." He shrugged. "Wasn't hard to find out where he kept his safe after that, and even zoom in for the combinations. It was all in the security recordings."

"You've kept him imprisoned down here because he didn't do what you wanted?" Owen said, pushing himself back up to his feet.

"You make it sound so petty," Fowen said. "I put him down here because Doyle gave up on the *greatest thing to ever happen to me*. Someone made up a whole story about *me*, Owen, and I needed to find out why, and who, and most importantly, what if it were actually real? I needed to meet Bethany, Owen. And if she really *was* real . . . then that left me only one option."

"Drown her?" Owen asked.

"You're so melodramatic," Fowen told him. "She was never

in any danger. I was watching her the whole time. I had to be, after all. I had Kiel's magic working on her."

Owen's eyes widened. "You were—"

"Magistering her? Yup. I was stealing her power, little by little. Took me a few minutes to locate the spell the Magister used in *Story Thieves*, but I found it and stole some of her power just like he did. I haven't tried it just yet, but I can't wait to!" Fowen looked straight up and sighed. "Can you imagine where I'm going to go? Fantasy lands, space, the past, the future, shrink down to the size of nothing . . . so many options."

"But why torture her?" Owen said. "Why almost drown her?"

Fowen shrugged. "I had to make her think I really wanted her to jump out, so she wouldn't. Reverse psychology, Owen. I suppose I could have just told her that, but death traps are so much more villainous, and she's going to need to believe Doyle's truly bad for all this to work."

"The Magister used up her power," Owen told him. "So will you. And then you'll be stuck in whatever book you jumped into."

"Nah," Fowen said. "Because she'll be close by whenever I need a charge." He turned to Owen and slowly grinned.

No. "You're not—"

"That's right!" Fowen shouted. "I'm taking over, Owen. I'm stealing your story. I'm going to be you, and you're staying here. Haven't you always wanted to live in a fictional world?" He frowned. "I do feel a little bad about the whole framing you for the library-burning-down thing, but I can't just have you running after me, or telling anyone what I did. So 'Doyle' will speak to the police. You're going to stay here, at the school, to pay for your crimes." He shook his head sadly. "Don't worry, though. You'll meet all kinds of interesting kids. It definitely won't be boring! And plus, I'll leave you a copy of all the fictional books. I can make one easily enough. I just needed them so I could pass for you, since you've read everything anyway."

This was all too much. How could it be real? How could he be doing this to himself?! "Why? Why would you do this to me?"

Fowen sighed. "Don't you see, Owen?" he said, giving him a pitying look. "You're wasting what could be the greatest life any person could ever live! You could keep jumping into stories with Bethany and Kiel forever, and having the biggest adventures possible. You could be a hero, you could learn magic, you could fly spaceships! But instead, you got all mopey because Charm was in danger and stories were hard, and suddenly you're not into it anymore?"

"I had just had my heart taken out," Owen pointed out quietly, wincing through the pain.

"I wouldn't have let that stop *me*," Fowen told him. "Look at what I was willing to do, Owen! I made Doyle a villain, I framed you and Kiel, I almost drowned Bethany, all so I could be the one to save everyone. Well, not save Doyle, but you get the point. I made up this story, and now I'm going to be its *hero*."

"But it's not just a story!" Owen shouted. "That's what I didn't get before. This is people's *lives*. You can't just go in and mess with them because it sounds fun. You need to take them seriously!"

Fowen leaned in and looked Owen straight in the eye. "*I burned down my mother's library*, Owen," he said. "You don't think I'm taking this seriously?" He stood back up, shaking his head. "It's honestly embarrassing, reading about you as the bumbling sidekick, the comic relief. I'll take care of things. I'll make a name for us both, a heroic one. And you can benefit too! Just tell people the book was written about you, and everyone will love you."

"I don't care about that. You're trying to steal my *life*!"

Fowen made a face. "I can, though. But don't worry. There aren't any hard feelings on my end. Really, I think this is all for the best."

Owen stared at him for a moment, then leaped straight at Fowen. Before he made it two feet, though, the band on his wrist sent a powerful jolt through his entire body. For a moment he completely forgot what was happening and just wondered why he couldn't stop jerking around on the floor. Somewhere close by he heard a muffled groan of pain, and something hit the floor, but he couldn't concentrate on that while he was twitching out of control.

He felt hands under his shoulders, and someone dragged him a short distance. Finally, Owen looked up to see Fowen close the cell door in front of him, with Doyle's unconscious body now outside. "Relax here for a bit," Fowen told him. "I have to go get the guards to help me carry this guy upstairs. You'll enjoy this . . . I'm going to have it set up in his office so when Bethany and Kiel finally get in, they'll see me, Owen, having just defeated Doyle all by myself. *I'll* be the hero that you never could be, and we'll go back to your home dimension and have the coolest, most awesome adventures ever. Maybe I'll even come back and tell you about them."

"*You're a monster,*" Owen whispered, struggling to sit up.

"No, I'm *you*," Fowen said, and grinned.

"You're not me," Owen said. "You're the *evil* version of me."

"I'm the *better* version of you," Fowen said. "Speaking of, I brought my cat, Spike, with me here. I couldn't bear to leave him home without me. Would you mind taking care of him? It's the least you can do."

"It's the *least* I can do?!"

Fowen gave him an annoyed look. "He's a *cat*. Don't take out your issues on him." He turned and started to drag Doyle to the door, then stopped. "Oh, one last thing. See if you can figure out *this* mystery, at least. Who actually wrote *Story Thieves*? Who's the real James Riley?" He grinned. "I'm pretty sure I know, but you'll have plenty of time here to figure it out. Let me know what you come up with!"

And with that, he took Doyle's unconscious body and closed the door behind him, locking it. Owen tried to call out Fowen's name, but an enormous pain hit him in the face like a hammer.

What, a flashback? Now?! NO, this was the *worst*—

MISSING CHAPTER 9

Yesterday...

*J*ust because Doyle let us in, doesn't mean we should trust him," Owen whispered to Bethany and Kiel as an enormous guard with an English accent led them down the full hallways of the Baker Street School for Irregular Children. Everywhere he looked, kids walked quickly to class, their eyes shifting nervously at the slightest sound.

"I don't like how scared they are," Kiel said. He stopped near one and stuck out his hand. "Hello," he said, grinning widely.

The boy, an enormous fourteen-year-old with more muscles in his arms than Owen had in his entire body, gave Kiel a terrified look, then sidestepped the magician and hurried away, not looking back.

Kiel frowned, his eyes going up to the moving cameras above them.

"Please don't speak to the children," the guard in front of them said. "It interferes with their rehabilitation efforts."

The guard turned around, and Kiel stuck out his tongue at him, which caused a nearby student to snort. The student immediately clamped her hands over her mouth, but it was too late. Something beeped, and a teacher stepped out of the nearest classroom, beckoning the student in. The girl dropped her head and followed, and the teacher, flashing a suspicious look at Kiel, Bethany, and Owen, quietly closed the door behind her.

"How exactly are they rehabilitated?" Bethany asked the guard.

"Very carefully," the guard said, then smiled. "Shouldn't keep Mr. Holmes waiting."

During the rest of the walk, Owen made sure not to even look at the students, for fear of getting them in trouble. Sure, these were all criminals of one kind or another, but still, he wasn't comfortable with any of it. None of this had been in the book.

And it didn't explain how Doyle was crossing over into other stories, either.

"Remember the plan," Owen whispered to the other two as they approached the double doors at the end of the hall, doors that said HEADMASTER'S OFFICE. "We grab him and jump out. No messing around. We'll deal with whatever he's done from the real world."

"Nonfictional world," Kiel murmured.

"Shh, both of you," Bethany said, shifting from foot to foot. "And forget the plan. Don't do anything until I say so, okay? I'll handle this."

Huh? Owen glanced over at her, but Bethany's eyes were focused on the door. This was odd. She had barely said a word when they were discussing how to handle Doyle—had just nodded along. And now she wanted to take care of things?

And why were her hands shaking?

The guard knocked lightly on the door, then opened it and waved for them to go in. All three stepped into the headmaster's office, and the guard closed the door gently behind them.

And then the lock clicked. *That* wasn't a great sign.

"Come in," said a voice from the far end of the room, and Owen turned his attention to the enormous wooden desk and a high-backed chair that was turned away from the door.

"Mr. Holmes?" Bethany said, stepping forward. "We'd like to speak to you about some of your latest . . . cases."

"I know why you're here, Bethany Sanderson."

Owen gasped at her name, but Bethany looked more . . . *guilty* than anything.

"Mr. Holmes," she whispered, "*please* tell me you found my father."

Owen's eyes widened. What had she done?

"*What* did you say?" Kiel asked, giving her a shocked look.

She didn't answer, her eyes fixed on the chair. "Tell me what you found, Mr. Holmes," she said, her voice wavering, her hands shaking even worse. "Everything else can wait."

Was *that* what this was all about? Doyle had crossed stories. Why would he do that if not looking for someone lost throughout the fictional world? Bethany had hired him to look for her father and caused this whole mess to begin with. Maybe her showing up here in the first place had done it. Doyle Holmes could probably tell she was half-fictional just by looking at her!

"I do have information for you," Doyle said, and he swiveled around in the chair, a boy wearing a question-mark mask, a Sherlock Holmes hat and coat. The books made it sound almost like a superhero costume, but in person it felt like something out of a horror movie. "But first, let's discuss the matter of my payment."

Payment? Not only had she broken *all* of her own rules, she'd promised to pay the guy?

"I brought what you asked for," Bethany said, reaching into her bag and pulling out a tiny black device. She laid it on the desk, while Doyle stared at her with his fingers steepled before reaching out and taking it.

"Before we continue, I'll need to confirm this is what you say it is," Doyle said, plugging the device into his desk.

Behind Doyle a bank of monitors had been showing classrooms full of kids. Now, though, the monitors began displaying book covers, *real* books, switching so fast that Owen could barely keep up. There were so many . . . what had Bethany given him?!

"It's a copy of every e-book that the library had," she said, sounding miserable, and Owen gasped loudly. She'd given a fictional character real books? But why? What use could he have for them? This was insane!

"Bethany, jump him out now!" Owen shouted, then moved to grab Doyle.

"I wouldn't," the detective said, raising a hand to stop him. "Not if Bethany wants to know what happened to her father."

The room went silent, and Owen slowly turned toward Bethany, who had grabbed his arm and was pulling him away from Doyle.

"Please," she said. "I need to know. I shouldn't have done this, *I know* I shouldn't have, but I *had* to. Don't you get it?"

Owen just stared at her. "No. I don't."

She looked away as Doyle stood up. "Payment accepted," he said. "However, I regret to inform you that I won't be handing over my findings."

"What?" Bethany said, pushing past Owen. "But I paid you! I did exactly what you asked!"

Doyle hit a button on his desk, and the door opened behind them. Guards flooded into the room, one grabbing Kiel and another grabbing Owen. Bethany, though, they left free.

"That you did," Doyle said. "But you're a *thief*, Bethany Sanderson. You steal from books, you trespass in stories that aren't your own, and you just paid me in stolen property. I can't encourage that, now, can I?"

"Let them go!" Bethany shouted, moving toward Doyle. Was she going to jump him out and leave the two of them behind? Owen tried to free himself, but he couldn't even budge in the guard's strong grip.

"Ah-ah," Doyle said to Bethany, and the guards holding Owen and Kiel began squeezing. Owen shouted in pain, while Kiel gritted his teeth. "Touch me, and your friends suffer. Now, let's discuss your punishment for your crimes."

"Punish me, but let them go," Bethany said, practically begging the detective. "They didn't do anything wrong!"

"Of course they did," Doyle snapped. "Owen stole Kiel's story. And Kiel was a thief for half of his life. *All of you* will be punished."

What? How did Doyle know all about them?

"Jump out, Bethany!" Kiel shouted. "Don't worry about us!"

"Worry about us a *little*!" Owen said. If she left them behind, Doyle might hide them somewhere. They might be stuck in the book forever!

Bethany turned to look at them and shook her head sadly. "I did this. This is my fault. I'm not going to just leave you two to pay for it."

"Remove her," Doyle told the guards, and they stepped

forward to grab Bethany by her shoulders. Kiel struggled again, but the guard just held him tight enough to make the magician groan in pain.

"I'm not leaving without you two," Bethany said as she passed between them, her eyes watering. "I *promise*."

And then she was gone, the doors slamming behind her.

"And now, Kiel," Doyle said, "you're going to do a little magic."

Magic? What was Doyle talking about?

"Gladly," Kiel said. "Let me go and I'll be happy to turn you into a toad and squish you."

Doyle sighed. "How charming. No, you're going to use your magic on yourself and Owen. You're going to wipe your memories, all the way back to when you first moved to the nonfictional world, Kiel. All of those memories were made by breaking the rules, and I don't intend to let you keep stolen property."

Owen gasped. He couldn't be serious. Their memories? "And why exactly would I do such a thing?" Kiel asked.

Doyle nodded at the guard holding Owen, and the guard squeezed until Owen almost burst. "And worse will happen to Bethany," Doyle said.

Pain filled Owen's head and he screamed, so he barely

heard Kiel yell for Doyle to stop. "I'll do it!" Kiel shouted. "Let him go!"

The guard stopped squeezing, and Owen would have collapsed to the ground if the enormous man hadn't still been holding him. "Perfect," Doyle said, then paused. "I shouldn't do this. I shouldn't gloat. It's not becoming. But I can't help it. You have to know. And besides, you won't remember any of this."

He gestured, and the guards holding Kiel and Owen both let go, then left the room. Owen, barely holding his feet, looked at Kiel. Should they attack?

Kiel barely shook his head. He was right. Doyle still had Bethany, and who knew what he'd do to her.

"You won't appreciate this right now," the detective said, his hands on his mask. "But trust me, I'm enjoying it enough for all of us."

And with that, he pulled his mask off, and Owen found himself looking in a mirror.

What? Was that . . . him? Was this some kind of evil weird future time travel thing? "Please tell me you're not my future self," Owen said, practically begging.

"Oh, I'm you," his other self said. "Just your fictional self. Impressed?"

Impressed? Owen could barely breathe! What was happening?

"How is this possible?" Kiel said, sounding as shocked as Owen felt.

"Life's a mystery, I suppose," Owen/Doyle said, putting his mask back on. "Now it's time for you two to forget." He held up a small button on a thin box. "If you say any spell other than the forget spell, or aim your wands at anyone besides yourself and Owen, then I push this button. You don't want me to push this button. *Bethany* doesn't want me to push this button."

Kiel gritted his teeth. "I'll find her. Her *and* you. And I'll make you pay for this."

Owen/Doyle shook his head. "No, actually, I don't believe you will. You're not the hero anymore, Kiel. Not this time. This story is *mine*, from start to finish. But you won't have to worry about that, not anymore."

Kiel gave Owen/Doyle a look of pure hatred, then turned to Owen, his wand in his hand. "We'll find her, Owen," he said quietly. "And we'll figure this all out. Trust me." And then he winked.

The wink was the last thing Owen remembered before the spell hit. The magic filled Owen's brain, and for some reason he lost control of his body, dropping to the floor. A familiar face leaned over him.

"Your story is *mine* now," his other self said.

"No!" Owen screamed, but his clone's hands reached for him, and then everything turned into a weird dreamlike fog.

The Amazing (But True!) Adventures of Owen Conners, the Unknown Chosen One

CHAPTER 132

Never wear a mask. That was the lesson of all of this.

"Put him right there, in the chair at the desk," Owen said, trying to suck in air through the stupid question-mark mask. The guards carried Doyle's limp body over to the chair and carefully arranged him in it so he didn't slide off.

"Perfect," Owen said, the mask changing his voice into the deeper, scarier version that he loved. Okay, so that part was awesome. "Now turn off the extra security. I'm going to have some visitors, and I want you to let them right in."

"Mr. Holmes, are you sure?" one of the guards said.

Did he just question a direct order? Owen slowly turned around, doing his best Doyle impression, and stared in the guard's general direction, not sure which had actually spoken. All four guards stared at the floor, silent. "Have I ever been unsure?" Owen said.

"Apologies, Mr. Holmes," one of the guards said, and all four bowed, then left quickly, closing the office door behind them.

Owen quickly pulled the stupid mask off and sucked in air. He hadn't been able to do that downstairs, while explaining everything to his nonfictional self, which had been annoying. But who else would appreciate his grand, complicated, amazing plan if not himself?

Well, he'd appreciate it after he'd calmed down a bit. When he realized how truly for the best it was.

Nowen (as Owen liked to call the nonfictional Owen in his head) couldn't do anything right! Before seeing him fail all over town, Owen had been convinced Nowen would be able to find Bethany instantly. *By the book*. They were in a *library*! What more of a clue did his other self need? Eventually he practically had to slap Nowen in the face with the clue.

Honestly. Other selves could just be such a letdown.

A noise from the desk chair made Owen turn. Doyle was stirring, moaning in pain.

Let's see how *he* liked his mask back.

Owen untied Doyle's gag as the detective tried to lift his head up, looking around in a daze. "Don't worry," Owen told him, sliding the mask down over his face. "In a minute, this is all going to be just a bad memory."

He could have done this before, of course. There'd been plenty of time since he'd taken Kiel's spell book and wands. But Owen wanted every detail just right for when Bethany and Kiel burst in to find that he, Owen, had just beaten Doyle. And that meant that Doyle had to still be woozy from getting his memory erased.

Taking the wands and shrunken spell book from his Sherlock Holmes coat pocket, he laid them on the desk, then draped the coat over Doyle. Getting the detective's arms into the coat was more annoying than Owen would have thought, but there wasn't a whole lot of choice in the matter.

By the time Owen popped the deerstalker hat above the mask, Doyle was starting to stand.

"*You,*" he said, his whole body shaking as he made it to his feet.

"Yup!" Owen shouted, his grin about as wide as his face. "Sorry about these last few weeks. Really. You didn't do much wrong, other than let me down completely. But like I said, you won't have to remember any of it, so it won't be *so* bad."

"You moronic *pustule* of an excuse for a human being," Doyle said, leaning heavily on his desk. "I will see you locked in the same cell you put me in for the rest of your days. I will *personally—*"

Then he paused abruptly and collapsed face-first onto the desk.

Owen put down the wand, having cast the memory spell. His eyes wide, he shook his head. "I can't believe I'm giving you guys up," he told the wand and spell book. "Seriously. I want to keep you forever."

Preparing himself, he tossed the wand into the air, caught it, and whirled around, expecting Bethany and Kiel to burst their way in, now that the school was open again.

Nothing happened.

He frowned. How bad exactly was their timing? Hadn't they been waiting at the gates? It couldn't have taken them *that* long to figure out they weren't in Doyle's office, like they thought they'd be when they jumped out of whatever book Owen had carried a page from. Why did they have to mess everything up?

A noise from outside made him stand up straight, and just as he thought the doors would open, Owen tossed Kiel's wand into the air again, then caught it.

No one came in.

What was the problem here? Why weren't they bursting in

already? Were even *they* tired of rescuing Nowen, so taking their sweet time?

Suddenly Owen felt a chill go down his spine. What if they *hadn't* been able to jump out of the unburned pages of that book? What if by setting that page on fire, Owen had actually *trapped* Bethany and Kiel in the book forever?

No, no, no, *no*. That couldn't have happened. He'd been so sure, and it'd been such a cool thing to do in front of Nowen! Sure, it wasn't the safest move, but honestly Nowen had surprised him a bit with the whole Trojan Horse plan. He'd assumed that all three would show up together, and he'd just use Kiel's magic to knock Bethany and Kiel out first, then when they woke up, he'd be the only Owen around, with a newly beaten Doyle. But no, Nowen had improvised and messed everything up.

"Nooooo," Owen whined, tapping his foot in annoyance. "Why does life have to be so hard?"

The doors burst open, and Bethany and Kiel stepped inside, followed by that annoying girl, Moira. Despite getting caught whining, Owen had to admit that their entrance was pretty cool. It was practically in slow motion, it was so awesome. If there'd just been an explosion behind them—

"Owen?" Bethany said, giving him a strange look as Moira closed the door, locking it. "*You* beat Doyle?"

Now *this*, Owen had planned for! He awesomely raised one eyebrow, tossed Kiel's wand up, then caught it. "*Someone* needed to do it. And it might as well have been me."

"Gasp!" Moira said, grinning widely. "Look at how cool my Sad Panda's gotten!"

Bethany flashed her a look, and Moira looked embarrassed, then shut her mouth. Bethany then turned back to Owen. "What did you do to him?"

"I just used Kiel's magic against him," Owen said, shrugging. "No big deal. He took our memories, I took his. It's called quid pro go."

"Not really!" Moira shouted, and got another look from Bethany. What was happening here?

"So he's forgotten everything?" Bethany asked as Kiel slowly stepped closer to Owen. "He doesn't remember me, or what I can do?"

"Not a thing," Owen said. Kiel reached out a hand, and Owen sadly handed over his wands and the spell book, which tried to bite both of them. Kiel shushed it, then began leafing through the book. Bethany watched him until he nodded, then sighed.

"Now," she said.

"Now?" Owen said, raising his other eyebrow.

"Now," said a familiar voice from right in front of him.

And then something punched Owen right in the face, so hard in the face that he spun around to land on the desk, staring right at the question-mark mask. He quickly looked over his shoulder. "Who did that?" he shouted.

"Just me," said the same voice, and from out of thin air, a zipper appeared, then pulled down, revealing a very, *very* angry Nowen.

"I can't believe you didn't figure it out, *Fowen,*" his non-fictional self said. "Guess who's here to take his *life* back?"

CHAPTER 39

Thirty minutes earlier . . .

*T*hese kinds of stories always need a double twist," Owen
said. "The plan has to look like it's failing, while actually
going exactly how you intended it to go."

Owen walked up to the gate of the Baker Street School,
holding an envelope with a book page in it.

At his side Bethany, Kiel, and Moira stood waiting in
silence, all wearing heat-masking invisibility suits from *Alpha
Predator*.

Owen reached out and pushed the intercom button.

"*Doyle thinks he knows everything,*" Owen said. "*So let's let him
think that. Let's give him a trick to see right through. Something
just a step below obvious, so he can think we really thought we were
getting away with something. He thinks we're that stupid anyway,
so let's just confirm it.*"

Doyle threw the envelope into the fire, and Owen, acting like he was truly horrified, leaped after it. Doyle tripped him, and through the suit's special goggles Bethany saw Kiel start forward, but she grabbed his arm and held him back. It wasn't time yet. Doyle hadn't opened his safe, and they still needed Kiel's wands and spell book. She watched as Doyle cruelly pulled Owen's arms behind his back.

Just one more thing he was going to pay for.

"All we have to do is let him beat us," Owen said. "Here's the idea. I take a page from some random book and hide it in an envelope. I'll tell Doyle that the envelope has, I don't know, terms of surrender or something, from Bethany. But it's going to look like I'm smuggling you in, like a Trojan horse. And that at the right moment, you're going to jump out."

"So let me see if I have the plan correct," Doyle said. "You come in, ostensibly surrendering, but carrying a page from a book that Bethany and friends are hiding within. At a designated time, right now, it sounds like, Bethany jumps out of that page to take me by surprise, bypassing all of my security in one swoop. Do I have it correct?"

"But instead, you're wearing the invisibility suits the whole time," Owen continued. "But it's not about just getting you guys

inside. It's about making Doyle think he's won, so he starts doing stupid things, like revealing his entire plan, and hopefully opening his safe."

"Don't be so melodramatic," Doyle said, using a poker to stir up the ashes from the book page. "It's not like they're trapped in that story. If they jump out now, they'll just end up back with the rest of the book."

Bethany narrowed her eyes. Was he right? Would they have been able to just jump back out of the other pages? Possibly, she guessed, but there was no way Doyle knew that for sure. Basically he'd just risked trapping them forever in that book, and that was something *else* he'd pay for.

Doyle bragged some more, and Bethany wanted to punch him. Open the safe, already! Show them how smart you were, and how little you had to worry about!

"Thought we'd get Kiel's wands and spell book off of you and then make you forget any of this ever happened," Owen told him, and Bethany grinned. That was genius of him, bringing that up. But would Doyle take the bait?

Doyle snorted beneath the mask. "You never had a chance, Mr. Conners. None of you did. I was two steps ahead of you this entire time. Three or four, for most of it."

And then he did exactly what they all hoped he'd do. He revealed the safe, and began opening it.

"This is the part I'm most worried about," Owen said. *"He's going to really have to think he's beaten us here, or there's no way he's just going to open his safe. It's like his most guarded secret. I'm going to have to be as convincing as possible that he just utterly destroyed us here."*

"And before you move, you might want to consider that countdown band on your wrist," Doyle said, his eyes on the combination locks. "Every student at the Baker Street School wears one. Most of the time it's just a watch, but within the school grounds it also works as a deterrent. Try to leave the school or act up in any way, and you'll be twitching on the ground in seconds."

Uh-oh. *That* wasn't part of the plan. She and Kiel looked down at the bands still on their wrists. But what if they just pulled them off?

Before Bethany could move, Owen touched his band, then began twitching and jerking, collapsing to the floor. She gasped, but the sound was covered by Owen's painful flailing, and this time Kiel held *her* back.

Doyle. Would. *Pay.*

As Owen writhed in pain, Doyle pulled Kiel's wands and spell book out of the safe. "Beautiful, aren't they?" he said. "I know they shouldn't exist, and that as a man of science I should reject them outright, but I simply can't put them down." The spell book tried to bite his head, but Doyle smacked it hard against the desk, and the book started whimpering.

"If he does reveal the spell book and wands, then we have him," Owen said. *"You guys just jump him invisibly, Kiel gets his magic back, and we wipe Doyle's memory for good. Done and done!"*

This was all getting to be too much. Bethany moved around behind Doyle, ready to grab him as Kiel silently got into place at her side, waiting for her signal. She nodded at him, then held up three fingers. Three . . . two . . .

"Come, let me show you something," Doyle said, and walked out of the office.

Owen got up and glanced at the safe, where Moira was standing, just as it closed, all fourteen locks whirring. Kiel and Bethany quickly followed Fowen and Owen, while Moira jogged to catch up. "Got you a present from the safe," she whispered to Bethany. "You're *welcome!*"

Great. What had she stolen now?

Doyle led them all into an elevator, where Kiel seemed ready to jump the detective, but Bethany shook her head. It was way too close a space. If they attacked now, they'd probably end up hitting each other and Owen as much as Doyle. Instead, the three of them flattened against the side walls in order to avoid touching Doyle or even Owen by accident, not wanting to startle him.

For a moment Owen looked right through Bethany at some articles on the wall behind her, which was eerie. But then Doyle started going on about how Bethany had ruined his family's reputation, and Owen played for time, trying to get details out of Doyle as much as possible.

In spite of the danger, Bethany couldn't help feeling proud of Owen. This was his plan, and he was doing everything right.

"If things go wrong, then we can improvise," Owen said. "But don't worry about me. Doyle's going to think of me as bait, so he won't do anything too bad to me. Just stay with us, and I'll try to get whatever I can out of him, no matter what."

Owen kept Doyle talking, though the detective seemed to think that revealing his plan painfully slowly was the only way to go. Finally, they came to a cell at the end of a long hallway, too shadowy to see into. Moira gleefully bounded forward and stared through the bars as Doyle beckoned Owen forward.

"I need you to see this," Doyle said. "I need you to understand what I've done."

Moira turned around, and even through her goggles Bethany could see her eyes were huge. What had she seen? She looked from Doyle to the cell and back, then quickly pulled Bethany and Kiel away.

"Something's wrong," she whispered. "There's a boy in that cell, and something's very wrong."

"This can't be," Owen said as he looked into the cell himself as Doyle backed away.

"Meet Doyle Holmes, Mr. Conners," said the boy in the mask. "I'm sure he'd like to introduce himself, but he's far too smart for me to take off that gag while I'm not wearing earplugs. I hate when he deduces strange things about me. It's creepy."

What? Doyle was in the cell? Then who was . . .

Doyle took off his mask, and Bethany wanted to scream.

Owen? The fictional Owen?!

Fowen proceeded to electrocute both the real Doyle and Owen, insulting Owen the entire time. Bethany's hands curled into fists, and she desperately wanted to attack, but this time Moira barred both Bethany's and Kiel's way. "This isn't what we thought," she whispered. "We need to know what he's doing."

"Magistering her?" Fowen said. "Yup. I was stealing her power, little by little. Took me a few minutes to locate the spell the Magister used in *Story Thieves*, but I found it and stole some of her power just like he did. I haven't tried it just yet, but I can't wait to!" Fowen looked straight up and sighed. "Can you imagine where I'm going to go? Fantasy lands, space, the past, the future, shrink down to the size of nothing . . . so many options."

Bethany surged forward, but again Moira held her back. "Not yet," she hissed at Bethany.

"That's right!" Fowen shouted. "I'm taking over, Owen. I'm stealing your story. I'm going to be you, and you're staying here. Haven't you always wanted to live in a fictional world?"

And there it was. The reason for all of this. Fictional Owen just wanted to have an adventure, so he'd written his own story for them to act out, for them to play the parts of victims, so he could be the hero.

Fowen dragged Doyle's unconscious body down the hallway, saying something about how the author of *Story Thieves* was some nobody. Kiel looked at Bethany, ready to attack, but Bethany held up a hand to wait.

So Fowen wanted to play the hero, huh? Well, they were going to let him.

"Moira, open that cell," Bethany said. "Kiel, give Owen the extra suit. We're going to go let Fowen have his win and be the hero. And then we're going to *tear his story apart*."

CHAPTER 40

T his can't be happening!" Fowen shouted. "You're messing up the whole story!"

"Apparently, that's what I do," Owen said, standing over his other self, trying to stay calm. After everything Fowen had done, all Owen felt like doing was hitting. Hitting and hitting and *more* hitting. "Now you're going to give up, and Kiel's going to wipe *your* memory."

Fowen glared at him, then snorted. "Not likely." He reached into a pocket and pulled out a small button, then pushed it over and over.

Immediately Owen, Kiel, Bethany, and Moira all collapsed to the ground, writhing in pain as electricity shot through the bands on their wrists.

Fowen wiped the back of his arm over his mouth, then stood up to his full height. "You really are the worst Owen, you know," he said to Owen, then kicked him. "This wasn't personal before. You could have just let me have your life. I rearranged *my* entire life for you, making it exciting and awesome. I built an entire mystery out of boringness, out of my regular everyday world. And you reject it?" He kicked him again. "No! You don't get to mess up *this* story, Nowen."

Owen tried to move, to think, to do anything, but the shock jolting his system wouldn't stop, and he kept jerking around on the floor as Fowen stepped over him.

"I'll be taking these back, then," Fowen said, grabbing Kiel's spell book and wands from the floor. "You all think you won. But I'm the one telling this story. And I say that if it doesn't end how I want it to, then we *start all over.*"

He opened the spell book to the forget spell page and held up a wand. "Don't worry," Fowen told them. "You won't remember any of this happening. We'll start from scratch, and this time, I'll know how Nowen's going to try to mess this up. We'll just keep going until it ends the right way. *My* way."

"No," Kiel groaned, but through the pain, Owen saw the spell fill Fowen with an unearthly light as he aimed a wand at Bethany.

And then, out of nowhere, the electricity stopped. And

though Owen's muscles still jerked out of his control, suddenly he could think again.

"What?" Fowen said, and jammed a hand into his pocket, then pulled it out empty. "Where did the button go?!"

"Someone didn't pay attention to the clues," said a voice behind him. Fowen whirled around to find Moira tossing the button into the air and catching it. "First, you should have remembered that I never had one of those wristbands. That was clue number *one*." She grinned, then threw the button as hard as she could into the wall, where it split into pieces.

All of their wristbands immediately unlocked and fell to the floor. Fowen gasped, turning his wand on Moira.

"Clue number two is that I'm smart enough to know when to act," Moira said, pulling out her Taser and zapping it a few times, sending electricity shooting out the top. "And clue number three? I'm a criminal genius. I could have picked your pocket before I knew how to walk."

Fowen began chanting, and Moira leaped for him, her Taser sparking.

But she was just a bit too far away.

The forget spell slammed into Moira face-first, and Owen could see the awareness of where she was disappearing from her eyes as she fell to the floor unconscious, just inches away from Fowen.

"You never belonged here anyway," Fowen spat at her, frantically trying to find the forget spell again in the spell book, since each spell could only be cast once before you had to relearn it.

Owen heard Kiel muttering words, but he couldn't make them out. Abruptly, though, the spell book began to grow in Fowen's hands. He dropped the book in surprise, but the spell book stayed exactly where it was in midair, getting bigger and bigger until it was almost the size of Fowen. It roared at the fictional boy, and Fowen screamed, running behind the desk to hide.

The enormous spell book turned toward Kiel and roared again, then picked up Kiel's wands in its pages and disappeared completely.

"What was *that*?" Fowen shouted. "What did you do?!"

"Set . . . it . . . free," Kiel said, slowly pushing himself off the floor. "Won't . . . let you . . . *have it*!"

Fowen gasped, his eyes wide in surprise. "Set it free? It's a book! You can't set a book free! Get it back here!"

"The magic's . . . gone, Fowen," Kiel said, just about at his feet. "Your story ends . . . now."

"You're going to get that book *back* for me," Fowen said, grabbing Moira's Taser and advancing on Kiel. "I don't care what it takes. I'm going to have that magic, and I'm going to redo this story until I'm the one living Owen's life. Me! I deserve this. I've waited my entire life to be the hero, and I made it happen. All it took was becoming the villain for a bit, but that's a small price to pay. Give me the life I deserve!"

Owen slowly pushed himself to his feet, his muscles beginning to actually listen to him again. Across the room Bethany was doing the same as Fowen advanced on Kiel.

"It's not coming back," Kiel told him, circling around Fowen just out of reach of the Taser. "And that was the only one I had. You're now just as magicless as the day you were born."

"Stop acting like you've won!" Fowen shouted, sparks shooting out of the Taser. "You don't get to win. This was *my* plan. I deserve Nowen's life, not him! He's wasting it. He's not good enough at it. I'd be the best Owen ever!"

Bethany kicked him in the back of the knees, and Fowen dropped to the floor, the Taser flying from his hands.

"That's what you don't get," Bethany said, standing over him. "Owen *is* Owen. No one gets to tell him how to live his life. Not you, not me, and not some author nobody. Owen gets to choose how his life story goes, and no one, let alone his idiot fictional self, gets to take that away from him."

"I think he's doing okay," Kiel said. "He won here, didn't he?"

"Because he had help!" Fowen shouted, quickly crawling away back toward the desk. "He couldn't have done any of this without his friends."

Owen took a slightly shaky step forward. "You're totally right," he said, trying to ignore the ache in his muscles. "I'm only here because of my friends. Just think what you might have done if you'd tried to be friends with them too, instead of manipulating them."

Bethany turned to Kiel. "We need to make him forget. Can you still do that?"

Kiel looked at her sadly. "No, I meant what I told Fowen. The spell book is gone." He paused, looking away. "I . . . I won't be doing magic anymore."

Owen tried to think of something to say to Kiel to help, but he realized now was probably not the time. "Then what do we do with Fowen?" he asked. "We can't just leave him here like this. He knows everything. And he's still got some of your power, Bethany."

"Oh, you're not going to do anything with me," Fowen said,

then ran between them, knocking Bethany and Kiel off their still-shaky feet. He barreled into Owen, pushing him hard into the wall, then stopped behind the desk and grabbed a book. "I *do* still have your power, Bethany," he said, practically spitting. "And there's always another way to take what should be mine."

And with that, he opened the book on the table to a specific page, then jumped in headfirst.

"No!" Owen shouted, and moved over to the desk as quickly as he could on his aching legs. He grabbed the book before the page could be lost, then gasped.

"This is bad," he said quietly. "Very, *very* bad."

"What book is it?" Bethany asked.

Owen held it up, not saying a word, and showed her the cover of a redheaded girl and a boy in a black cape jumping into a book. "It's *our* book," he said quietly. "It's *Story Thieves*."

Bethany stared at him for a moment, then nodded. "Hold it open," she said.

"What?" Owen said, just as she ran straight at him. He opened the book wide in front of him, and Bethany dove right in.

The Amazing (But True!) Adventures of Owen Conners, the Unknown Chosen One

CHAPTER 134

As her fingers touched the page, they melted and re-formed, becoming various words like "knuckles" and "fingernail" and "thumb," all describing whatever part they'd been. Those words then spread over the page like brownie batter, absorbing right into the book. Finally, she just shoved her arm in up to her shoulder.

"I'm wriggling my fingers at you right now in Wonderland," she told him.

Owen laughed oddly, then made a weird face and fell backward to the floor, unconscious.

Bethany sighed, shaking her head. "Alien invasions and rocking-horse-flies are fine, but *this* you faint at?"

Owen watched Bethany nervously look around, wishing he could electrocute her some more. But instead, she just gave his nonfictional, unconscious self an apologetic look, then ran off into the library.

"Owen?" his mom said from the front. "Are you almost done?"

Owen stepped out from behind some shelves, staring at Nowen on the ground. "Oh, not going to answer your mom?" he whispered. "Guess I'll help you out, just this once." Then louder, "Give me, like, two minutes, Mom!"

"Don't think I forgot about your homework!" his mom shouted back. "I'll be done soon, so get to it!"

Owen nodded, then looked around for an appropriate book. His eyes settled on one, and he grinned. "Don't like mysteries, huh?" he said, opening the book. "Guess you won't enjoy your time in this one, then."

And with that, he took the book and ran it over Nowen's unconscious body, using Bethany's power to send Nowen into the pages. Then, with his other self gone, he cleaned up the children's section a bit, and went back to the front of the library.

He had homework to do, after all.

Later that night, lying in a bedroom that looked creepily familiar, Owen ran through the next day. He couldn't remember everything his other self had said in the next chapter, but that was okay. He'd get close enough. And as soon as *he* met Bethany, he'd be the only Owen she ever knew about.

Story officially stolen.

He turned over in bed, a contented look on his face. Sure, he might end up jeopardizing all of existence with some sort of time travel paradox, but that was the risk you took. And if reality *did* fall apart, then wasn't it really Bethany and Nowen's fault? He'd tried to take over Nowen's life in the present, but *noooooo*. They had to insist he take the riskier approach.

The only truly horrible part was that he could never tell them how badly he'd beaten them. He closed his eyes, drifting off to sleep, imagining how it'd go.

"You did what?" Bethany would say.

"I'm actually the Owen from the fictional world," he'd tell her, bragging. "I completely stole nonfictional Owen's story out from under him. You had no idea!"

"Ha-ha," she'd laugh. "You're so smart!"

"I sure am," he'd say.

The daydream was so nice that it was all the more jarring when his eyes flew open. What was *that*?

Had something just . . . skittered across the floor?

Owen slowly sat up in bed, trying to see something in the

dark bedroom. The curtains shut out even the moonlight, though, and all he could make out were dark shapes. There was his desk, and his bookshelves overflowing with broken books missing their covers, and—

Wait, *something just moved*!

"Hello?" he said quietly, flailing a hand for his light, not taking his eyes off the spot where he'd seen . . . whatever. "Is someone there?"

Nothing answered, but on his other side, he heard the skittering again.

"Hello?" he said again, his voice barely above a squeak.

"Little boy," said a high-pitched voice. "You've been baaaaaaaaad."

Owen's eyes widened, and he frantically pawed at the lamp, trying to turn it on, only to knock it to the ground. He almost screamed in frustration and fright, but instead dove after it, desperate to turn it on, his body hanging over the side of his bed.

His fingers closed around the lamp's knob, and he switched it on, light flooding the room.

Upside down, Owen looked beneath his bed to the other side. There he saw two red shoes about the size of doll's feet. And then slowly, ever so slowly, something on the other side of the bed bent down.

It was a doll. A clown doll.

A clown doll with teeth that smiled at him.

"Little boYYYYyyyy," it said, "I've COOOOME for you . . ."

Owen started to scream for all he was worth, only to have an enormous book come out of nowhere and slam into his head. He instantly crashed to the ground, falling the rest of the way off the bed, and watched in horror as the clown doll came skittering at him.

"Bad boys get EEEATEN!" the clown said, and Owen covered his eyes in terror.

But nothing happened.

Finally, he opened his eyes one by one and found something even worse than a clown doll standing over him.

Bethany dropped an enormous book of horror stories right onto his stomach, knocking the air out of him. As Owen struggled to breathe, she bent down and smiled. "Welcome to every night for the rest of your life," she whispered to him. "I know where you live, Fowen. And I know what you've done. I don't care how much it changes my story, my past, none of it. I will make sure you *pay* each and every night for the rest of your life. You'll never get a wink of sleep. Every time you close your eyes, I'll be there. And there's a whole horror section in the library, with new books coming in all the time."

"No," he moaned, covering his eyes again. "No, *please*."

"Where's my Owen?" Bethany asked him.

He opened his eyes again. "*I'm* your Owen. . . ."

Bethany grabbed the horror book and began leafing through its pages. "Oooh, ghosts. I'll probably have a harder time getting those out before they drive you insane, since they're so hard to touch and all. Want to try?"

"He's in there!" Fowen shouted, pointing at a book on his shelf. "I swear, he's in there. Just grab him from page four, he won't have been in too long if you take him from there."

Bethany glanced at the book, then glared at Fowen. Without pausing, she reached her head and hand into the book, then pulled her head back out and walked the book over to Owen's bed. There she pulled her arm out and gently ran the book down the length of the bed, spilling a still fainted Nowen out onto his bed.

"He wakes up there in the next chapter," Fowen told her, still squeaking a bit. "I didn't even change the book. Please . . . no more!"

"Sorry, Fowen," Bethany said. "You know too much, and now there are no forget spells to take care of that. You're going into the horror book!"

"No, please!"

"It's either that, or this one," she said, holding up the book he'd stuck Nowen in. "You put your other self in there, it's only fair."

Owen glanced between the two books for a second, then sighed, tapping the second one.

"Good choice," Bethany said. "Now, I know you can jump out on your own until my powers you stole wear off, so I just want to warn you: I see that cover lift even an inch, and you're clown food. We understand each other?"

Owen nodded sadly and held out his hand.

"And just so you know," she said, shoving him into the book, "you're the worst Owen *ever*."

CHAPTER 41

S o what now?" Bethany asked as she, Kiel, and Owen stood in Doyle's office.

Owen shook his head. What *did* they do now? So much had just happened that he could barely take it all in. Fowen was trapped in a book, which Bethany held close to her, ready to grab him if he tried escaping. It'd only be a day or so before his power ran out, though, and then he'd just be stuck there.

"We should tell Fowen's mother where he is," Kiel said.

Owen shook his head, walking over to the still-unconscious Doyle. "I think I have a better idea." He pulled the mask off and saw the voice changer inside. "Let me make a quick phone call."

Two minutes later Inspector Brown had been informed by "Doyle" that Owen Conners would now be attending the Baker Street School for Irregular Children to be rehabilitated over setting fire to his mother's library. Inspector Brown promised to inform Fowen's mother, and thanked "Doyle" for taking care of all of this. Owen then buzzed a guard and asked to have Fowen's cat, Spike, brought up from wherever he'd hidden him.

He might be Fowen's, but his other self had been right about one thing: It wasn't the cat's fault that his owner was evil. And Owen wasn't going to just leave the cat here.

While Owen retrieved the cat in his carrier from the guard, Kiel and Bethany stood over Moira.

"What about her?" Kiel asked. "She won't remember anything she's done here."

"No, she won't," Bethany said. "But we still owe her. I'll take care of it. We'll bring her back with us." She bent down to grab the hand of the unconscious criminal genius, then paused. "What's this?"

A curled-up piece of paper stuck out of Moira's back pocket. Bethany pulled it out and unrolled it, then went deathly white.

"It's from Doyle's file," she said, her voice barely above a whisper. "The one on my dad."

Kiel and Owen both kneeled down next to her, watching in silence as she read it. Finally, she began shaking, and dropped the paper. She immediately threw her arms around Kiel and shoved her face into his shoulder, her back heaving.

Owen picked up the paper and quickly read it. Doyle had actually been fairly thorough, investigating pretty much the entire fictional real world. And at the bottom in bold was his conclusion.

Client's father is presumed dead. There is no record nor trace of him anywhere. Case closed.

A few minutes went by in silence, with Bethany crying into Kiel's shoulder, and Kiel hugging her close. Finally, she pulled away, sniffing loudly and wiping her face on her sleeve. "Let's get out of here," she said. "I never want to see this place again."

"Agreed," Kiel said, not looking much happier than Bethany.

"I can't believe you did that," Owen told him, taking Bethany's hand. "You gave up all your magic to save us. I don't even know what to say."

Kiel nodded. "I suppose I could always find a new master and go through the trial of wills and courage to bind a new book to my service." He shrugged. "Right now, I just want to sleep."

"Me too," Bethany said quietly, then took Kiel's hand. Together, Kiel and Owen grabbed both of Moira's hands, with Owen's other hand on the cat carrier, Fowen's terrified cat watching them all with fright. And then Bethany jumped them all out of the book.

"Moira, you're still asleep?" someone yelled. Moira's eyes flew open, and she immediately sat up in bed. Wait, she was asleep? Hadn't she just been somewhere else? Somewhere more incredibly fun?

Her father stood over her, shaking his head. "Promising to be good includes being on time to school, kiddo."

"I'm up," she said, stifling a yawn as her eyelids slid closed again. So tired. So very, very tired. What had she been doing all night?

"By the way, this came for you," her father said, and she felt something light hit her in the lap. She made a face and opened her eyes to find a letter from some school. "Looks like I'm not the only one keeping an eye on you."

Moira glanced at the letter, suddenly feeling more awake. The Baker Street School for Irregular Children? That was the place all the teenage criminals were so afraid of being sent off to. She wrinkled her nose. How bad could a boarding school really be, though?

"I'll pass," she said, handing the letter back to her father as she slid out of bed. She kissed his cheek, then went to her closet to find some clothes for school.

Her father grunted. "Just keep your promise and neither of us will have to worry about this," he said, pointing at the envelope. "You *have* been good, right?"

"Dad," Moira said, her hand on the closet doorknob. "It's me! Of *course* I've been good. Angel-like, even! Future civilizations will mark this moment as the goodest anyone's ever been. In fact, I've been *better* than good. I've been *best*!"

Her dad gave her a suspicious look for a moment, then smiled despite himself. "Get dressed, I'll make breakfast." With that, he left her room, closing the door behind him.

The Baker Street School. Moira rolled her eyes. Like she'd ever get caught doing something bad enough to get sent *there*.

She opened her closet door . . . and found herself staring at ten overflowing bags of gold coins.

Huh.

Moira reached quietly out and closed the closet door, her hands shaking both from excitement and panic. Not getting caught was suddenly going to be a *lot* more interesting.

CHAPTER 42

Owen didn't see Kiel or Bethany for a week after returning home, apart from school. After everything that had happened, none of them even brought it up. They all needed a chance to breathe and to decide exactly how to feel about everything that had happened.

Finally, Bethany tossed a note at Owen in Mr. Barberry's class, and Owen saw one hit Kiel, too.

Library tonight?
—B

Owen crumpled up the note and gave the slightest nod back to Bethany. Even knowing it wouldn't happen for hours, his palms began to sweat. He had so much to say, but it all just made him so nervous. Would he really be able to go through with it?

For the rest of the school day, Owen avoided looking at either Kiel or Bethany, not wanting them to see how anxious he was. That wasn't really fair to them, not after everything they'd been through.

Working at the library that night before it closed, Owen wandered around the shelves, looking at all the different books they'd visited. The Narnia books, Sherlock Holmes, and so many more. Finally, he took down *Kiel Gnomenfoot and the Source of Magic* and flipped through, going straight to the end as he usually did.

Reading about Charm just made everything better.

Finally, time came for the library to close, and he walked back to his house with his mother, carrying a pile of books that were too broken to keep lending out, so were destined for the book graveyard in Owen's bedroom.

"Don't read those all tonight," his mother warned him. "I saw that you didn't do any homework at the library, so that gets done first."

"I know," Owen said, thinking for the first time that homework might actually be a good distraction.

Needless to say, it wasn't, and was just as horrible as every other time he'd done homework. *Some* things, at least, didn't change.

Eventually his mother turned off her light long after Owen had pretended to go to sleep himself, his new cat, Spike, lying on his chest. Either Spike thought Owen was Fowen, or the cat had decided Owen was close enough, as he followed Owen around everywhere.

A fictional cat now lived in his house. That went well with his robotic heart.

Owen gave his mother another hour to fall asleep, just lying in his bed and petting Spike, wondering how Bethany and Kiel were going to take things tonight.

Several times during that hour, he considered not going. It could wait, after all. But getting it over with seemed like the smarter thing to do, and didn't he owe them the truth, at least?

In his mind, Fowen mocked him. "You're so useless, you're scared to tell your friends what you're thinking," he said, giving Owen a disgusted look.

"Don't listen to him," said a different voice in Owen's head, and Charm's robot hand exploded out of her arm, punching Fowen right in the face. "You'll always be the best Kiel ever, Owen." Then she sighed. "But I'm not real. I'm just you telling yourself these things, so maybe don't listen to me."

Owen shook the daydream out of his head, sighed, and got up.

It was time. Probably past time. He'd be late if he didn't hurry.

He *didn't* hurry. In fact, he was even later than he'd thought he'd be.

Kiel and Bethany were both waiting inside, having used the keys Owen had given them months ago. Neither one was speaking when he walked in, and for a second he wondered if they were nervous about tonight too.

Then Kiel winked, and Owen immediately felt better. Whatever funk had come over Kiel during their time in *The Baker Street School for Irregular Children* seemed to have disappeared, so that was good news.

"Sorry I'm late," Owen mumbled, taking his seat at their usual table. "What's the plan tonight? Back into looking for your father, or just having fun?"

Bethany didn't look at him. "Neither. I have something to tell you both."

"Me too," Owen said quietly.

"I do, as well," Kiel said. "But you two can go first."

Bethany glanced up at both of them, and shook her head. "No no, you go."

Kiel waved her on. "I insist."

They continued doing this for another few seconds until

Owen slapped the table. "I'll go first," he said, not looking at either of them. "I just wanted to tell you both that . . . I'm done. I'm done with all of this. I'm not jumping into books anymore. We're messing with a whole other world, and I just can't take it anymore."

Kiel and Bethany both went absolutely silent, and Owen could actually hear his heart beating in his ears. Granted, it was going a mile a minute, but still. Finally, he looked up at both of them.

Weirdly, neither looked surprised.

"I'm finished as well," Kiel said. "It's time I went back home." He sighed. "I don't know who I am anymore. Without my magic, what am I? Fowen was right about that, at least. I need to find what life has in store for me now, and I think the place to start is back where I belong." He looked up at Bethany. "I came here tonight to ask you to take me back into my books."

Bethany just stared at him sadly for a moment, then nodded. "I was going to tell you that I had to take you back tonight too, Kiel. Because I'm done *too*, too."

Both Kiel and Owen stared at her in surprise. "But your father!" Owen said.

"Doyle's file was wrong," Kiel told her. "You can't just give up!"

"You know he's out there, Bethany," Owen said. "Doyle couldn't explore *all* the worlds . . ."

"I can't keep letting this make me crazy," she said, staring at the table. "I've been looking for him for, like, half my life, and I'm no closer now than when I started. It's just too big a world, and I've got no leads. But beyond that, *look what I did*. I almost set loose a horrible, evil boy on the entire fictional world." Realizing what she said, she blushed deeply, then gave Owen an embarrassed look. "Sorry. You know what I mean."

"No, he's the worst," Owen said.

"I don't hate *anyone*, and I hated him," Kiel admitted.

"I'm so with you on that!" Bethany said, almost smiling.

"Okay, we get the point," Owen said, trying not to sound as irritated as he felt. "Can we get back to your dad? You're really going to just let it go?"

"I think it's past time," Bethany told him. "It's like Kiel said. I'm not sure I even know who I am without that. I can't just keep living the same story. I have to find my own now."

She went silent, and for a moment no one spoke.

"I was actually thinking about writing, maybe," Owen said.

"About Charm?" Kiel asked, raising an eyebrow.

"*No?*" Owen said, probably a bit too fast to be believable. "I have some other ideas. Maybe they already exist on some fictional world somewhere, and maybe they don't. But I thought it'd be fun to just see what happened, see where a story in my head goes for a change. Hopefully, I won't mess up too many fictional characters' lives *that* way. Or at least in any way they're not meant to be."

Bethany smiled. "You're definitely going to have to let me read it."

That idea sent a chill down Owen's spine. "Uh, we'll see."

Bethany turned to Kiel, and for a moment it looked like she wanted to say something. Finally, she just shook her head. "When do you want to go back?"

Kiel's face dropped, and he looked more miserable than Owen had ever seen him. "Right now, if that's okay. I'm not sure waiting will help."

Bethany nodded slowly and stood up. "I'll go get the book."

As she walked away, Owen reached out and hugged Kiel, who hugged him right back even harder.

"I'm going to miss you," Owen told him. "You're always going to be my favorite hero."

"You're a true friend, and I couldn't ask for a better one," Kiel said. "You've lived my life, Owen Conners, and that connects us. Like brothers, only closer. I hope you read of my adventures someday and imagine yourself by my side, as that's what I'll be doing."

Owen sat back, his eyes wide. "That's . . . a good way to say good-bye."

Kiel just winked.

When Bethany returned, Kiel stood up, and together they walked farther back into the library. Owen let them go, giving them a chance to say good-bye by themselves. At one point he thought he heard the book hit the floor, but it was several minutes before Bethany returned, her eyes wet. She didn't bother sitting, instead nodding toward the front door.

"Let's just go," she said. "I don't really want to be here anymore."

Owen nodded and led them outside. As he locked the library door, he glanced up at Bethany, who was crying without any sort of embarrassment now. "You okay?"

She nodded, then shook her head. Owen stood up and hugged her tightly until she let go, then stepped back. "We don't have to jump into books to be friends, you know."

She smiled, sniffing through her tears. "Of course we don't. Our friendship just won't mess up anybody's stories from now on. Maybe we can just see some movies and do normal things for once."

"Video games too," Owen said.

Bethany laughed at that. "Just no jumping into them."

Owen's eyes widened. "Can you . . . do that?"

Bethany's laugh died, and she gave him a death look. "Owen Conners, do *not* even think about it!"

CHAPTER 43

Bethany sat in her bedroom, collecting all the books she'd accumulated over the years. Some she'd be keeping, like *Goodnight Moon* and *The Little Prince*, just for emergencies. Most, though, she was going to give to Owen for the library.

She didn't need the temptation.

Still, there was *one* last thing she had to do. She still owed someone a thank-you.

The green sun of Argon VI warmed Bethany up as she slowly floated to the ground behind EarthGirl. "Hey," she said quietly, knowing Gwen could hear her from miles away.

EarthGirl turned around faster than the speed of sound and shouted in joy. "Bethany!" She immediately hugged Bethany hard enough to crack a mountain in half. "You're back! Did you find your father?"

"No," Bethany said quickly. "But I did realize I had something that might help *you*."

"Help *me*?" EarthGirl said, giving her a curious look. "But how?"

Bethany took Gwen's hand in hers, smiled, then jumped them both out of the book.

The two of them landed on Bethany's bed, and Bethany turned to the shocked Gwen with a finger over her mouth. Gwen looked like she wanted to scream in surprise, but she just nodded silently.

Bethany went to the door and listened to hear if her mom was still up. She could hear the TV still on downstairs, so Bethany grabbed Gwen's hand and walked her quietly down the stairs, then out into the kitchen.

"You're still up, Beth?" her mom said from the living room at the front of the house.

"Yeah, just going to get a snack and look at the stars for a bit," Bethany said loudly.

"Okay, but only for a minute. You've got school," her mom said.

Bethany started to leave but realized Gwen was staring in the direction of the living room in amazement. Right. Bethany quietly led her to the door, where they could both see Bethany's mother sitting on their old couch, watching some late-night news show. Gwen's eyes began to water, and Bethany quickly pulled her back into the kitchen, then out the back door into her fenced-in yard and the cool night air.

"This is . . . this is Earth?" Gwen said, one tear slowly sliding down her cheek. "But how?"

"I'm a time traveler, remember?" she said. "I sometimes visit here. That's my . . . my adopted mom. I just thought you'd want to see what your home planet looked like."

Gwen swallowed hard, tears flowing quicker now. "Would . . . would *my* parents—"

"*No,*" Bethany said, probably a little too quickly. "No," she repeated, more gently this time. "This is still a hundred years before your time."

"But . . . but we can save them, then!" Gwen said, gesturing to the houses all around them. "We can save *everyone!*"

Bethany sighed. *Of course* EarthGirl would want to save her planet. Who wouldn't? "It's already happened in your future. If we changed it, then you wouldn't exist to help me save it, you know? It'd be a paradox, and that'd explode the entire universe."

Gwen shook her head. "I don't accept that. There's *always*

a way, Bethany. We just have to find it! You traveled through time, and we both have superpowers—"

"Not here," Bethany pointed out. "Try flying."

Gwen gave her an odd look, then leaped into the air, only to immediately drop back down to the ground. "No green sun?" she said.

"It's yellow, actually," Bethany told her. "I need to take you back now, but I just wanted you to see what Earth was like. It's not much, but I hope it helps."

Gwen reluctantly nodded, then faster than Bethany could react, Gwen threw her arms around her and hugged her tightly. "I can't *begin* to thank you for this," she said. "Not even a little bit."

Bethany nodded, getting choked up herself, then led Gwen back into the house.

"Get some sleep now," Bethany's mom said, and Gwen froze in place.

Bethany looked at her, then gestured for her to go ahead.

"Okay, I will," Gwen said, just loud enough for Bethany's mom to hear.

"Okay, good night then, sweetie," Bethany's mom said, and Gwen almost giggled, even as tears fell down her face.

349

Bethany quietly walked them both back upstairs, then took Gwen's hand. "Close your eyes," she told EarthGirl, and when she had, Bethany touched the open page of the book and jumped them back to Argon VI.

As the heat of the green sun beat down on them again, Gwen opened her eyes, and floated into the air, twirling slowly in circles. Finally, she hugged herself tightly, then turned to Bethany. "I can never repay you," EarthGirl told her. "Never ever, Bethany. But let me at least show you *my* home here."

"I . . . I need to get back to my own time," Bethany lied. "Got to get to bed. You heard my mom." She smiled.

Gwen nodded. "If you ever want help looking for your father . . . or with anything at all, you don't even need to ask. I'm there. *Always.* We're partners now, like detectives. And partners support each other."

"I think I'm good, actually," Bethany said, looking up at the bright-green sun in the sky. "I don't know why, but all of a sudden . . . I think things will be okay."

UNCHAPTERED

Nobody wrote "The End" in Story Thieves: *The Stolen Chapters*, and placed it on his shelf. While that was taken care of, things were progressing much faster than he'd like, and he needed to be prepared.

And that meant taking another quick trip.

He turned the page, pulling fictional reality apart, then stepped through to what he knew was just another story, but looked like an entirely new world, this one foggy, with cobblestone streets and gas lamps smelling of kerosene. The *clip-clop* of horses alerted him to someone coming, so he quickly created clothes and a face, making himself resemble an average citizen of Victorian England, then stepped out of the street.

It didn't take long for him to find who he was looking for.

A man in a deerstalker hat and brown coat was speaking to a group of children, mostly young ones, but a few a bit older.

Right in the middle was a boy covered in dirt, whispering something into the man's ear. The man dropped some coins in the boy's hand, and the boy quickly burst out of the group as the other children gathered around the man, hoping for more of the same.

Nobody stepped into the way of the boy with the coins and grabbed him by the back of his shirt, pulling him to a stop.

"You would be one of Sherlock Holmes's irregulars, would you not?" he asked quietly.

The boy stopped in the middle of the sidewalk and gave him a suspicious look. "No one here knows that name."

"Neither of us are from around here, are we, Owen Conners," Nobody said, and for just an instant flashed his normal, feature-less face at Owen before returning to his Victorian disguise.

"*Nobody,*" the fictional Owen Conners said, his eyes lighting up. "I was wondering when you'd show up!"

"You knew I'd come?" Nobody asked, a hint of a smile playing over his reforming face.

"*Of course,*" Owen said. "I saw you walking away with the Magister's textbook at the end of *Story Thieves,* so of course you'd come for me, too. I mean, it didn't say for sure that it was the Magister's textbook, but it had to be. And that meant I was next!"

"And why would you think I'd do that?" Nobody asked.

Owen just smiled. "We're not in the book right now, are we?"

Nobody looked up, directly at you, the reader, then turned back to Owen and shook his head. "No one can see you."

"Then I think you're not Bethany's father, because you're secretly her enemy," Owen said, whispering in spite of Nobody's assurances. "I think you're putting together a group of her worst enemies to take her down. Like the Avengers or the Justice League or something, only evil."

"And you would want to fight against her, then?" Nobody asked, raising an eyebrow.

"As long as I get to take down my nonfictional self, too," Owen said, his eyes narrowing. "I owe Nowen big time. Him and that idiot, Kiel."

"So you've learned nothing," Nobody said, and reached out to the boy. Owen just watched in confusion as Nobody's hand touched his arm, at which point he screamed. The scream cut off instantly as Owen's mouth closed on itself, while his flailing arms and legs began to retract into his body.

Moments later Nobody held just a small ball in his hand, which he put into his pocket. "Of the two Owens, I thought I'd be doing this to your nonfictional self a lot sooner than to you," he said, almost sadly. "You disappointed me, fictional Owen."

With that, he stepped into an alley, then pulled the pages of Victorian England apart, and stepped back into his own library. He deposited the fictional Owen Conners into a jar on a shelf, next to a copy of a math textbook, before sighing.

"Things are happening much too fast, Bethany," he said, staring at the copy of Story Thieves: *The Stolen Chapters*. "You're causing more trouble than I can keep hidden." He sighed, then opened a new, empty book titled Story Thieves: *Secret Origins*, and put his pen onto the first page.

"I suppose there's nothing for it. It's time that you meet your father."

ACKNOWLEDGMENTS

Liesa Abrams Mignogna stared at the pages, wondering what James Riley could be thinking. Was he actually saying that he was a character in the Story Thieves books? Was he crazy? Was this some sort of ego thing, putting himself in a book?

Did he really believe it?

And the acknowledgments page was even stranger than the rest of the book. "He's writing about *me*?" she said, straightening her Batman cape across her shoulders. "Is this . . . a joke?"

Apparently, Acknowledgments-Liesa was thinking the same thing, as "'Is this . . . a joke?' asked Liesa" was right there at the top.

Sometimes being an editor was a lot harder than anyone knew. Especially with *this* author.

"Did you see this?" Liesa said to Emma Sector, her coeditor on the books. "*This* is what I've been dealing with since *Half Upon a Time*."

Emma shook her head. "He's got you going over a list of everyone he's thanking. Look."

Liesa glanced down and saw that Acknowledgments-Liesa was running over a list of who James had thanked: Michael Bourret, his agent; Mara Anastas and Mary Marotta, his publishers; Carolyn Swerdloff, Teresa Ronquillo, Matt Pantoliano, and Lucille Rettino in marketing; Faye Bi, his publicist; Katherine Devendorf in managing editorial; Adam Smith, the copy editor; Sara Berko in production; Laura Lyn DiSiena, who designed the book; Chris Eliopoulos, his interior illustrator, and Vivienne To, his cover artist; Michelle Leo and the education/library team; Christina Pecorale and the rest of the sales team; and Stephanie Voros and the subrights group. All the people who worked really hard, basically to give James the chance to narcissistically insert himself into his own book.

Those poor, poor people, Acknowledgments-Liesa thought.

Real Liesa shook her head, wondering again why she put up with this. Why did *everything* have to be so meta with James? "Can't he do it the easy way, just once?" she murmured. And how was he going to thank his friends and family, his loved ones, if this was all written from her perspective? She shook her head.

Her e-mail beeped, as it did every 1.2 seconds, and she

thankfully turned away from the acknowledgments to look over at her computer.

Except, of course, it was him. It was *always* him.

> Subject: Whoops!
>
> LIESA!!!!!
>
> I totally forgot to add in all my friends and family and loved ones! Obviously, I need Corinne in there, like, right at the top of everything. And my parents, who probably still wonder what they did wrong. My family. Everyone who's supported me. The Laird family, Katie, Heather, Mark, and Kim. My readers, ESPECIALLY my readers, who are the greatest, most kindest, wonderfulest people ever.
>
> Also can we put a thank-you in to J. K. Rowling as if she and I are friends? Something like "and most importantly, thanks to J. K. Rowling (or Jo, as I call her) for all those long talks we had over coffee, where we just laughed together over nothing." That's legal, right?
>
> James

Liesa banged her head against her desk twice, took a deep breath, then hit reply.

> Subject: Re: Whoops!
>
> Hey,
>
> No, that would be sort of odd, since you don't know

her. Speaking of odd, why don't you just maybe write your acknowledgments in a more normal way? Then you don't have to confuse everyone even more, especially right when they're finishing the book.

Speaking of confusing, are you actually trying to say you're Nobody in this book?

The reply came just seconds later.

Subject: Re: Whoops!

;)

"And NOPE!" Liesa shouted, shutting her computer down. "It's OVER! It's just OVER!" She grabbed the acknowledgments, planning on ripping them up, then glanced down at the pages and saw that Acknowledgments-Liesa was doing exactly that too.

"ARRRGH!" she shouted, both in real life and on the page, then collapsed into a heap on her desk, shuddering every few seconds. *Why? Why do I do this?!*

"Writers," Emma said quietly from the doorway as she clicked off the light, then closed Liesa's door. "They really *are* just pure evil."